Street Justice

Charlie's Angel

Samantha Fury

Street Justice Charlie's Angel

This is a work of fiction. Names, characters, places and events are products of the author's imagination or are used fictitiously. Any resemblance to actual persons, living or dead, locales or events is entirely coincidental.

Cover image adapted from photographs from:
Dreamstime © John Kershner
Dreamstime @ Jason Stitt
iStockphoto © Luis Alvarez

ISBN 1440485526
EAN-13 9781440485527.

Contact Samantha and read free chapters @
http://www.samfury.webs.com/
jacksgirl@suddenlink.net

I would like to thank my Heavenly Father
for the great imagination He gave me.
My husband for marrying me,
my family for putting up with me,
my dogs for trying to leave
me alone while I was so busy.
My Great-Aunt Deane, who's already
asked for a copy!
Thanks to everyone who helped
me in this process.
The good folks at
Christian Writers have been a huge help.

A Heart-Felt Thank You To My Editors!

Ursula Dingess
Willa Thompson
&
Carol Robinson

Without these three women this book
would not be what it is today.

Sincerely
Samantha Fury
AKA
Jack's Girl

John 3:16-17

[16] For God so loved the world,
that he gave his only begotten Son,
that whosoever believeth in him
should not perish,
but have everlasting life.

[17] For God sent not his Son
into the world
to condemn the world;
but that the world through him
might be saved.

Psalm 125 :1

[1] They that trust in the LORD
shall be as Mount Zion,
which cannot be removed,
but abideth for ever.

Chapter 1
Charlie

Charlie sat on the floor leaning against the kitchen cabinet. She glanced at the gun and the crimson on her hands and shirt. Was it her blood or Benny's?

Everything happened so fast. She didn't know Benny's temper could escalate like that, and she never thought he would attack her.

From the first day Charlie moved in she knew Benny couldn't be trusted. She tried to make Tammy see, but her sister was in denial. Charlie sighed, why didn't she see this coming? She should have left the first time she caught her sister's boyfriend watching her.

Today's trouble began as she came home from work with supper. She set the pizza on the table and took out her cell phone. Benny came out of nowhere and snatched it out of her hand. "You don't need to call Tammy. She's gone. She won't be back 'til Monday." Benny stepped back smiling.

"Give me my phone."

"Take it."

"Benny!"

"I paid for it." Benny sneered.

"You did not. Give me my phone." Charlie reached as he held it out, but Benny tossed it over his shoulder. He grabbed her wrist and leered. She couldn't help but smell his breath.

"Are you drunk?"

"Who me?" Benny laughed, gesturing at the bottle of whiskey on the table.

"I'm tired of you Benny!" Charlie turned.

"No, you don't! Come here! Don't you know what this means? We're finally alone." Benny grabbed her wrist.

"I'm not staying with you," Charlie spat out.

Benny yanked her close, picked her up and turned her around. "Let's dance."

Charlie pushed, but Benny held on, laughing. Out of anger and frustration, she slapped him hard.

Benny stepped back; he raised a brow and wiped his lip with the back of his hand. He looked at the blood, shaking his head. "You shouldn't have done that."

"Let me go Benny!"

"You're not going anywhere. I'm tired of your skinny sister. I want you!" Benny stood in front of the back door taunting Charlie. She turned and ran to the front door. Benny followed, caught her, and slammed her against the wall.

"You can't get away from me!" Benny slapped Charlie twice and laughed as tears streamed down her face.

"Let me go!" Charlie screamed.

"No! You're mine now!" Benny leaned in, kissing Charlie on the neck.

"Stop it! Get off me!" Charlie pulled a picture frame from the wall and hit Benny as hard as she could. He fell back, cursing, momentarily dazed. She pushed him and ran, but didn't get far before she felt Benny's hand pull her down.

She fell with a thud, and winced at the pain. They wrestled on the floor. "No woman's gonna get the best of me."

Charlie fought, kicking and hitting with all her might. Benny tried to kiss her again, but she turned away.

He straddled her, laughing. "I know what you need." He stood, dragging Charlie into the kitchen pushing her into a chair.

Charlie tried to get away, but Benny forced her back down. He picked up the bottle of whiskey and slammed it on the table. "Drink it!"

Charlie looked up, her mind frantically working out a plan. "I said drink it!" Benny pushed the bottle into her hand and yelled, "Now!"

"Okay, okay. I'll do it." Charlie nodded and steadied herself. Would it work? It might be her last chance. "I don't like to drink." She looked up at Benny and smiled. He was drunk. Maybe she could con him. "I guess I could give it a try."

"Sure, take a swig." Benny's drunken smirk convinced Charlie her plan might work. She twisted her wrist backwards, picked up the bottle in an awkward manner, and then brought it to her lips.

Charlie tilted her head, keeping Benny in her peripheral vision. She let the dark liquid flow into her mouth, asking the Lord; *please don't let this kill him*. She then swung her arm, striking Benny on the side of the head with the bottle of Jim Beam.

As she spat out the vile tasting whiskey, she kicked the chair away and scurried to the kitchen. She stuck her hand in the cookie jar and sank to the floor, holding Benny's gun in her hand. Charlie leaned back. Her body was trying to recover from the shock of the beating and the sound of the bottle hitting Benny's head.

Charlie froze for a few seconds and sat holding the gun. She looked down at the blood on her hands and wanted to scream. Her hands and legs trembled, but she willed herself to calm down. She huddled, listening, her lips moving in a silent prayer.

She kept the gun in one hand, crawled to the end of the bar, and peeped into the dining area. Benny lay close to the back door. The thought of him grabbing her leg as she walked by caused her heart to race. "If I can get out of the house, I'll be okay."

Charlie stood on wobbly legs and dug into the cookie jar again. Benny's poker stash would come in handy. She'd given Tammy money for weeks; it was time for payback. She shoved the money and the 9mm Kel-Tec in her pocket, said a prayer, and hurried over top of Benny. She grabbed her jacket and purse from the coat rack and ran out the back door.

Once she made it to the sidewalk she stopped and looked back, Benny wasn't following. Had she hit him too hard? Charlie took a deep breath and looked around.

She didn't want to be in South Bend, Indiana. She wanted to forget these last three months and go back home to Ohio, but she couldn't. Two months after she turned twenty, she left home because of her dad.

Since the accident at work, he no longer allowed her to go to church. He started drinking, and blamed most of his problems on God. Charlie knew her dad's pain had put them in a tense situation. He needed relief. If he could get the insurance company to approve his surgery, maybe things would change.

Charlie felt anger rise. She looked to the sky. "Why did you send me here? What good did it do me? I'm no better off. I'm kicked out in the cold, beaten and bleeding!" Charlie looked around feeling lost.

"Now what? I'm too broke for a hotel. I can't go home. That just leaves . . . Aunt Verla, in Chicago." An idea began to form and Charlie started pacing. She looked down at her shirt; she needed to hide the blood. She slipped into her jacket and zipped it up.

Her hands had stopped shaking, but her lip ached. She pulled out some tissues and tried to wipe the blood away. When Charlie heard a noise she looked up. She could see Benny's shadow moving around inside the house.

"I can't let him catch me."

Charlie looked up and down the street and noticed Benny's neighbor, Sam, leaving for church. She ran across the street, calling to him as he unlocked his truck. "Can you give me a lift?"

Sam looked toward Benny's house and his brow furrowed. "Where to?"

"The bus station."

"Sure, come on, I'll take you." Sam didn't mention the fact that she was a mess, or ask her about the blood that was on her hands and face. Five minutes later as he dropped her off at the ticket office, he turned and finally broached the subject.

"Are you okay?"

"I will be."

"Do I need to call the police?"

Charlie shrugged." Maybe you should, to be sure Benny's okay."

Sam nodded, "I can do that, but I was worried about you, not Benny.

Charlie glanced up. "I hit him pretty hard, but I saw him walking inside the house."

"Don't worry about Benny; he's got a hard head. What about you? Are you sure you don't need help? I can take you to the doctor.

"No. I'm fine. I'm going to see my aunt."

"Well, you be careful. I'll be praying for you. Here, take this."

"I don't need to . . ." Charlie tried to protest but Sam interrupted.

"It ain't much. I forgot my wallet at the house, but it might come in handy. Take it." Charlie nodded and took the money putting it in her pocket.

"Take care, missy."

"I will."

After closing the truck door Charlie walked into the building. Her pace quickened and she went to the bathroom, stepped into a stall, and pulled out the gun.

She checked the chamber as quietly as possible. It was empty. Next she took the clip out; there were five rounds left. She pushed the clip deep into her jeans pocket, and slid the gun into her jacket.

She counted her money; it added up to seventy dollars. That would get her to Chicago. She stepped to the sink and washed up, looking at her reflection.

"I'm a mess."

She could see a bruise close to her eye, and a busted lip. She patted her face dry, hoping her lip wouldn't start bleeding again. After brushing her tousled hair, she tucked in her shirt, managing to hide most of the blood. Charlie checked her appearance and then headed out to look at the bus schedule.

Twenty minutes later she boarded a bus to Chicago. Charlie sat in the second seat back and prayed for guidance. She glanced at the strangers around her. They seemed lost in their own thoughts.

How many of them were running from something, too? Charlie settled down and tried not to think about what awaited her in Chicago or what might be following behind her.

Chapter 2
Chicago

"A city on a hill can not be hidden . . . Matthew 5:14." The smile Charlie got from the bus driver when he turned to look at her seemed phony. Maybe he didn't like people talking to themselves. She didn't care. She smiled on, mesmerized by the Chicago skyline.

The bus rolled into the Midway Terminal at nine-thirty. Charlie didn't expect the station to be busy at this time of night. People hurried by, pushing and shoving. It made her feel lost and out of place.

It took an hour to get off the bus, find a bathroom and get a cup of coffee. She spent another thirty minutes looking for an English-speaking cabby. She needed a quote on how much it would cost to take her to 2029 Kolin Avenue.

The first guy shook his head. 'K-Town not at this time of night.' The next three either couldn't speak English or didn't want to take the time to see what she wanted. She sighed deeply out of frustration.

"I'll take you to 'K-Town', but it'll cost you forty."

Charlie turned, startled. She nodded to the young man; he didn't look old enough to drive. "You will?"

"Yep. I'll take you to Kolin. My cab's down the street. You got forty?" The young man seemed to be looking her over. Charlie knew with her black eye and busted lip she must look a sight.

"I have it."

"I'll take half up front; call me Willie. Stay here, I'll get the cab."

Once in the car, Charlie handed the young man a twenty. He stuffed it into his pocket and spoke. "A lot of cabbies don't come to K-town this time of night."

"Is it a rough neighborhood?"

"It's not the best; but also I'm not going to get a return fare. That's why I charged you for both ways."

"I see. Should I have waited until tomorrow?"

"Nah, just watch your step. Don't be hanging out on the streets and you'll be fine."

"Thanks. The only place I'm going is to see my aunt."

"Are you staying long?"

"I'm not sure yet."

Willie handed a card over the back seat and Charlie took it. "Call me if you need a cab. I'll take you anywhere you need to go."

"Thanks. I'll keep that in mind."

Willie and Charlie chatted until he made the turn onto Kolin Avenue and brought the cab to a stop. Charlie handed him the other twenty, said her goodnights, and stepped out into a light rain.

Charlie watched the cab's taillights disappear down the street, then turned, looking at the line of houses. The building Aunt Verla lived in stood four stories high with a white fence surrounding the entire complex.

After trying the door, Charlie realized she needed a key to get inside. If she couldn't stay with her Aunt Verla, she didn't know what she would do. She spent most of her money on getting to Chicago.

She could call the police, and confess to stealing Benny's gun. They'd be more than happy to put her up for the night.

As if she didn't have enough troubles, the rain started to fall harder. She moved close to the building, standing under the small awning. Five minutes later a young woman with an umbrella came hurrying down the street and started up the steps. Even in the dim light Charlie could see she didn't look happy.

"Look! I know it's raining, but you can't stay here."

Charlie's brow furrowed and she gestured at the door. "I'm here to see my aunt."

"Sure you are. Now go on before I call the cops." The young woman took out her cell phone. "I *will* call them."

"My aunt really lives in this building. Verla King, she's in apartment 5B."

"Verla isn't here! She's gone to Florida."

"Florida?" Charlie sighed.

"You should have known that, since you're her niece. How did you get her name? Did you go through our trash?"

"No! She's my aunt. I'm from Indiana. I didn't know. We don't talk to each other that much." This bit of news hit Charlie hard. Eight dollars wouldn't get her back to Indiana, and since she didn't have a credit card, there would be no use in looking for a motel room.

"Look, I need to go. I don't know if she's your aunt or not. What I do know is that you can't stay here. I'm not going to let you in."

"I don't have anywhere to go."

"That's not my problem."

The rain greeted Charlie by pelting her in the face. It stung her lip, and she fought back tears. She hurried down the street to an all-night diner that Willie suggested.

She stood under the small canopy gathering her thoughts. Did she dare spend her last few dollars on something to eat? Willie warned her to stay off the streets.

Charlie stepped inside the diner, shaking off as much rain as she could before entering. At least she'd be warm and dry. She moved to a small booth, sat down and picked up the menu. The warm room felt good, but she was chilled from being in the rain.

She pulled out her money, counting the few dollars in her purse, eight dollars and change. Charlie knew she shouldn't spend it all on one meal; she'd have to find something cheap, and take it from there.

"Hey, lady, what do you want?" A man yelled from the counter. "We don't have a waitress tonight."

Charlie moved to sit at the bar. She glanced at a menu, and when the man stepped closer she spoke. "I'll have a cup of hot tea and some toast with butter, please."

"Sure thing." The man raised a brow and gave her a nod. She could tell he wanted to mention her busted lip and the bruises on her hand, but he didn't.

Instead he took her money, laid her change on the table and with a nod, said her order would be ready in a minute.

When her order arrived, she picked up the tea and small saucer that held the toast, and went back to the booth to stay away from the cold air.

She added sugar and cream to her tea as she stole glances at her surroundings. Three people sat scattered over the diner. One man dined alone as he chatted on his cell phone.

Across the room were two women; one reading the paper while drinking a coffee, the other sat looking at a menu. She glanced up now and then as if waiting on someone.

None of them seemed to even notice Charlie, and for that she was thankful.

Around ten-thirty a handful of people came wandering in, and for about an hour, the place stayed busy. Charlie sat watching the natives come and go, thinking and praying, not sure what she should do. The hot tea helped her feel better, and as she ate the toast she longed for the pizza she'd left sitting on Benny's table.

She tried not to make any direct eye contact with the patrons, and she tensed when a rough looking crowd came in; they looked to be what her dad would call thugs. They ate, laughed, and talked loud, but left causing no trouble.

Midnight came and went. Around two a.m., Charlie glanced at her watch. She wondered if the man at the counter would care if she stayed all night.

He looked tired, and when she ordered her second cup of tea, much to her surprise, he spoke.

"Here, I need to get rid of these. Take two if you want." The man pushed a covered tray of doughnuts in her direction and she smiled.

"Thank you."

"Ah, you're welcome." He finally said in a tired tone, waving his hand, and going back to a book he was reading.

Charlie went back to her booth and thanked the Lord for the doughnuts. She picked up a jelly filled delight, but looked up as the door flew open. A young woman came rushing in, glancing over her shoulder.

Charlie raised a brow as she scrutinized the woman's clothes. She wore a red mini skirt that contrasted well with her dark skin, a blue tube top and a white jacket. As she walked by, she unzipped her purse and locked eyes with Charlie before heading down a back hall.

Seconds later Charlie turned her attention back to the front door. A policeman rushed in, looked around, and then left hurrying on down the street.

Charlie pushed the last bite of the jelly doughnut into her mouth, and glanced up as the young woman slid into her booth. She smiled at Charlie as if she knew some great secret. The change in the girl was dramatic, but the beauty was still there.

The woman looked better without the blonde wig and the outlandish make-up. How could she change clothes so fast?

"Hey there. Can I buy you breakfast?" The woman smiled, then turned to the man behind the counter, "Stan, fix an early-bird special for my new cousin."

"Sure thing Allie."

Charlie raised a brow. "Why do you want to buy me breakfast?"

"Well, you do me the favor of being my cousin, and I'll do you the favor of buying you something to eat."

As the door flew open once more, and the officer came back in, things began to make sense to Charlie. The officer tapped his foot for a moment; let the door close, then moved toward their table.

"What about it?" Allie whispered.

Charlie didn't have much time to make up her mind. She didn't want to lie, but she didn't want to sleep on the street either. She saw the policeman getting closer, and decided to jump at the opportunity.

"Ok, but I need a place to sleep worse than I need something to eat."

"You got it. Now what's your name?"

"Charlie Anderson. I'm from South Bend, Indiana."

"Okay, Charlie, now don't look so worried. Smile."

Charlie forced a smile, and then looked toward the policeman as he spoke.

"Ok, young lady. You're under arrest. I know it was you I chased for three blocks. I think it's time we go downtown."

Charlie looked at the woman, and then to the officer. She thought it might look better if she spoke first. "Can I help you, Officer?"

"Ma'am, do you know this woman?" Charlie knew the officer was looking her over. Her jacket was zipped so he couldn't see the blood, but she'd bet by now there were bruises on her face.

"I sure hope so. I'm spending the night with her. I came all the way from South Bend for a visit."

"From South Bend. I assume you can prove this."

"I can prove I'm from Indiana." Charlie reached into her purse, pulling out her ID, as she recalled the gun in her pocket. "I'm here for a few weeks. I might stay longer, if I find a good job." *Or, if I get put in jail for carrying a handgun.* Charlie hoped the officer didn't ask to look through her purse. If so, he might find the clip.

The officer took the ID and looked it over. The man's brow rose and then a scowl appeared. He didn't seem to like it much that Charlie's ID matched her story. After a minute he turned and looked toward the owner of the restaurant, as the man spoke.

"They're telling the truth. I know these girls."

The officer nodded, giving Charlie her identification. "Well, I guess I made a mistake."

"Don't you mean you think all black women look alike?"

Charlie moved her hand out to the woman across the table and touched her gently. "I don't think that's what he meant." Charlie glanced at the officer and smiled. "She's had a bad night. I'm sorry; she didn't mean anything."

"I'm sure she didn't." The officer glared at the two girls. He might have said something else, but the old man behind the counter called to him.

"Officer, would you like a hot cup of coffee before you go back on the street?"

Charlie sighed as the man turned and went to the counter. Once he sat down, she turned her attention back to her new cousin. Allie stared at the man with a definite look of irritation on her pretty face. Charlie didn't want to offend her new friend because she really did need a place to stay. She spoke, trying to keep her tone soft.

"I know we just scammed him, and it's really none of my business, but . . . did you break the law?"

Allie turned, looked at Charlie and smiled. "I know you may not be from a big city like Chicago, but I think you can figure out which law I broke."

"I have an idea."

Allie leaned back and smiled, "I'll bet it's the right one."

"Like I said, it's none of my business."

"Well, so you'll know. I'm not a mass murderer, or anything close. I don't even steal," the girl leaned forward and smiled at Charlie, "unless you call taking money from a man for kissing his feet for an hour stealing."

Charlie made a face. The girl leaned back laughing, keeping her voice low. "I made him wash 'em first, and I made eight hundred dollars. It was the easiest money I've made in a long time."

17

"Not many people I know can say they make eight hundred dollars an hour."

"You got that right, honey."

Both girls grew quiet as the old man sat two plates down on the table. The man winked at Allie. The officer was gone now, so he spoke freely as he walked back to the bar.

"You got away with it again, Allie. You snow em' every time."

"I couldn't do it without you, Stan."

"Well, if you weren't one of Rico's best girls, I wouldn't put up with it."

"Oh hush, you know you love the excitement."

"Just eat up and get out of here. Your cousin looks like she needs some rest."

Chapter 3
Allie

Around three-fifteen, the two girls walked into Allie's apartment on Komensky Avenue. Charlie would be spending the night only a few blocks from where Aunt Verla lived. When Allie turned on the lights Charlie looked around. The apartment seemed spotless. Allie shook her head, and crossed her arms.

"Do you think all working girls live in a rat hole? I make good money and I don't mind spending it on myself."

"You've got a nice place. I just didn't expect it to look like this. As far as working girls go, I only know what I see in movies."

"Well, some of it's right and some of it's *way* off. I work for a clean guy; but then again as Stan said, I'm one of Rico's favorite girls. He gives me more of a cut. I've been with him a while and he knows he can trust me with the big clients."

"I guess that's a good thing."

"Yeah. It's a real good thing! Don't get me wrong. I didn't always live like this. I've lived, and slept, in the gutter. I don't want to go back. Rico got me a deal with the manager, and I buy almost everything second hand. I just make sure it looks good."

"Well, you did a great job furnishing your apartment."

"Thanks." Allie walked over to look out the window. "I hate to rush off, but the rain's quit, and I have a party to go to. Make yourself at home, and I mean that. If you get hungry rummage till you find what you want. There's a second bedroom down the hall. I don't think anyone's ever slept in there, so things may be dusty, but they're clean."

"I really appreciate this. I ran off from my sister's house; her boyfriend tried to rape me."

"Wow! That's a bummer, but it explains the busted-up look. Take a load off and kick back. You can stay a few days, as long as you're quiet in the mornings."

"Yes, ma'am. I can do that."

"Call me Allie, or Alice."

"Ok, Allie. Call me Charlie."

Allie walked over and picked up a T-shirt from a basket of clothes on the couch and handed it to Charlie. She took Charlie by the chin, looking at her busted lip. "I don't think you need stitches, but it's gonna hurt a while. Rummage through the meds in the bathroom, find some antibiotic cream, and get some rest."

"I'll try. Is this a good neighborhood?"

"Oh, yeah. You don't have to worry about the crime here." Allie stepped to the door laughing; she paused before stepping out the door. "Well, there's crime, but Rico's the one in control, and he never lets anyone come near *his* girls."

Charlie's body ached as she walked into the bathroom. She found some cream for her lip and changed into the white T-shirt. She folded her clothes over her arm and went to the extra bedroom. After closing the door and laying her clothes over a chair, she walked around the room.

A full-sized bed rested against the left wall. A dresser with a mirror and two small nightstands gave the room a homey feel. Charlie pulled the covers back and laid the gun under the pillow. The room looked clean and unused. She left her socks on, placed her shoes by the bed and lay down.

Her body ached, but she couldn't sleep. She sat up, sighed and decided it would be a good time to pray. She rose and stepped to the window and looked out. She could see the skyline in the distance. "What a beautiful sight."

Charlie touched her finger to her bruised lip and her mind went to her family. Should she call her mom or wait until morning? After a few moments she decided she'd have to wait. She couldn't pay Allie for a long distance call. She also didn't want to call collect and upset her parents at this time of night.

If things went the way she hoped; her parents wouldn't learn about her trouble with Benny until Tammy came home. Charlie paced while praying. After some time she looked around the room, smiling when she found a small radio.

She carried it to the bed, plugged it in, and set it on the nightstand. She turned the dial until she found an all night gospel station. She laid down, and with the sounds of good gospel music, managed to drift off to sleep.

Charlie sat up, forgetting for a few seconds she'd slept in a strange bed. When she began to move she felt the effects of Benny's handy-work. Her back ached, and she could see bruises all over her body. She glanced at her watch to see, six-thirty. She stretched gingerly and moved to peek out the door. The shirt Allie gave her came above her knees, and she didn't want anyone but Allie to see her.

She needed to talk to Allie, to see if she could stay longer than a few days. She wanted to get a job and make some money for the trip home. She slipped out of the bedroom and saw Allie sitting on the couch taking off her shoes.

Charlie smelled the *pot* before she saw the smoke. Benny used it often enough for her to know that odor. Her nose wrinkled as she walked down the hall. Charlie stopped in her tracks and thought about backing into the bedroom and avoiding Allie. Why did God lead her here? Charlie didn't know people like this girl. She went to church. She didn't even curse and now this happens.

She could handle this situation in two ways. Accept Allie and then try to witness to her, or pretend she didn't notice anything and distance herself from the girl. If she ended up staying, would she sink to her level, or would she be able to bring Allie to a higher plain? Charlie closed her eyes for a moment and said a quick prayer. She knew she needed to get her life back on track, and this situation was a reminder of that fact. It was time for a definite change.

"Lord, I don't know why I'm here or what I should do, but please help me. Lead my steps and my words and turn me into a person who can be a great light to Allie and others. Amen."

Charlie walked into the room and sat down in a chair. After a few moments Allie spoke, but she didn't open her eyes. "I know I shouldn't smoke this stuff, but it's something I do after a rough night. Don't think I'm a pot head, 'cause I'm not."

"I try not to judge people."

"Judge . . . that sounds like a church word."

"Well, I go to church most of the time."

Allie opened her eyes. "Really? You go to church? But you spent the night here with *me*?"

"I needed your help. You didn't find me in the street, beaten, but you were my Good Samaritan."

"I know that story. My aunt goes to church; she read it to me once. So tell me Charlie, what brings you to my door?"

"I guess God."

This made Allie laugh and she leaned back and shook her head. "God gave up on me a long time back."

"Nah. He's waiting for you to come back where He can reach you again."

"Reach me? He wouldn't touch me with a ten foot pole."

"I'm sure if you ask He'd wrap His arms around you and let you cry on His shoulder. We just don't give Him the chance."

Allie shrugged, closed her eyes, as if thinking something through. She sat up, put out the joint and let the smoke roll out before she spoke. "If you have so much faith, how did you end up here?"

"I don't know. Maybe God sent me to help you; to show you He really does care. Maybe He sent me here to teach me something. It's hard to tell what the Lord has up His sleeve. He lets us go through stuff in order to teach us a lesson."

"And you don't care? I never did understand that. If He loves us so much, why does He let people hurt?"

"Well, the Bible gives us one example. God let Job suffer to prove to the devil his servant wouldn't turn his back on his Maker, even when terrible things happened to him."

"So you think this could be a test?"

"It could be. Or maybe I'm here to help you, or someone else I haven't met. I won't know, maybe for months. I may never know why this happened. I may not want to know why I got chased by my sister's boyfriend, and why God let my dad lose his job and grow hateful to me."

"Did your sister know about this? Did she kick you out?"

"No. I ran away. I can't stay with my parents now. My dad's in a tight spot; he blames God for everything. He doesn't understand how I can be so faithful when God's allowed *him* to be in so much pain."

"Why *do* you still love Him?"

Charlie smiled. "That's easy. I love Him because He loves me. No matter what I do, I can go to Him and He'll be there."

"How is He here for you now? You're on the street. You can't go home."

"Well, He helped me find the diner and He sent you to feed me. He knew we'd meet, and He put me in a place where I could help you. He led me here because He knew you'd take me in.

"Well, however you got here, I'm glad I could help . . ."

"Me too. But, will you let me stay another night? Maybe several?"

"I don't know. Are you going to preach at me?"

"If I feel God wants me to."

Allie laughed, shaking her head in dismay. "Why do you want to stay here? Look at how I live. I sleep with men for a living; I smoke pot in the morning to help me forget what I do at night. This ain't no place for you."

"Well, that's kind of what I thought. But Jesus hung out with all kinds of people. They called Him names because He hung out with prostitutes and drunks. A woman like you came one day and washed His feet with her tears, and dried His feet with her hair. The rulers back then said if He was a prophet He'd know what kind of woman was washing His feet."

"I don't remember that story," Allie rose to go to her room.

"I'll read it to you some time. But I'll tell you, Jesus knew all about her. He knew what kind of woman she was. He could sense her regret and sorrow, and He forgave her."

Allie nodded as she walked down the hall. "You can stay, but I may ask you to do things now and then."

"I won't sleep with men for you." Charlie laughed, shaking her head no.

Allie turned with a smile on her face. "That's my job. But I can't cook so maybe if you want to stay for a few weeks you'll have supper on the table around five this evening. There's some money in the sugar bowl if you need to go out and get some groceries."

"What about a key to the apartment?"

"It's on the peg by the front door. Whatever you do," Allie stated, "please do it quietly."

Chapter 4
Settling In

The first evening Charlie cooked a beef roast with potatoes. It was one of many meals they would share over the next few weeks. Charlie would rise at dawn, talk with Allie about her night, and plan a menu for the next day.

Allie wanted Charlie to feel at home. It was fine if she wanted to use the phone, and she could stay forever, as long as she kept cooking those fine meals. She could also use the key to come and go as she pleased, as long as she kept quiet in the mornings.

The day after she moved in, Charlie called her mother to say she would be spending some time with a friend in Chicago. She found out Benny survived her right hook, and that Tammy didn't want to hear her side of the story.

She promised to keep in touch but didn't mention Allie. Her mother would not approve of her new environment.

Since she'd moved in with Allie, things were changing. Some mornings Allie didn't smoke pot but instead Charlie would rub her shoulders and tell her a Bible story. They were getting to know each other and they were becoming good friends. Charlie decided to stay, so she found a job at a restaurant a couple of miles away. She didn't like riding the bus, but she was getting used to the system, and learning her way around town.

Each evening Charlie arrived home in time to cook supper. They would sit laughing and talking, forgetting their problems for a while. Allie didn't discuss her profession, but Charlie knew it was stressful. A couple of times she came home crying.

Charlie tried to talk Allie into quitting and getting a better job. One night during a thunderstorm while they sat in the dark waiting for the power to come back on, Allie confessed she wanted to move to Florida. She spoke about the move as if it was a distant dream. Charlie told her all dreams felt distant at first, but it was no reason to give up on them.

One Friday evening, a few days before Halloween, Allie walked in and sat a small box in the center of the table. "What's that?" Charlie asked as she set a kettle of hot pasta on the table.

"It's a small present I picked up. Today makes two weeks since you moved in. You can call it an anniversary present. I hope you like it."

"Thank you; I love presents." Charlie sat down looking at the small box. "What is it?"

"It's our dream box. I know you don't want to live here forever and I don't either. This is our way to a better life."

"I like that idea."

"Me too. My dream is to take my aunt and move to Florida. If you want, you can join us or you can have a dream of your own. We'll each have our own envelope. I'll be putting as much money in as I can and I thought you might want to join me."

"This sounds like fun."

"It will be. And don't forget, you're welcome to join me and my aunt in Florida. I haven't told her about it yet. I want to save enough money for the trip first and maybe even go down, look around, find an apartment and get a job."

"This is great! I got paid today so here's my first ten dollars on my dream."

"I'll match it." Allie pulled a ten out of her pocket and they sat down to eat supper.

Over the two weeks of living with Allie, Charlie started saying a blessing over their meals. She knew Allie felt uncomfortable at first, but soon softened to the idea.

A couple of times, as she went out the door for the night, she'd even asked Charlie to pray for some of her friends. They were becoming close and both of them were glad for the night they'd met.

This night as Allie headed out the door, she stopped and looked at Charlie. "I need you to pray about something, but I'm not sure how to ask."

"What is it?"

"Well. I met this guy the other night; at one of Rico's parties. He's so good looking, and not like most of the men I meet. He kept watching me. I'm sure he knew why I was there, but we had a nice talk and *only* a talk."

"That's great."

"So far, but he's going to be at this party tonight. I'm so nervous. I don't want him to be one of the guys . . . you know . . . I like him but not that way. I'd hate to have to . . ."

"Don't worry. I'll spend some serious time in prayer. Just look for it to work out the way God wants it to."

"I'll try. Also pray for me 'cause I get nervous when I'm around him. I don't know why, but there's something about this man I *really* like."

"I'll pray."

"I know you will." Although it wasn't normal for Allie, she hugged her new friend. Charlie could see tears in Allie's eyes as she turned to go out the door.

Charlie headed to her room to pray for Allie. The tears flowed for her friend. She knew down deep Allie hated her job. Charlie even hated to think of it as a job; it wasn't. Although Allie made money, it seemed more like a prison than a job.

After praying, Charlie called to check on her dad. His surgery had been postponed again, but thankfully his pain and stress levels were lower. Charlie didn't keep her mother on the phone long but wanted to let her know things were well. They never spoke about Tammy or Benny. Charlie wanted to ask how her sister was, but didn't. She knew if anything serious happened, her mother would let her know.

After saying goodnight to her mother, Charlie slipped into her nightgown. Her body ached from working such long hours.

She glanced at the Bible the young pastor gave her and sighed. For the second time, she missed going to the new church over on Park Ave. She turned the lights off and looked out the window on the city, thinking about her new job.

Charlie liked her boss, Jim. Since she was the new girl, he kept picking her for overtime. She didn't mind filling in when others wanted some time off. It helped her add more money to the dream box.

The tips she made from waiting tables paid better than she thought possible, but at times the men could be hard to deal with. They wanted to paw her, smack her on the rear, or tell her a dirty joke. It made her think of Allie.

Charlie couldn't understand how Allie could live like that, going out and working the streets night after night. Sometimes the construction workers came in for lunch; they made kissy faces and called her sweetheart. Whenever she became embarrassed or mad, she thought of Allie.

Charlie began to pace thinking about Allie and her new love interest. Maybe all the men who hung out with Rico weren't immoral. She found it hard to believe a man would deal with a pimp, and not be in the same line of work.

She heard the rain begin to fall and turned, watching as the raindrops hit against the window. She went over and looked at the skyline. No matter where she went after living here, she knew she would miss this view.

She sat down in a chair and looked out over the city. She began praying for those working and living on the streets. There seemed to be a lot of police out tonight, but then again, it was closing in on Halloween.

Hopefully she wouldn't have to work that night. She wanted to talk Allie into helping out at one of the local churches. Several of them would be handing out candy to the children for Trick or Treat. She hoped and prayed Allie would go with her.

Chapter 5
Angel

Sirens flashed and Angel cringed as the rookie pressed his face against the back of the cruiser. The cop holding him laughed and pressed down as he took out his cuffs.

"You're not getting away from me, punk." The rookie sounded a little too sure of himself. Angel wanted to pull his badge and tell the kid, 'hands off,' but he couldn't. Some of Rico's guys were sitting right behind him.

He might get away from this rookie, but the kid looked trigger-happy and Angel didn't want to take a chance on getting shot. He grimaced as the kid once again pressed his face against the car as he tried to cuff him.

"You pretty boys are all the same! You think you can get away with anything. Well, let me tell you. You won't get away with anything on my watch!"

"I can see that." Angel's tone won him another slam into the car. After the kid got the cuffs on, he pushed Angel down to sit on the sidewalk. Now and then a cop would come along, pick one of them up, push them into a car and head to the station.

Angel sat for fifteen minutes before someone came along, grabbed him from the back, and pushed him to a cruiser. "Watch your head," the cop warned as he forced Angel into the car. Angel glared out the window at the kid that cuffed him. Some day he'd get the chance to properly introduce himself.

The man behind the wheel of the cruiser took off a blond wig and a pair of glasses, tossing them aside. He put the car into drive and pulled out.

"It took you long enough," Angel glared at Joe, a man who seemed more like a good friend than a brother.

"Hey! I got here as fast as I could. You should have called sooner."

"I took a chance calling you when I did."

"Well, just be glad you didn't get a free ride downtown to booking. You're lucky I was close by, passing out candy with Nyssa."

"You call this lucky," Angel leaned forward showing Joe a cut on the side of his face.

"You'll live. I don't think it'll affect your looks any. Don't be a cry baby."

"Hey, who went to hold your hand at the dentist last month?"

"I was getting two teeth pulled. That's a lot more serious then a small cut on your face."

"Speaking of bad teeth, you got any candy?" Angel looked over the seat.

"Nope. I got a couple of sandwiches you can have. I can get more when I go back to help clean up. Where do you want me to drop you off?"

"It doesn't matter. I can walk to my apartment from here. This is Rico's part of town you know. I'm hoping this will win me some brownie points with his boys.

"So you think you might get to meet Rico soon?"

"I'm still working with some of his punks. It's really hard to break into the inner workings of this group. But I don't think it should take much longer. I showed them tonight I'm willing to fight the cops. I told the guys I needed the work. I'm hoping they'll contact me soon."

"The chief said to keep the apartment for another month. I got some money for you, too."

Joe pulled the car to the corner and Angel bent around so Joe could take the cuffs off. Once his hands were free he reached for a small bag and laughed at the smiling pumpkin on the front.

"Did you take the kids out trick or treating?" Angel began rummaging through the bag.

"Nyssa took them to church for some apple-bobbing and pin the smile on the pumpkin. We didn't take them out; there was plenty of candy at the party."

"You went too?"

"Yeah, Nyssa put her foot down. She wanted me to see the kids in the play. They did a good job. I'm glad I went." Joe turned in the seat and handed Angel another bag. "Here's a few other things."

"A new phone already?" Angel took a couple of bites of one of the sandwiches.

"Yeah, this one comes with a tracking device."

"I'm not sure I like the amount of faith they have in me."

"You're new. No one here knows you but me."

"I know. I like to complain. Here's the old phone."

Joe took the phone and tossed it into the glove box. "I'll drive you around the street and then you can jump out."

"Works for me. I'll try not to get arrested this time."

"Do that, and keep your nose clean. I've got a wife, unlike some people. I don't need to be babysitting you every time I turn around." With this comment, Joe checked the mirrors and slowed the car. Angel opened the door, and in the shadows of the side street, he slipped out to make his way back to his apartment.

It was half past ten when Angel walked across Maple and Lincoln. A streetlight flickered, but he paid it no mind. He was taking out his phone to learn the features when someone jumped out, holding a knife. Angel looked at the punk and, speaking in a weary tone said, "It's been a long day. Is this really necessary?"

"Trick or treat," the kid sneered and Angel could see another knife blade in the moonlight.

"Will this night ever end?" He slipped his phone back into his pocket . . .or tried to. As he moved his hand he felt the hit. He almost passed out. He closed his eyes and fell to his knees. The phone flipped out of his hand and went scooting across the ground to the kid with the knife.

31

As Angel scrambled to his feet, the leader of the gang put his knife away and bent over to pick up the phone. Angel knew he was out-numbered; there were at least three of them, not counting the punk on the stairs.

He threw a few punches and put up a good fight, but after a few minutes, it was over. He felt them looking through his pockets, and barely knew when one of them pulled out his ID. He was out cold when the youngest kid ripped away the gun that was strapped to his ankle.

The tallest kid opened a small bag, but when he found two sandwiches, he tossed it over his shoulder.

"Someone's coming." The kid by the stairs yelled. "Throw him in the bushes and run."

Chapter 6
Good Samaritan

Charlie couldn't talk Allie into going to the church festival, so she went alone. When she arrived and heard they were going to be short-handed, she jumped at the opportunity to help. The puppet show started at six and ended at eight, so they could have everything wrapped up before it got too late. Halloween night on the back streets of Chicago could get scary.

It was nine forty-five when Charlie, Nyssa, Joe, Tracy and Donna finished cleaning up and locked the church doors. They walked to the parking lot and stood talking.

"We sure appreciate all your hard work." Pastor Tracy once again shook Charlie's hand, and then turned to his wife and smiled, "I guess we should go pick up the kids." Donna nodded and the two walked off leaving Nyssa, Joe and Charlie to say their goodnights.

"We need to get our kids, too. I'm sure glad Nyssa's folks volunteered to take them home so we could help clean up." Joe moved to his cruiser and motioned to his wife. "I'll follow you home. No speeding! I'd hate to pull you over and give you a ticket." Joe started to leave but turned as his wife spoke.

"You better not give me a ticket, Joe Morganson. I'll give you a trick instead of a treat." Nyssa laughed and winked at Charlie as she unlocked the minivan. She and Charlie got in, buckled up and were on their way.

It was a short ride from the church to Allie's apartment, so Charlie and Nyssa were in no hurry to part ways. They were talking about next week's service, and when Joe flashed his lights, Nyssa laughed. "Well, I better get moving. Joe's tired, and I don't want to push my luck. He's not usually willing to help me do anything at church, so I was thankful he came."

"Well, he picked a good night to go. You guys did a great job tonight. I loved the play."

"Thanks. I hope you can come again. If you need a ride, call. The church owns a bus, and the number's on the pamphlet the ushers passed out."

"That's good to know. Taking cabs can get expensive." Charlie glanced into the mirror. "I better let you go. Thanks again for the ride." Charlie opened the door and climbed out of the van.

"Anytime," Nyssa added as Charlie closed the door.

Charlie walked up the stairs and was stepping into the building as Joe and Nyssa left. She turned when she heard a rustling sound. She glanced down the stairs and saw something white in the bushes.

She leaned over the rail peeking down into the dark shrubs. There, with its head stuck in a bag, was a snow-white cat. "Hey there. What are you eating?"

Charlie pulled out a flashlight, shining it in the direction of the cat and couldn't help but notice the orange pumpkin smiling back at her. She hurried down the steps and walked around to the shrubs. She knelt down, reached in, and pulled the bag off kitty's head, confirming it came from the church.

She took the sandwiches out, stuffed the bag into her pocket and laid the scraps on the ground for the kitten. The cat purred as she stroked its soft fur. Charlie quickly remembered she was on the streets of Chicago, and not in the suburbs of Ohio, so she glanced over her shoulder.

She was about to stand when once again she heard a rustling sound. Thinking it might be another cat; she moved the beam of light from side to side. When she saw a man's hand, she fell backwards and screamed. For a moment she sat there, inches away from the fallen man.

It came to her as she began to move; this man was at church tonight. The bag had been inches from his hand. "Hey! Are you okay?" She moved to get on her knees as she began to pray. It was tempting to run inside the building and call the police.

As she was thinking about leaving, the story of The Good Samaritan came to her mind. She couldn't just leave him there alone. "Sir. Wake up."

After a moment she could see the man's hand start to move. "Are you okay, do you need an ambulance?" She watched as he tried to rise to his knees. She hurried to her feet and helped him to stand.

In the process, she dropped her flashlight. She left it lying in the bushes and helped the man out of the shrubs.

"If you can walk, I'll help you into the building, then we can call the police." She still couldn't see his face, but by his build and clothes she could tell he wasn't an elderly person.

"I need to get some of this mud off. I don't need the police now. I was mugged, I'll be fine."

Charlie looked up and down the street, *Could the muggers still be around?* She looked at the man. As he moved toward the light she could see him better.

His face was bleeding and caked in mud. "You don't look okay to me."

"I will be. I need to wash up and be on my way."

The idea of taking a stranger into the apartment was intimidating but she couldn't leave him alone. He was bleeding and he'd be a good target for another mugging. She wondered for a moment if The Good Samaritan wanted to run and hide instead of help.

Charlie hesitated at the door, praying, wondering what should she do. The bag with the smiling pumpkin came to her mind, and as she pulled it out of her pocket she asked. "Did you drop this?"

Then man looked down and Charlie moved the bag upward, where the streetlight would give him light to see. "Yes," he said after a moment, "it came from the church."

This was the answer Charlie needed to feel safe. "Come on. Let's get you inside where we can see what's wrong with you."

"Thanks. I appreciate your help."

Charlie managed to get the young man upstairs and to the kitchen. She pulled out a chair and helped him to sit down. She ran the water until it was warm and then took a towel and began to clean his face.

He was dressed rather nicely in new jeans, a black leather coat and a western cut shirt. She noticed a fancy looking watch on his arm and a tiger's eye ring on his finger.

She also noticed under all the blood and dirt was a very handsome young man. He seemed to be mostly out of it as she cleaned him up, but he managed to stay in the chair. Now and then he'd moan, though she was trying not to cause him pain.

Under the mud she found a cut on his cheek, a small scrape above his brow, and he looked like he'd soon have a black eye. As she kept working, she found a red scratch on the edge of his face, and another light cut on his neck.

Most of the mud was on his cheek, but she also checked inside his shirtfront and found some dried blood spattered on his chest. She took all the leaves out of his hair, and then managed to get his coat off.

It was here she found a cut in the sleeve of his coat. Once she laid the jacket aside, she looked over his arm. "This looks ugly." Since he wasn't talking, and he didn't want to go to the hospital she cleaned his arm the best she could, and bandaged the cut. It wasn't bleeding by the time she finished wrapping the wound.

Forty-five minutes and a few bandages later, the man looked human again. Charlie stood, placing her hand on his shoulder, wondering if he was okay. "Are you awake? I think you should see a doctor."

"I'll be fine." When he spoke her brow rose in wonder, *so he is coherent.*

"Are you sure?" She asked.

"My side hurts and I have a headache. Other than that I'm fine."

"Your head hurts?" Charlie's brow rose.

"Yeah, some punk hit me in the back of the head."

Charlie moved behind the man and looked him over to see if there were any more wounds.

Finally she found a place on the back of his head. She pulled his hair back and though there was no blood, it looked painful. She stepped back and came to stand in front of him and spoke in a soft tone.

"You took a good hit to the back of your head." The man opened his eyes and looked up. He squinted at the light but seemed to focus

"I'm fine. I just need some rest. My side is aching."

"Are you sure?

"I'm sure. Can I crash on your couch for a while?" Charlie looked at the clock and knew Allie shouldn't be home until six the next morning, so she nodded and put her hand on his shoulder.

"You can lay down on the bed. My roommate won't like it if she comes home and finds a man on her couch."

"I can leave if it's going to cause you trouble."

"No. She shouldn't be home until the a.m., but just in case you can rest in my room. Come on. I'll help you."

It was a slow process but Charlie helped her patient into the bed. She then took off his shoes and pulled a blanket to his waist. He was out like a light. She sat on the window seat, looking at the handsome man before her. Was he lying about being at the service tonight? Could she have missed him in the crowd?

He didn't have a beard, and his dark hair and dark eyes would catch her attention with ease. Charlie sighed and decided it didn't matter. She glanced back and forth from the window to her patient.

After thirty minutes she rose, heading to the couch to read. Most of the time the man seemed restful, but now and then he'd moan and hold to his side. "I wonder if he has a broken rib."

37

Charlie hoped her patient didn't regret not calling an ambulance. Many people didn't have insurance these days; maybe he couldn't afford it.

Since he was sleeping peacefully, Charlie decided he was going to be okay. She turned quickly, looking at the stranger in her bed. *What if he wakes up and wants to rob me?* This wasn't a good idea, but it was too late to change her mind.

She closed the door and glanced around. There was no way to lock him in so she sat a chair in front of the door. If he came out while she was reading, at least he wouldn't sneak up on her.

Chapter 7
The Patient

Charlie sat up with a start when she heard Allie coming up the steps. "Allie's singing. Well, that's different." Charlie glanced at her watch and shook her head. "Seven-thirty? Allie's never this late."

She rose and went to her room, moving the chair and closing the door behind her. She walked over to the bed; her patient was still sleeping. She took her hand and put two fingers on his wrist. He seemed to have a strong pulse and even opened his eyes and looked at her.

"I'm alive, nurse."

"Well, that's a relief." Charlie let go of his wrist as he tried to move. The man moaned as he raised his hand to rub the back of his head.

"Do you feel better or worse?"

"I'm not sure. How did I feel when I laid down?" The man gave her a flirtatious smile.

"I doubt if you felt very good."

"Then I guess I'm doing okay."

Charlie glanced toward the door. The expression on her face must have shown worry, for her patient spoke.

"What's wrong? Is someone out there I need to worry about?"

"Not really," Charlie began, "It's my roommate, Allie. She won't be happy if she finds you in here."

"Why? Are you gay?"

"No. Of course not," Charlie smiled. "This is her place. Well, I think it belongs to Rico."

"Rico? Is he here?" The man sat up, trying to ignore the pain, but stopped moving when Charlie answered.

"No. But he's her boss. I think he's tough to deal with." Charlie paused and glanced toward the door and then back to her patient. "She won't like it when she finds out you're here."

"I see." The man gave her a knowing nod. "I know the kind of man Rico is. He owns this part of town."

"So I've heard." Charlie's brow rose as the man looked around the room.

"Was I wearing a jacket?"

"Yes. It's in the closet." Charlie retrieved the jacket, reaching it to the man. She studied him as he looked through his pockets. "I didn't take anything."

"I didn't think you did." The man's tone showed irritation in not finding something. He continued his search. Charlie studied the man as he pulled up his pants leg; he cursed when he found a small holster empty. She stepped back as he pushed his pants back down and asked, "Did they take my shoes, too?"

"No. I took them off." Charlie wondered if she should yell for Allie. Could her patient be carrying another gun? She moved to get his shoes and set them by the bed, wondering what kind of man this was.

"Do you work for Rico?" Charlie found herself asking and the man looked at her. He didn't answer but sat on the edge of the bed trying to put on his shoes. He bent over but sat up holding his side. She could see the pain in his brown eyes.

Pity won over the apprehension she felt. "Let me do that." Charlie knelt, putting one shoe on, then the other. Her hair fell over her shoulders as she slipped on the second loafer.

*****

"I don't work for Rico," Angel smiled. He enjoyed being pampered for a change. This young lady was gorgeous but she didn't look like a hooker. "I'm sorry, but I have to get out of here. I think I can help you with your problem."

His nurse looked at him like she wasn't sure what he was talking about. He took her by the hand and helped her to her feet, though it caused him some pain.

Angel pulled out the envelope, rummaged through his money and took out two one hundred dollar bills. He smiled as he put the envelope back into his pocket. "The little punks missed this."

"They missed your ring and watch too. Are you sure you were mugged?"

Angel's brow rose and he gestured out with his hands, "Do you think I beat myself up?

"No, I guess not."

"Trust me, I was mugged. Something must have scared them off before they were done. Luckily for you and me I still have my money. I'll give you a couple hundred since I stayed the whole night. Tell your room-mate whatever you want, but I think the money will solve your problem."

Angel pushed the money into her hand when it seemed she didn't want to take it.

"I can't take your money." Angel ignored the cute redhead, slipped into his jacket and walked over to the door. She was by his side looking at him, holding out the money. "Take this."

"No. You keep that. I appreciate your help. Most people would have left me lying in the mud."

"You should thank the white kitten. I went to rescue her and then I found you"

Angel smiled and studied the girl's face for a moment. "What's your name, beautiful?" He knew it sounded like some corny line from a bad B movie, but he didn't care. He liked the smile that came to her lips.

"Charlie." She pushed the money at him again, "I don't want your money. You keep it."

"There's plenty more where that came from." Angel paused for a moment and then moved to the door. He stepped out into the living room. Charlie was right on his heels. As he walked to the front door, a young lady sitting on the couch rose. She looked angry.

"What are you doing? You know I can't have men in here. You know what Rico said."

*****

Charlie nodded, moving to stand by her patient. She looked at the man, and then to Allie. She wasn't sure what to say. The man turned and looked at her, then spoke.

"I don't mind paying more. I don't want to cause you girls any trouble with Rico.

The man took out the envelope, tossing another three hundred dollars on the coffee table. "I don't want to get on Rico's bad side; I know he's a shrewd business man." The man turned to Charlie and stepped closer. He probably thought he was doing her a favor, but he wasn't. He leaned in, kissing her softly on the lips, winked and walked to the door.

"I'll see you ladies again, I hope."

With this comment he left. When Charlie turned to face Allie she could see irritation on her friend's face. The money she was holding didn't help matters any.

"I know what this looks like. I promise you, I didn't sleep with him. I found him in the bushes beaten up, and I knew you'd have a cow if you found him here. I told him Rico owned the place, and the next thing I know he's trying to make you think he slept with me."

"So you're saying." Allie said as she took the money out of Charlie's hand and added it to the money on the table, "that Mr. Moneybags paid five hundred dollars for nothing?"

"I didn't sleep with him. I promise." Charlie knew Allie didn't look convinced.

"Well, *whatever* you did, that's a lot of money," Allie shrugged her shoulders. "You must have impressed him."

"All I did was help him clean up, and let him sleep in my bed."

"*Sure,*" Allie handed Charlie the money. "I believe you." Before Charlie could speak Allie held up one hand. "I have to get some sleep but first I have to tell you something." Allie took

Charlie by the shoulders and pushed her to the couch and they sat down.

"Do you believe me?" Charlie interrupted.

"Yes, of course. You don't lie. I know that, so forget it. Besides, he looked pretty beat up. Now listen. You know that cute guy I told you about, William?"

"Yes." Charlie sighed.

"Well, last night I was hanging out at one of Rico's parties. William came up to me, smiled a wicked smile and asked me what I would charge for the whole night."

"What did you tell him?"

"I told him eight hundred dollars, because I didn't want to sleep with him. He smiled and pulled out a credit card. I told him I didn't take plastic; he laughed and we walked out. He took me out to eat, then we went dancing, then we went for a long walk at the arena. We talked for hours and then around five this morning, he took me out for breakfast, then he brought me home."

"That's great!" Charlie hugged Allie and leaned back, looking at her as she went on.

"I really like this guy. The strange thing is, he knows what I do for a living and he didn't even try to kiss me. We just talked. I don't know what to think. But I know I want out of this life quick."

"I know you do." Charlie nodded thanking God for the huge change in her friend over the last few weeks.

"I have an idea." Allie glanced at the money and then back to Charlie. "You really should think about coming to work for Rico as one of his dancing girls. Your looks would get attention. You'd get a lot of men to dance with you. If you can get that guy to pay you five hundred dollars for a couple of band aids and a little TLC, just think what you could make in one night!"

"You want out, but you're trying to get me in?"

"Yes, so we can get more money and get out sooner."

"I could never do that. I've seen women on TV do lap dances. There is no way I could . . ."

"You don't have to. All the girls don't do that kind of thing. Some of them dance, or sit and listen to the men talk about their troubles. Listen, I'm tired. Just think about it. It pays good, and we could get our money faster for our dream box."

"I don't know." Charlie watched Allie get up and head to her bedroom and before she closed the door, she said one last thing.

"Just think on it."

Chapter 8
Undercover

Angel hailed a cab and headed to the precinct. The chief wasn't going to be happy. His wallet was missing, so that meant new credit cards and a new ID.

Placing his hand on his jacket, Angel looked down at his arm. Though he was thankful the leather coat took the brunt of the cut, he still hated that the jacket was ruined. The cab driver hit another pothole and Angel shot him a dirty look. His side ached, and he felt every bump on the ride.

Once close to the station, he paid the cabby, and eased out of the car. He made a purchase at a busy café to be sure he didn't have someone following, and then went to find Joe. When he walked in he got an unexpected greeting.

Joe rose from his desk and began to curse a blue streak, and it was all directed at him. Something about half of Chicago's finest out on the streets, and how dare he just waltz in.

"I'm happy to see you, too." Angel forced a smile.

"Where were you? I just knew some punk took your phone and left you bleeding on the street."

"That's about what happened." Angel cringed as he sat down; his side throbbed. "Did you get my phone or ID back?"

"We got the phone when the kids started using it last night; by using the tracking device in the phone, we got one kid. Your two credit cards were picked up at a local department store this morning." Joe sat down shaking his head. "Why didn't you check in?"

"I was kind of out of it. But I'll live. Thanks for asking."

Joe picked up his coffee mug, started to take a drink, and then set it back down. "This is why I don't do undercover work. I hate not knowing."

"It's what I'm good at. It's what I trained for."

"Well, I don't have to like it." Joe leaned back holding his coffee. "We checked the apartment. Where were you?

"In a bed, sleeping off being knocked in the head. The punks took my piece, my ID and my phone. It seems you already know that."

Joe took a sip of coffee. "Well, at least you're okay. I won't have to explain to Dad how I got you killed."

Angel looked up. He couldn't recall the last time Joe said 'Dad' instead of Stephan, but he didn't mention it. "I took a beating, but I'll make it."

Joe gave a slight nod of recognition then went on complaining. "Well, so you'll know, when I got the call saying they'd found your phone, I went out looking. I didn't get much sleep, and you cost me a night of romance with Nyssa."

"Sorry about that." Angel winced as he moved to get comfortable. For a few moments they were silent, then Joe spoke.

"I'll have them cancel the phone, call off the search party and inform the chief that you're still alive," Joe glared at Angel again.

"I was out cold. If I could have called, I would have. Get me another gun, too, while you're at it, and some aspirin."

"Anything else?"

"Since you asked, I need five hundred dollars and a new ID. Also, cancel those two credit cards."

"We did that when those punks tried to buy a big screen TV. I wonder if they work for Rico."

"I think everyone in that part of town works for Rico." Angel thought back to the two women in the apartment. He wondered if he should tell his brother where he'd spent the night. As long as Joe didn't press the issue, he'd keep that part of the story to himself.

Angel wondered if Joe and Nyssa knew the young lady that bandaged his wounds. Through the fog of last night he remembered her asking about the sandwich bag. She'd mentioned the festival, too.

When Joe came back to the desk with a new gun, ID, a glass of water and two aspirins, Angel brought up the subject.

"How did the festival go last night?"

"It was nice."

"I lost the sandwiches." Angel tossed back the aspirin and drank some of the water.

"They were good. The ladies at church are great cooks. Nyssa brings me food all the time from their dinners and parties."

"Any single ladies I might be interested in?"

"Are you looking to settle down? Most women that attend church don't bar-hop or party."

"I don't party that much."

"They don't party *at all*," Joe shook his head, looking back at his paper work.

"So, there's no available young woman at your church?"

"It's not my church."

"Nyssa's church?"

Joe looked up quick. Angel could see the irritation on his brother's face. Finally, Joe leaned back in his chair.

"Are you serious? You know if you date some woman from church and break her heart, Nyssa will kill me. Then, come looking for you."

"I'm willing to take that chance. It's time I dated someone with some class." Joe nodded and tapped his pen on the desk. After a second he shrugged.

"Well, I don't go often, so I don't know many of them. Matter of fact, I only know one. She's some new girl Nyssa met. We took her home last night."

"Is she nice-looking?"

"Yeah, she's pretty. Red hair, nice figure, but she's not from around here. She doesn't have a city accent and I'm sure she's not your type."

47

"Why not?"

"She goes to church. Girls like that don't date people like you."

"What about Nyssa? She married you."

"I got lucky. She fell in love and followed her heart, not her upbringing."

"What do you mean?"

Joe sighed and leaned back. "Most people who go to church don't marry those who don't. Something about being unevenly yoked."

Angel shrugged. He started to mention he hadn't gone to church much, but talking about their past, and his mother, usually ended up in an argument.

Joe went back to his paper work.

"So that's it. You won't introduce me?"

"I'll think about it. When this case is over."

"Can't I at least know her name?"

Joe looked up and shrugged. Angel knew exactly what he was going to say.

"Charlie."

While waiting on his new credit cards and money, Angel went to his desk. He began looking through the latest fliers, missing wives and children, burglaries and stolen cars. The usual.

Thumbing through the most recent, he stopped and looked at one sheet. He laid the others aside and read the small print, amazed at how this young woman could pop into his life twice in less than twenty-four hours.

It seemed Charlie Anderson was missing from South Bend, Indiana. Someone accused her of stealing a gun and eighty dollars. The person who filed didn't seem to be a family member. A small FYI at the bottom of the page caught Angel's attention.

Benny Fitch is dating Charlie's sister. He claims she stole his money and his gun. None of her family seemed to think she was missing.

Angel could tell Benny sounded like trouble. He filed the paper away in his desk and tossed the others in a tray. He looked up as Joe walked in; he smiled as his brother tossed down two credit cards.

"Try not to lose these."

"I'll do my best, but I didn't have much choice in the matter."

"I guess not. You need to be careful. I wish the chief would allow someone to go undercover with you."

"Would you say that . . . if I wasn't your brother?"

"I doubt it."

"I didn't think so." Angel picked up the cards and placed them in his wallet. "After last night, I'm hoping I'll be invited to meet Rico."

"Well, I wish you luck. I think you should take a day to rest, and the way you're holding your side, maybe you should have your ribs checked."

"I will. I hope they're only bruised. I can't afford to lose any time on this case."

Two hours later, a grumpy looking nurse gave Angel a clean bill of health. "They're bruised, not broken," she mumbled, reaching him his paper work. She didn't seem to like her job any more than the nurse that gave him the five stitches on his right arm.

Angel paid his bill with a credit card, signed the name Angelo Blackwell on the release papers and picked up some medication for infection and pain. He stepped out into the cool air, happy to be out and away from people with needles and cold instruments.

He called a cab, picked up some take-out, and headed back to his apartment to begin the waiting game. He hoped one of

Rico's men would call soon. The waiting was tough and boring. He kicked back in his chair after eating, smiling as he held his new Glock 27. His thoughts were crowded with the events of the past day.

An hour later he kicked back on the couch; one thought kept coming back. Looking at one of the small band-aids on his hand, his mind wandered to a very appealing young lady named Charlie Anderson. He was intrigued by her and couldn't wait until their paths crossed again.

Chapter 9
Rico

Charlie's shift started at eight, and the day was dragging by. She was thinking about the five hundred dollars the young man left that morning. *All money should come so easy.* Charlie took off her apron and went to clock out.

"Where are you going?" Jim's tone was grouchy and that was unlike him.

"To take my lunch."

"No. Not yet. I want you to wait on table five."

"I'm tired and hungry. Can't one of the other girls do it?"

"No! Go on over and take their order."

"Do you mind telling me why?"

Jim's brow furrowed as he glanced across the room. He sighed and his tone sounded angry though he kept his voice low. "Because you're the best looking waitress I've got and that man could ruin me if he wanted to. Now go over there, and *if* you value your job, you'll make his visit unforgettable."

Charlie didn't know what to think. She'd never seen Jim so edgy and it made her nervous. She liked being on her own and she needed this job, so she did as he told her.

She picked up two menus and walked over to a couple of well-dressed men. They both were nice looking, but there was just something about them that didn't seem right. The younger of the two men checked her out as she approached and the older man watched in irritation.

"Can I get you something . . . to drink?" Charlie added after the young man gave her *a look*.

"Good thing you clarified that beautiful I was considering what my first request would be." Charlie didn't know what to say. She moved her attention to the older man and he shook his head as he spoke.

"Ignore my nephew; he's spoiled and disrespectful. Bring us two iced teas and we'll look over the menu."

"Yes sir." Charlie headed into the kitchen and, to her surprise, she found Jim watching. "Who is that?"

Her boss stood there for a moment and turned about the time she was ready to head back with two glasses of tea. "It's Rico DeLusa. Whatever you do, *don't* make him angry."

"Rico? *The . . . Rico,*" her voice lowered, *"the pimp?"*

"Don't you dare let him hear you say that!" Jim glanced toward the two men. "The man owns this part of town. His dad was in charge, but he's in jail now. Rico took over, but he isn't from the old school. He has his own way of running things. He's not top man by any means, but he's on his way up. Now, go and be polite."

Charlie took the tea over, trying to be calm. What if she spilled something on Rico, or said the wrong thing. He watched her in a way that made her tense.

Rico smiled as she came back to the table, "May I say, I think your talents are being wasted here. Why don't you think about coming to work for me?"

"Don't bother the young lady, Rico. Can't you see you're making her nervous?"

"This is my Uncle Alfredo," Rico gestured across the table. "Is he right? Do I make you nervous?"

"A little."

"There's no need for that." Rico took Charlie's hand and kissed it. "I'm trying to help you move up in stature. I can put you to work in a place where you'll wear the best clothes and never want for anything."

"Rico. Leave the girl alone."

"You don't order me around. You're only my uncle! Don't forget that." Rico let go of Charlie's hand and glared at the man across the table.

"Since Jerry's in jail it's my duty to be here for you."

"I'm old enough to take care of myself." Rico turned his attention back to Charlie. "Be a doll and bring me some lemon for my tea." Charlie nodded and walked away from the table.

*****

Rico's uncle shook his head in disgust. "Don't you know how to treat anyone with respect?"

"Sure I do. I'm good to all my women."

"You're a glorified pimp."

"I'm not a pimp. I help women better themselves. I see to it they go to the doctor, and I treat them well. If it wasn't for me, many of them would be on the streets, going hungry or freezing."

Alfredo looked at Rico. He wanted to lean across the table and give his nephew a good shake. Rico hadn't been taught right from wrong, and Jerry spoiled him way too much, but he should know better than to assume his dad's role. Why couldn't he see it would only lead him to jail? Jerry saw the light, but only after prison brought him to his knees. "Please don't follow in my brother's footsteps."

"I won't. I'm not going to jail."

"That's not what I meant, and yes, sooner or later, you will be behind bars. I only wish you could see how low you're stooping in treating women in this manner."

"I'll say it one more time. I'm good to these girls. They live well. I don't beat them. They can quit any time they want. Keep your opinions to yourself, old man. You're not going to change me, so why don't you go home and pray or something."

"I pray for you every day."

"Good! Maybe that's why I'm so prosperous."

"God doesn't approve of what you're doing, and He sure isn't going to bless anything you put dirty hands into."

"I'm getting along fine the way I am. Go home! I've got some business to attend to."

Alfredo rose from the table the moment the waitress returned. He put his hand on the young woman's shoulder and looked her in the eye. He only hoped his few words would sink into her mind.

"Don't let my nephew talk you into working for him. You have a good job; keep it. Stay away from Rico; he'll lead you down the wrong path." The man looked at his nephew and then turned and went out the door.

*****

Charlie wasn't sure what to think. She set the lemons on the table and was going to walk away but Rico took her hand.

"Would you sit down? I need to ask you a question."

"I shouldn't. I'm on duty."

Charlie glanced into the kitchen; Jim looked at her and then at Rico. "Take your lunch, Charlie. Laura, get over there and take their order."

Charlie wasn't sure what to do. She wanted to keep her job, so she joined the man and ordered a cola, chicken strips and fries. Rico ordered a steak and a salad. Charlie took a drink of her cola; Rico looked at her and smiled as she spoke. "What did you want to ask me?"

"I want to know if you'd like to come work for me. I can get you a lot more money than you'll ever make here. Good money. You need to understand your beauty won't last forever. In life we have to use our gifts while we've got them. You need to come and work for me. You look smart; you can invest what you make and be set for life."

Charlie sat her cola down and forced herself to look at Rico. His cool blue eyes were attractive, but intimidating. How did she tell him she didn't want to work for him without offending him? Jim said Rico owned this part of town. She sure didn't want to get on Rico's bad side

"Sir . . ."

"Call me Rico."

"Okay, Rico. I don't mean to offend you, but I have a good idea what you're asking me to do. I could never . . ."

Rico held up his hand and shook his head no, then placed his hand over hers. "I do have ladies who work in the profession you're alluding to, but I also have women who work in some very nice circumstances. I've learned there are many lonely men in this town, and some of them are very wealthy."

"I'm a good judge of character. I could put you in a position where you'd be making five hundred to a thousand dollars a night. There would be nothing involved but dancing, laughing, and maybe dinner. All of this would take place in one of my nicer clubs downtown. You would never have to do anything you didn't want to do, and the men never expect anything. It's a date . . . nothing more."

Charlie moved her hand, shaking her head. "I find it hard to believe a man would pay that kind of money to talk." As she said this, she thought back to Mr. Moneybags. He didn't seem to have any qualms about dropping five hundred for not much at all. She looked back at Rico as he went on with his proposal.

"Then, my dear, you're very mistaken. It happens every night. This city is full of rich, lonely men who don't want to have to worry about someone trying to steal everything they have. Not all men want the same thing. You should consider my offer. Working for me can have great advantages."

"I appreciate your offer . . ." Charlie was about to say, 'but,' and Rico seemed to perceive her answer. He reached across the table and placed his finger over her lips.

"I don't like that word . . . it's akin to another word I don't like." With this comment his phone rang and he moved his hand to take the call. He was on the phone for about five minutes, and then he hung up and turned to the kitchen and called, "Jim, make mine to go." Rico turned back to Charlie and smiled. "You'll have to forgive me, but I have an important matter to attend to. I hope you'll consider my offer."

Charlie nodded and watched as Rico walked to the counter where he picked up his lunch. He gave a slight nod of his head and a gentleman who was sitting at a nearby table rose and walked to the door. The man, who Charlie assumed was Rico's bodyguard, held the door open as Rico walked out. She watched as a long black limo pulled up to the door; the two men climbed in and the car pulled away.

Chapter 10
Good News and Bad News

The alarm clock went off for three minutes before Charlie managed to hear it. She'd stayed up late the night before talking to Allie and her mother. She stretched lazily. A few minutes later she climbed out of bed and took a quick shower.

By the time she sat down to eat breakfast it was after nine. Allie was sleeping in as usual, so she sat thinking about the conversation she had with her mother. It seemed, once again, the surgery would be postponed because of insurance problems.

Since her dad had been laid off before his last premium was paid, the hospital wouldn't take him in for the surgery unless he came up with a percentage of the cost of the operation.

That wasn't going to happen. She looked at the dream box on the table; her small amount wouldn't help much. Rico's job offer came to her mind.

"What am I thinking?" Charlie ran her fingers through her hair and envisioned five hundred dollars a night coming into her dream box. She mentally did the math. In thirty day's she'd have more than enough for a down payment for the hospital.

"I can't do it." Charlie knew getting involved with a man like Rico would take her down the wrong path; it would be nothing but trouble.

After washing the breakfast dishes, Charlie headed to Jim's Diner to begin her shift. By noon the place was packed and she was too busy to think about the phone call from her mother. The customers, as usual, were hurrying in and out, most of them leaving good tips.

When the clock hit two, and the crowd thinned out, Charlie took a break in one of the back booths. Chili, fries and a coke made up her lunch. She sat eating, her mind deep in thought. When she felt the booth shake she glanced up to see Rico sitting down.

"Hey beautiful. How are you today? You look tired."

"I'm exhausted. This place *is* busy."

"You can give all this up, and come work for me."

"I don't think that's going to happen."

"It's easy work and good pay."

Charlie glanced up, shaking her head no. "I have a job."

"True but, I have an important client coming in this weekend. I need a girl and you'd be perfect."

"I can't do it. It goes against my values."

"Sure you can. It's a date." Rico leaned back with a smug smile.

"Just a date?" Charlie laughed. "Why don't I believe you?"

"I don't know. You should. I'm telling the truth. I have some important clients and trust me, the last thing they want to see is their name on the front of a paper for doing something that's against the law."

"I'll have to thank you, but refuse your offer."

Rico shook his head and leaned forward before he stood. His expression showed his disappointment. "We'll see about that." Rico's blue eyes mocked her. He rose from the booth and gave her a knowing smile.

Charlie turned in the seat, watching Rico as he walked back to the front of the diner where he joined two other men. A sigh came from deep within. This was all she needed, being hounded by a pimp. She finished her lunch and went back to waiting tables.

Jim once again sent her to wait on Rico, but today he paid her no mind. He was too busy with his meeting. The two men with Rico didn't look like the type to hang out with a man of his stature. She wondered what other kinds of business ventures Rico was delving into.

The bodyguard kept an eye on her and, as usual, sat a few tables away. She noticed he never ate but he often ordered a cup of coffee. When they were gone, and she was picking up the tips, she hoped she would never see either of them again.

Charlie didn't get her wish. Rico and his bodyguard came to Jim's diner for three straight days. Every day, like clockwork, he came in, dining with different guests. The calls from her mother also came like clockwork, informing her of the latest tale of woe about the insurance company.

It was Thursday morning when things began to change. Charlie was getting ready to head out to work when the phone rang. She sighed when she saw the caller ID. It was her mother. She paused, and then answered. "Hi, Mom."

"Oh, Charlie, I have the best news! I don't know why, but they agreed to do the surgery."

"That's great! So you got the insurance problems worked out?"

"No. The hospital called and informed us to come in for some blood work. They didn't explain anything, but they're going to do the surgery. I didn't ask them why, but we have an appointment tomorrow. Your dad is in such a good mood; I can't tell you how relieved I am."

"Mom, this is great. I wish I could talk longer, but I'm running late for work."

"That's fine. I wanted you to know what was going on. You have a good day, honey. I hope you'll think about coming home soon. I miss you."

"I miss you too, Mom. I'll call you later."

"Bye, honey."

Charlie hung up the phone and headed to work. It was easier today to smile at the customers as they came in. She was in a great mood. Not even the sight of Rico in his white suit could dampen her spirits.

She picked up two menus and headed over to his table. The bodyguard sat down in his usual seat and she dropped off a menu to him on the way to Rico.

"Good morning," Charlie smiled.

"You're in a good mood. Did you get some good news?"

This seemingly idle comment made Charlie pause for a moment as she laid the menu on the table. "Yes. I did."

"Well that's great! Why don't you join me and tell me *all* about it?" Charlie sat down; her good mood slipped away as she wondered why Rico looked so smug. He glanced her way picking up the menu and then spoke.

"Now tell me, what time *did* you get the phone call?"

Charlie's expression showed dismay and disbelief. She leaned back in the booth, not sure what to say. Rico raised a brow at her silence and went on speaking.

"I did some investigating the other day and discovered you were in need of some help. You'll learn fast that I take care of my employees. I treat the people who work for me like they're family."

Rico closed the menu and studied Charlie's expression. "You may think because you're attractive and young that I'm interested in you for myself. Don't be offended, but I'm not. I'm a business man and the business comes first."

Charlie didn't know what to say. She looked at Rico, knowing what he expected. He was spying on her! Did he have the phone tapped? "But I *don't* work for you."

"Yet . . ." he added, as he smiled, "I need a favor from you. I have an opportunity that will be good for both of us. I'm going to ask you to consider going out on a date with a man in his late 40's. He's got a very important awards ceremony to attend. He wants someone like you on his arm. He trusts me to pick a perfect lady for this event."

"I told you. I can't do it."

"Can't or won't?"

"It doesn't matter. I'm not going to do it." Charlie started to rise from the table but Rico put his hand on her arm and when he spoke, she sank down into the booth. For the first time she saw anger in those blue eyes.

"You want your dad to have that surgery, don't you?"

"Of course I do. Did you tap my phone?" Charlie's voice cracked and Rico smiled and moved his hand.

"No, of course not."

"Then how did you know?"

"I told you, I take great interest in the people who work for me. I know your dad needs that surgery, and I know why you left South Bend."

Charlie leaned back in the seat and looked at Rico. "I don't understand."

"I'm an important man. When I ask questions, I get answers. When I make a few phone calls, people listen." Rico leaned forward and looked Charlie in the eye.

"You need to listen to me, young lady. I've done you a big favor because I like you. An associate of mine made a call to St. John's Hospital on behalf of your dad. The surgery will go through as planned as long as they don't receive another call."

"You talked them into doing the surgery?"

"You could say that. Now, if you want to keep things going in the right direction, you'll do me this favor." Charlie was speechless. When Rico handed her an envelope, she didn't know what else to do but take it.

Rico stood up and gave Charlie a stern look, "I'll expect you to follow those instructions, and don't be late."

*****

Rico left Charlie with her thoughts and walked to the counter. He motioned for Jim to step closer. Rico leaned forward keeping his tone low and asked Jim for a personal favor. Rico smiled as Jim's brow shot up at his request, but the man nodded, agreeing.

Seconds later, Rico walked out the door and climbed into his limo. He left his bodyguard, John, behind to watch Charlie. Maybe she needed a little more convincing that he was serious.

The bit of news Rico gleaned from the dirty cop, Lloyd, had turned out to be useful. The trip to South Bend netted them quite a bit of information.

Rico learned that Charlie left home to live with her sister a few months back. According to Benny Fitch, the girl couldn't leave soon enough. Lloyd, Rico's informant, didn't put much stock in what Benny said. He seemed, in Lloyd's words, to be lazy and shiftless.

Rico didn't care what Benny said or did; he was happy for more information on Charlie. She would be the perfect match for his new client. This bit of information could be used against Charlie if necessary. John, his bodyguard, would drive her to the beauty parlor and the mall where she could pick out something suitable to wear.

He hated stooping to blackmail to get what he wanted. It wasn't his style. Most of the time all he needed to do was dangle some cash and his *employees* would do what he asked. This girl was different.

She wasn't from the streets; she was from the suburbs. Her character, and where she came from, was what made her a perfect date for an up-and-coming Senator.

*****

Charlie sat looking at the white envelope. Did this man have enough clout to call a hospital and get her dad into surgery without any insurance or money? All these thoughts were going through her mind as Jim came over and sat down.

At first, he wouldn't look her in the eye. He sighed deeply and put his hands on the table. She straightened and leaned forward, speaking to him in a soft tone.

"What's wrong?" Jim took a moment, and when he spoke, she could tell he was uncomfortable.

"I don't know how to say this. I like you Charlie, and I don't want to fire you 'cause it'll look bad on your record. But you have to go. You can't work here anymore."

"What . . . Why? I don't understand."

"You're not from the city, but you have to know Rico is *very* powerful."

"I'm learning that."

"Well, I don't know any other way to say this . . . so here goes. You have to leave. I have to do this. Rico has some kind of fixation on you. I'm sorry. You're a great worker, but I have to do what he says." Jim rose and started to move, but he turned and looked at Charlie when she spoke.

"Did he tell you to fire me?"

"Yes, he did."

Charlie sighed and looked across the room as Rico's bodyguard rose, walked over and sat down. He looked at her and shrugged. "Let me explain something to you. The boss is like a kid at times, and you're his new toy. One day he'll learn he can't do this and get away with it."

"You sound like you don't agree with what he's doing."

"I don't."

"Then why do you work for him?"

"Because he pays good, and I've made some dumb mistakes. This job is digging me out of some old gambling debts. I've kicked the habit and in a few months I'll be free of my debt, and Rico. Till then, I'm one of his right hand men. I'm here to take you shopping."

"Really? Do I look like the kind of person to get in a car with a total stranger?"

The man forced a smile. "My name's John . . . and I've got a job to do, and that job is to take you shopping. You may not want to go, but understand this. Rico's not as cruel as some, but he has a temper. You should do as he says."

"My dad needs back surgery. Rico's pulled some strings and Dad's getting the surgery he needs."

John leaned on the table and gave Charlie a stern look. "I can guarantee you, if he got the surgery scheduled, he can have it cancelled. Are you willing to let one date stop your dad from getting this operation?"

"No."

"Then let's go."

The shopping didn't take long. Charlie picked out some clothes and went to the beauty parlor while her bodyguard, John, waited in the car. She bought the most conservative items she could find, and, as the note instructed, she bought three complete outfits.

Three hours later they were on their way back to Allie's apartment. John parked the car and spoke. "So you'll know, I'll be waiting here. Put away the things you bought and get dressed. You can kill about an hour, then come back down ready for your date."

"Do you have a picture of this man? How am I supposed to know him when I see him?" Charlie looked at John.

"You'll get with the driver at the club, and then head over to pick up your date. I've never seen him, but I know he's close to fifty; he's a politician and you're to be window dressing.

You won't speak unless you're spoken to, smile a lot, seem as if you're having a great time. If anyone asks where you met, tell them you met at a dinner party last month."

Charlie nodded and when the car stopped, she reached for the door handle. John took her wrist and when she met his gaze he spoke. "I want you back in this car no later than quarter after six."

"I won't be late." Charlie waited for him to turn loose. She ignored the urge to run and with as much grace as she could muster, climbed from the car and crossed the street walking up the stairs.

She unlocked the door, laid her things on the sofa and sank down into the chair, wondering what she was getting into. She sighed, hoping she was doing the right thing.

Around six she was walking toward the door to leave when Allie came out of her room, still wearing her robe from her evening shower.

"Where in the world are you going?" Allie walked over looking at Charlie. "Wow, that's a fine looking dress."

"I don't have much time to explain. I left you a note. The long and short of it is . . . I'm working for Rico tonight. He's blackmailing me into going out on a date with some soon-to-be politician."

"What? Why you? I could have done that. What's he paying you?"

"I don't know. I'm not doing this for the money. It's so my dad can get the surgery he needs. I have to do this. I wish he did want you instead of me."

"I don't understand. Why would he do this? I'm supposed to be his best girl."

"Allie . . . he's a pimp. He doesn't care about you. When are you going to understand that he does what he does to make money? It's not because he cares for you." Charlie shook her head and opened the door. "I'm sorry; I have to go."

With this Charlie headed out the door, a few tears trying to sting her eyes. She didn't want her make-up to be smudged so she forced herself not to cry, but to be angry. It was really hard to pray but she tried. She couldn't understand why she was in this situation.

All she'd ever wanted was to live a normal life, go to church and see her family saved. Why did she have to go through such lengths to have what some people took for granted? Pushing these thoughts out of her mind, she climbed into the front seat of the car and looked at John. "I'm ready to go. Let's get this over with."

"Yes Ma'am. You look great. Rico sure can pick 'em."

Charlie knew better than to speak at that moment. She closed her eyes and steadied herself for what was going to happen. She began to pray for guidance and strength. Opening her eyes, she looked ahead to the street and let out a sigh.

She didn't want to know what she'd do if push came to shove. She loved her dad more than words could say, but how far would she be willing to go for him to get the help he needed?

Chapter 11
The Oasis

Angel climbed into his car and started to put his seatbelt on, then stopped. Sometimes it was the little things that messed you up. Being safety conscious wouldn't be something a rough bodyguard would think of.

Sitting at the red light, Angel glanced at his watch. He'd be at The Oasis in ten minutes if traffic kept moving along. Two hours earlier he'd informed Joe he'd be working for Rico later that night.

Angel exhaled a deep breath. Finally, after six long weeks, he'd worked his way into meeting Rico. Escorting a couple to a fancy party didn't sound like much, but it would get him in the door. He wondered if this was all a waste of time, but he couldn't turn down the position.

He dressed the part, wearing a dark blue suit, a white shirt and a dark blue tie. He wore shiny dress shoes and his brown hair was pulled back in a ponytail.

Angel pressed the brake as he turned into the drive of The Oasis. He spotted Juan running out to meet him. The kid was barely sixteen and Angel hated to see him getting mixed up with this crowd.

He'd met Juan on the streets four weeks ago. Angel liked the kid a lot. He worked doing odd jobs for Rico, making money to help keep a roof over his family's head. Several times Angel wanted to warn the kid he was working for the wrong man.

Angel slowed the car as the kid flagged him down. Juan wanted something, so he stopped the car and climbed out leaving the door ajar.

"You won't need your ride tonight. Rico's rented a white limo. He wants to show off to this hot shot. The guy's gonna' run for senator or something and Rico wants to grease him up."

Angel handed Juan the keys to the car. "I guess it's a stretch?"

"You bet. It's out back. It's a beauty. I went down with John when he picked it up. He let me drive it for a few blocks. I'll bring it out in a bit. Go on in, the girl's here already."

"What girl?"

"The date Rico's arranged for this rich dude. She's a real beauty. She's got her red hair all pulled up in tight curls."

"Red head?"

"Yeah. She looks like a million bucks. She's got this fancy dress on. John brought her in just before we went down to get the car."

"Is she one of Rico's girls?"

"Nooo. This one's clean. I can tell. She's so nervous. John took her shopping this evening. He said he even had to take her out to get her hair fixed."

"I bet he liked that."

"He said he'd baby sat her for half the day."

"This date must really be important."

"It is, but I don't know why he got a girl with a guy's name. He should call her something else." Juan shook his head, with a disgusted look on his face as he slid into Angel's car. "I mean, what guy wants to kiss a girl named Charlie."

Angel stopped in his tracks and turned, looking at Juan. "Did you say Charlie?"

"Yeah, what kind of name is that for a girl? Listen, you better go on in. Rico wants to give you two the same spiel. She's at the bar. Go on. I'll park your car out back."

"Alright," Angel turned walking inside. He didn't know what was going on, or why his pretty nurse was working for

Rico. He knew one thing; if Rico was involved, it couldn't be a good thing for Charlie.

Angel walked into the club. He didn't need any help finding Rico. He knew what the man looked like. He moved closer to where his new employer and the young lady stood. Rico held to the girl's arm while talking to her in a soft voice. Angel heard only the last few words of their conversation.

"You make this evening a success and we'll call that deal with your dad done."

Angel didn't approach, but when Rico acknowledged him with a nod, he stepped forward and spoke. "I'm your new driver Angel Blackwell." Angel glanced to the young woman and did his best to hide the fact that he'd met her before.

"Well, you don't look like an Angel!" Rico laughed, "I think you and Charlie here . . . should . . . hey I know what you are." Rico laughed a booming laugh. "You're Charlie's Angel."

"I remember that show." Angel forced a smile.

"Me too. All those babes. I wouldn't mind getting arrested by those girls." Rico said with a grin. Angel smiled at the remark and waited for the man to speak. "Charlie, I have a few business matters I need to discuss with Angel. You have a seat at the bar."

*****

Happy to get away from Rico, Charlie moved to a barstool and sat down. Using the mirror behind the bar, she looked at the man named Angel. Did he recognize her? She knew who he was. When did he start working for Rico? Did he lie to her? Maybe he'd worked for Rico all along.

She recalled the way he looked and found it hard to believe that he would let someone beat him up so he could spy on her. As she studied him, she could see the cut on his face was still visible.

"Hey, honey. I love that dress," a strange voice called. Charlie turned and did a double take. *Was that a man?* The look on her face said it all, and the person smiled at her.

"I know I make a nice-looking woman, but I can't do a thing with this voice."

"Yes, it is deep." Charlie was at a loss for words. She forced a smile. The person was wearing a long blond wig and looked like a woman. Charlie knew people like this existed, but she never thought she'd meet one of them.

"Are you one of Rico's new *Barbie's?*"

"I'm new, but I'm not sure what you're talking about."

"Well, his Barbie dolls is something new he came up with. They're part of an escort service he's starting, but they don't . . . you know . . . hook."

"Well, I guess that's me. I'm here for a date."

"Sure nice to meet you. They call me Rosie."

"My name's Charlie." Rosie held out his hand and they shook hands. The man wasn't feminine; no soft hands, and he didn't look like a woman.

"You can call me Sam. That's my real name."

"Good, cause you don't look like a Rosie."

Sam laughed and shook his head no. "I hate this job but it pays good."

"This is your job?"

"Yeah, I know. It's a crazy job, but it pays the bills. I'm going to college so I need all the money I can get. The tips are great and though I'm not gay . . ."

"You're not gay?"

"No! It would be easier if I were."

Charlie shook her head in wonder. She didn't want to think about it. She couldn't wait to get back to her life and get out of this Oz-like place.

"I know. It's crazy," Sam shrugged, "but when you need money you do what you have to. None of my regular crowd would ever come here, so they have no clue. They know I have a job that keeps me busy, and that it pays good."

"Do you sleep with men?" Charlie leaned forward keeping her tone low.

Sam shook his head, a look of disgust on his face. "No way. I'm a dancer. A good one, but I stay on the stage. I don't go out into the audience."

"Why don't you dance for women, if you like women?"

"Women come to the club, too. You'd be surprised at how they wine and dine me, trying to turn me back to women."

Charlie couldn't help but smile at this comment. "So, you make money off the women who want you to become straight, and money off the men who think you're gay. I guess you do get a lot of tips.

"Honey, you have no idea," Sam shook his head, "Sorry, it's hard to talk like Sam when I'm dressed like Rosie. I need to head out and go finish my wigs. I'll be a red head later; one of the girls is curling my wig."

Charlie raised a brow and nodded her head, looking at Sam. The man gave her a smile and picked up a bottle of water. "I know it's a strange life, but I make great money. I'll more than likely pay my way through college doing this."

"But is it worth it?"

"I think so. I don't sleep with anyone; I don't do drugs. Why, I don't even drink. It's a job. People take me as I am. Some day I'll have a better job and I hope to look back on this and laugh."

With this comment, Sam went to curl his wigs. *What a strange occupation.* Charlie shook her head; it was a little better than what Allie did for a living. Still, Charlie knew flipping burgers or working in a restaurant would be a more stable position.

There was too much temptation in this job to do the wrong thing or go down the wrong path.

Charlie smiled as she watched Sam walk away. Finally, she could see why God brought her to this place. There were so many people around that needed God in their lives.

Did He send her here to show someone there were other roads to choose from? At first she felt angry with God for putting her in this situation, but as she watched Sam walk away, she realized what a great opportunity this could be.

Now, what would she do? Run because she was afraid of her own limitations, or would she dive in and try to be a light in a dark world?

Whatever she chose, she was going to pray harder and start reading her Bible more, so when the time came she'd be armed and ready to step out on her faith.

Chapter 12
Born Again

Angel stood outside the Oasis, waiting by the limousine. Rico asked him to go outside while he spoke to Charlie. When she stepped out five minutes later, he opened the door and she slipped into the back seat, not giving him a second glance. If she recognized him, it wasn't showing.

He closed the door and moved around to the front of the vehicle, getting in behind the wheel. The window partition was down, so he stole glances at his passenger. She looked beautiful, but his mind went back to the facts.

Juan's words came floating back; he talked about how John had baby sat Charlie and took her out shopping. As he looked at her red hair pulled up in a stylish way, he wondered why was she here.

When they were stopped at a red light Angel gave a quick glance over his shoulder. "I guess you remember me?"

"Yes. I know who you are."

Angel positioned the mirror that allowed him to see his passengers. He stole glances at Charlie as he drove. "I don't think we should tell Rico we've met."

"Why? Do you think he would care?"

"Who knows with Rico? Just in case, I don't want to mess things up. I need this job."

"I won't mention it."

Charlie's tone was short and Angel looked up. He could see anger in those pretty eyes, and he wondered if it was directed at him. He let the silence hang in the air for a moment before he spoke.

"I'm not sure why, but you seem miffed. Did I do something?"

Charlie met Angel's gaze in the small mirror; she hesitated and then spoke. "I thought you told me you didn't work for Rico."

Angel nodded. "That's what I said. I didn't; this is my first job with the man."

"So you haven't worked for him, before today?"

"No. I must admit I wanted to work for him, but I didn't have the job secured then."

Charlie broke off the eye contact and looked out the window. "I don't know why so many people want to work for that man. He can be cruel."

"True, but I could ask you the same question. If you dislike him so much, then why are you here?"

The look Angel saw on Charlie's face made him regret the question. She didn't answer for a few moments. She kept her gaze out the window, but finally she spoke. "This is just temporary."

"I see." Angel wanted to ask more, but he didn't want to seem too nosey. He was trying to think of something to say when she spoke again.

"So you hired on as a driver?"

"For now. I hope to move up." This comment won him a dirty look, and Angel had to look down to hide the smile on his face.

Seconds later the phone rang interrupting their conversation. Angel answered his cell; it was Rico. He listened for a moment and then pulled the car into a nearby mini-mall. He glanced in the mirror at the young woman while listening to Rico.

"I see. I'm not far from there. I can pick him up."

Angel took out a pen and jotted down some directions and then wrapped up the conversation with Rico. He pushed the phone back inside his jacket and turned in the seat looking at Charlie, "We have a change of plans."

"What do you mean?"

Angel gestured the small piece of paper in her direction. "I hope you didn't have your heart set on going out?"

Charlie sat up leaning forward. "Why? What happened?"

"Was this a blind date?" Angel rested his arm on the back seat.

"Kind of."

"So you'd never met this guy?"

"No."

"Well that explains it." Angel started to turn in the seat but Charlie leaned forward more, and put her hand on his arm.

"Explains what?" Charlie's brow furrowed.

Angel smiled. "It explains how this guy could stand you up. Any man that had ever met you wouldn't dare do that."

Charlie flashed Angel a shy smile, and then looked away as she leaned back in her seat. "I thought I heard you say we're picking someone up."

"I did and we are. Rico's dad." Angel glanced at the directions. "We're to pick him up, take him to his new apartment, and see he gets settled in."

"Really?"

Charlie's voice sounded so relieved that Angel turned to face her. "You don't sound disappointed."

"I'm not. I didn't want to go on this date, but I didn't have a choice."

Angel could see Charlie regretted the last part of that statement. "Rico can be persuasive."

"I shouldn't have said that."

"Don't worry. I won't mention you were delighted his plans fell through, but I'm not sure taking care of his dad will be any better. You know what they say about little apples."

"Yes, they don't fall far from the tree."

Angel turned and put the car into drive. "I heard a rumor that Jerry got religion in jail. Maybe he'll be a changed man."

When they arrived at the airport to pick up Jerry, Angel leaned over the back of the seat and looked at his pretty passenger. She was wearing a long red dress that was elegant yet modest. Her hair was swept up in a classy 'do with a few soft ringlets cascading around her face and neck.

"Since there didn't seem to be any time earlier for a proper introduction, here goes. My name's Angelo, but I prefer Angel."

"Call me Charlie." She reached her hand out he took it, held it for a brief moment then let go.

"I'll go round up Jerry. You're a bit over dressed to be wandering around the airport, so if you don't mind you can stay in the car."

"Oh, I don't mind,"

"Good. It shouldn't take long."

Angel went in and waited by the counter. A few minutes later a man came walking up. He immediately stuck out his hand and gave Angel a firm shake. "Jerry DeLusa here. Did Rico send you?"

"Yes, sir. The car's waiting outside."

"Good. I'm ready to start my new life."

"Ready when you are, sir."

"Then let's go."

"I can get your bags, sir."

"This is all I have. You don't have to worry about much luggage when you've just left Camp Waterport Correctional Facility."

"I suppose not." Angel shrugged.

"Nope. Nothing in here but a few shirts and two Bibles."

"I guess the rumors about you finding religion in prison are true."

"Oh yes, son, I'm a changed man! They call it getting 'born again.' Nothing like it! You'll have to try it. I never understood what life was about until I found Jesus."

Angel nodded as he opened the back door of the car. Jerry took one look inside, shut the door and looked at Angel, "I hope my son didn't send her for me. I don't do those kinds of things anymore."

"No, sir," Angel grappled for words. "I was taking her to a party and her date cancelled. She's only along for the ride."

"Good to know, son." Jerry stated and once again Angel opened the door and Jerry slid in to sit beside Charlie.

"Jerry DeLusa. Nice to meet you," Jerry held out his hand.

"Charlie Anderson. Nice to meet you, sir."

*****

After the driver pulled out onto the highway, Jerry turned and looked at the young woman by his side. What was his son into now? He turned in the seat and studied the woman for a moment before speaking.

"So, do you work for my son, Rico?"

"Yes, only on a temporary basis."

"Well that's good. If he hasn't changed his ways since I last saw him, I'm sure he has you up to no good." The girl's brow furrowed and she smiled.

"That's a strange comment for a man to make about his son."

"I guess it is, but tell me, am I right?"

The girl didn't have to speak; he could guess from her expression what her answer would be. Jerry nodded, "I see he's following in my footsteps. I've learned so much over the last few weeks. I'm going to have to make some big changes. My son and I need to get out of the business of hurting folks and get into the business of saving their souls."

"Wow! It sounds like you have changed."

"Yes, young lady, I have. There's nothing like serving God, and being a Christian. It gives you a feeling that words can't describe. To be honest, this is all new to me, but I must say that it helps to read God's word daily. Do you have a Bible?"

"Yes, sir, I do."

"Good." Jerry turned to face the young woman. "I just started reading in Acts where the apostles prayed down the Holy Spirit, and I'm so intrigued. I can't wait to learn more."

"Some people think you have to pray to be filled with the Spirit, others think you get it automatically when you get saved."

"Really, that's so fascinating." Jerry smiled and all the way to the apartment they chatted about the Bible and church. Jerry found it mesmerizing that the young woman before him was baptized in a creek, at the age of ten. He also informed her he wanted to talk to her more. "Do you think you can help me find a good church?"

"Yes, sir. I just started going to a small church in K-town. I think you'd like it."

"Good. When are the next services?"

"This Saturday."

"Great. Will you still be working for Rico? If not, I'll pay you to take me."

"I don't know if I'll be working for him or not."

"I'll talk to him about it. Why don't I do that now? Angel, drive us to The Oasis. I might as well face my son. No use in putting it off any longer."

*****

"Yes, sir." Angel wasn't sure what Rico was going to say about all of this, or what Jerry was going to do when he found out his son was now in the prostitution business.

Chapter 13
New Beginnings

Angel drove to the club, eavesdropping on Jerry and Charlie as they talked about church and Bible study. They were still chatting when he parked the car. They were getting along well and it seemed that Jerry *had* changed.

Getting out of the vehicle, Angel held open the door. Charlie followed Jerry into the club through the back entrance. Jerry then sent Charlie and Angel to the bar so he could have a few minutes alone with his son.

The office door closed and Angel led Charlie to a booth, instead of the bar, where they could talk. Once seated, he leaned forward in confidence.

"This isn't going to go over well. I can see trouble coming."

"I don't think so either. Jerry's still on a high from being saved, but he's not going to sway Rico as easily as he thinks."

"I don't think he'll sway him at all."

"What about Jerry? What if he wants to start running things again? Can he?"

"That's a good question," Angel straightened and gestured with his hand. "Jerry's been in jail a while and I'm not sure how much power Rico's going to relinquish. I couldn't help but overhear some of the things Jerry said. I don't see his old cronies turning things over to a man who's going to destroy their way of life."

"I think you're right."

Angel couldn't help but notice Charlie's scrutiny of his ponytail; he shook his head and removed the band holding his hair back. His hair wasn't long, but Rico wanted him to cut it, or pull it back, for the fancy party he was supposed to attend.

"I hate that thing," Angel tossed down the band and ran his fingers through his hair, "but I wasn't about to cut my hair for one night."

"It didn't suit you," Charlie smiled looking away.

Angel knew she was embarrassed for staring, but he didn't mind. He looked at her and commented, trying to make her feel at ease.

"I like it when you wear your hair down, too." This comment won him a smile.

"Thanks. I wouldn't wear mine like this either," Charlie gestured. "I couldn't do it myself, and I wouldn't have the money to keep it fixed this way."

The conversation slowed and after a moment Angel changed the subject. "You and Jerry really hit it off. Tell me, how did you get mixed up with Rico? I didn't mean to eavesdrop, but it was hard not to listen."

"I can see now this whole thing with Rico might end on a good note, but at first it didn't look promising. Rico saw me at a diner and thought I'd be perfect for this date. He wouldn't leave me alone."

"He can be persuasive. He's a lot like Jerry. That's one reason he kept moving ahead when Jerry went to jail."

"What happened to the business then?" Charlie glanced toward Rico's office as she waited for Angel to answer. When Angel spoke, she looked back.

"Jerry signed everything over to Rico years before he went to jail. He can get money from Rico by just asking, but the running of the business? I'm not so sure about that."

"Well, you heard him. He wants to build shelters for the homeless and help get the women off the streets. Rico wants to ignore the homeless and make money using those same women."

"I know. It's not going to go well."

As if on cue, Jerry came walking out of the office and he didn't look happy. He went to the bar and sat down. Charlie and Angel exchanged a glance and then Charlie spoke. "I hope he doesn't get angry and fall off the wagon."

Angel shrugged. "I don't know if he ever drank. But his son may cause him to *start* drinking."

*****

Charlie rose and walked to the bar; she could easily see Jerry's anger. Praying before she spoke would help. Getting back into her old routine of a good prayer life was like any other task; it required effort.

She never turned her back on God during her time of troubles, but she lost some of her good habits. After saying a quick prayer, she put her hand on Jerry's shoulder before speaking.

"I know it seems like he won't change right now, but you can't give up. You have to work on him little by little."

Jerry let out a sigh. "I know. I can't help but think that I made him what he is today. I led him down this road, and I feel like there's nothing I can do to stop him or turn him around."

"Well, I'm not going to give you some apple pie story that everything will work out fine. But I will tell you that things won't change if you give up. There will be times, like this, where you're so frustrated you don't know what to do."

"You're right. I want to give up."

"That's the devil talking to you."

Jerry turned, a look of disbelief on his face. "You mean he still talks to me? I'm saved now."

"Oh, yes. He's going to talk to you more now than he ever did. Back then you were no threat to him. He may have talked to you now and then before you got saved, trying to get you to do this or that. But let me tell you, he's really going to work on you now. He'll try to get you to give up and turn back."

"I guess you're right. I'm so new at this I need someone like you to keep me in line."

"That's why it's so important to go to church and Bible study. It's why we need to surround ourselves with Christian friends. When we get down or discouraged, we can turn to them for guidance and encouragement."

"I'll remember that. But there's so much to learn, and I've wasted so much of my life doing the wrong things."

"We all waste time, but we have to learn from those mistakes and pick ourselves up and go on."

"What do you think I should do about Rico? He doesn't want to even hear my suggestions."

"Right now there's not a lot you can do. But there's no reason you can't start showing him you're serious. You made lots of money and made things happen when you were sinning."

"True, but I lied, cheated and stole from people; I can't do that now."

"I know, but you have talents and ideas and now you'll want to use them for God. You can do this. I know you can. You have the excitement of a new love for Jesus in your heart, and you need to keep it alive and work while it's day."

Jerry smiled. "I read that a few days ago."

"Reading the Bible is one of the most important things we can do. If you can't read all the time, there's other ways. You can get the Bible on CD or on an MP3 player. Get that Word in your heart so when you need it to be there, it will be."

"How can you be so smart and be so young?"

Charlie laughed, "I don't know as much as I should."

"Well, you know more than I do. I'm glad you were working for Rico, but I'm going to steal you away. You're going to be working for me now, if you want to."

"Doing what? I don't have much experience."

"You got the kind of expertise I'm looking for. If you're willing, I'll hire you as my personal assistant. You'll run errands for me; help me find these Bible studies and services to go to. I always did have people around me advising me and helping me in my business. Now I'm going to do the same thing, but this time I'm going to be doing *His* business."

With this, Jerry pointed up to the ceiling and smiled at Charlie. "I want you to have Angel take you home so you can pack your bags. You're moving in with me."

"What?" Charlie laughed.

"You heard me right. I need you close by. The apartment Rico rented has at least two bedrooms. One of them is yours. Angel can take you home, help you pack, and you can move in before the night's over."

"Are you sure that's what you want?"

"Yes, I'm certain."

"I guess it would be okay." Jerry could tell Charlie seemed unsure.

"It won't be a permanent situation, but for now it will do. Also, just so you'll know. You don't have to worry about me; I'm not going to try any hanky-panky stuff." Jerry could see Charlie relax some so he went on.

"You're my new assistant. I'm looking for a woman, but I want a woman my age. I won't be doing anything I shouldn't. You'll be safe with me."

"I suppose I could give it a try."

"Why, sure you can."

"What about Rico?"

"I may not have control of the business yet, but he's still my son. You let me worry about Rico."

✳✳✳✳✳

Jerry motioned and Angel rose, moving to the bar. Jerry told Angel he would be in need of his services. The man listened, and when he glanced at Rico's office, Jerry spoke.

"I'll tell you like I told Charlie. Let me worry about Rico."

"Yes, sir." Angel agreed, and Jerry went on with his instructions.

"I want you to take Charlie home, help her get packed, and then take her on to my apartment. If she needs help carrying anything, be sure and make yourself useful."

"Yes, sir. I will."

"Also, stay with her at the apartment until I get there." Jerry took out his wallet and handed Angel two hundred dollars. "If she tells you she needs anything, see to it that she gets it."

Angel took the money, stuffed it into his pocket. "Will do, sir."

"That's too much . . ." Charlie tried to reply but Jerry shook his head.

"I've got a lot planned and I want it done right. You let me worry about the expenses. I may be saved, but I still know how to pour out a little wrath of my own."

"You'll hear no arguments from me," Angel replied. Jerry glanced at Charlie and raised a brow.

Charlie nodded and lifted her hands in defeat, saying. "You're the boss."

"Good. Now you two go on. I'll inform Rico that things around here are going to be changing, whether he likes it or not."

Chapter 14
Roommates

Charlie and Angel were quiet on the ride to Allie's apartment. Since the limo belonged to Rico, they were now riding in Angel's car. Charlie felt, for the first time in a while, that she was starting down the right path.

She finally understood what brought her to this place, and it gave her a peaceful feeling for a change. Talking to Jerry renewed her faith, and she prayed that somehow she'd do what the Lord wanted her to do.

Could she help Allie find her way, or give Jerry the boost he needed or maybe help Rico find the Lord? Any or all of them was a possibility.

"You're being too quiet." Angel said breaking the silence.

"I'm thinking and praying." Charlie turned in the seat, looking at the young man that had abruptly come into her life. "Do you ever pray, Angel?"

"I suppose we all pray now and then. When I was young Mom taught me the . . . 'Now I lay me down to sleep' prayer."

"I ask the Lord my soul to keep. If I should die before I wake, I ask the Lord my soul to take," Charlie finished the thought.

"Yeah, that's it. I don't remember when I stopped saying it. But I did."

"Sometimes we can get complacent, especially if we feel we've reached some spot we can't get past. But then, out of the dark, a light appears and we see God is still there, waiting for us to realize we need Him all over again."

*****

Angel looked at Charlie and found her looking back. He wondered if she found him attractive or did she only want to save his soul? When she spoke, he decided it was the latter.

"That night I found you in the bushes, I started praying for you."

Angel laughed, "Why?"

"I don't know. I guess I felt sorry for you. I was afraid those guys would come back for you."

"Maybe your prayers worked; they didn't come back. I guess I owe you. You can pray for me anytime. My work can be dangerous."

"Well, this should be a good night then. I don't pose much of a threat to you."

"I don't know about that." Angel flashed Charlie a smile. "One can never be too careful around a beautiful woman."

"Thanks, though I never thought of myself as beautiful."

Charlie's comment brought a laugh from Angel. "Don't they have mirrors where you come from?"

Charlie gave Angel a shy smile. "I guess I was too busy to take the time to look."

"I would never be that busy." Angel glanced back. He could feel electricity stirring between them. That wasn't necessarily a good thing. He needed to keep his mind on getting Rico, not on the beauty sitting beside him.

Turning his attention back to the road, he made the last right turn and soon they were on Komensky Avenue. They got out of the car and he thought Charlie looked beautiful in the moonlight wearing that red dress.

They headed toward the apartment and he felt a twinge as he walked past the place where the muggers dumped him that night, but it left when Charlie gently touched his hand.

"Don't think about that night. I found you."

Angel smiled and thought that phrase sounded like something out of one of those corny love stories his mother used to read. But for some reason, it didn't feel corny. He reminded himself he wasn't on a date; he was working, and when she moved her hand from his, they walked into the building.

*****

When Charlie opened the door, she saw Allie sitting on the couch. Her roommate looked angry and it was obvious Allie knew Charlie was leaving.

"I just got off the phone with Rico," Allie snapped.

"I guessed as much." Charlie felt Angel step closer and he placed his hands on her waist.

"I see you brought that dirty scoundrel with you, that spy for Rico."

"Angel's not a spy. Neither of us work for Rico now."

"I don't care who he is, or what the two of you do. I want the both of you out of my apartment," Allie stood up quickly.

"What's wrong, Allie?" Charlie started to move forward, but Angel pulled her back and spoke in a low tone.

"She's too angry; don't approach her."

Allie shook her head, pacing, before turning to look at Charlie. "I trusted you. I took you into my home and now this. You threw yourself at Rico and stole this job right out from under me. How could you do that to me?"

"What? I didn't know anything about this. I didn't want this job. Rico blackmailed me into doing it."

"Sure he did!" Allie dismissed Charlie with a look and turned her attention to Angel, pointing her finger at the two of them. "Get her and her junk out of here. NOW!"

Allie stomped off to her room, slamming the door closed as Charlie stood by, tears brimming in her eyes. She looked at her belongings stuffed into boxes; some of her clothes still on the hangers. She wanted to go after her friend, to explain. Was this part of God's plan? Did Allie have to feel betrayed?

Charlie took one step toward Allie's door, but felt Angel's steady hands on her waist.

"We should go. You can talk to her another time. She's not in any mood to deal with this now."

"I know." Charlie moved to pick up a few boxes and Angel carried the rest. She took one look around her temporary home and turned to go.

Charlie managed to hold off the tears until her things were packed in the trunk. The darkness of the streets helped to hide her pain. She thought of Allie as a sister. She never meant to hurt her.

How in the world could she convince Allie she didn't go behind her back? How could she prove it? She said a prayer and the tears began to fall harder. Charlie placed her hand over her lips and closed her eyes, giving her troubles to God and praying that the progress Allie had made would not be lost.

*****

Angel didn't look in Charlie's direction, but he knew she was crying. He wanted to reach out to her in some way but they barely knew each other. There was a spark, which in time could turn into something, but should he pursue it?

Rain started to fall lightly, but by the time he pulled into the parking garage, it stopped. He found a parking space, took out the key to the apartment, and headed up to Jerry's new home. With both of them carrying boxes, one trip did it. When Angel put the key into the lock, his police training kicked in.

"Stay here at the door. I need to make sure the place is secure. After all, we are dealing with Jerry DeLusa. It's hard to tell who might want to leave him a surprise."

"I guess you're right." Charlie's soft tone took Angel off guard and he glanced back. He didn't see any tears now.

Charlie stayed at the door until he returned. Angel noticed her studying his gun as he placed it in the holster. He could tell she wanted to ask something so he looked at her, and waited.

"Do you have a permit for that?" Her tone seemed unconcerned, so he couldn't tell if she was teasing. He smiled and shrugged.

"What do you think?"

"I doubt it."

Angel smiled. "You don't seem all that upset. Are you used to strange men brandishing guns at the drop of a hat?"

Charlie shook her head no. "Not really, but these last few months, I just take it as it comes, and try to make it through the day."

She gave him a quick smile and walked past him. Angel was surprised at her comments. For the first time, he wondered what she would think if she found out he was a cop, working undercover. Would that make her like him more or less? One could never tell when it came to women.

*****

Charlie looked over the apartment, amazed by it's size and beauty. As she went from room to room, she thought of Allie. Did Allie know about this job with Jerry, or was she only angry about the blind date. A sigh escaped Charlie from deep within.

Charlie thanked the Lord again. She didn't know why the guy canceled; she didn't really care. She wondered would it be over, or would Rico set up another date.

As she walked through the apartment looking around she prayed for Allie. She prayed her anger would subside and that soon she would listen to reason. She turned to Angel; he was looking over one of the phones.

"This place is huge! Look at this kitchen."

"Yeah, it's okay."

Charlie knew he wasn't listening. His thoughts were on the phone and the security of the apartment. After a moment, he put down the phone and looked up and spoke.

"What?"

"Is your place this nice?"

"No, it's not. But I'm not the one moving in. I guess I'm not as impressed as you. Come on, lets see if we can find the room you'll be staying in."

Angel put his hands on her shoulders and pushed her towards a room next to the kitchen.

Charlie glanced over her shoulder as she put her hand on the doorknob. "Go on in. This is the smaller of the two rooms. I'm sure it's yours."

She opened the door, peeping in at first, and then pushed the door open wide. "Woooowwww!!! Charlie smiled as she moved into the room and began to look around. "This is some apartment. I have my own personal bathroom!"

*****

"So it seems." Angel leaned on the doorway, then stepped back as she walked past him into the kitchen. He smiled. It was a joy to watch her moving around the room, ooing or ahhing over some little thing he would never notice.

She is beautiful. Angel smiled as Charlie walked out to stand on the terrace.

"How can he afford something like this? Wasn't he in jail?" Charlie turned, the red dress sparkling in the moonlight. She shivered and stepped back inside. Angel followed Charlie, speaking as she walked past him again.

"Jerry went to jail for selling drugs. They couldn't take all of his money. He's a smart man; he signed most everything over to Rico years ago. I guess he knew some day he'd go to jail for something."

"Well, I think he learned his lesson." Charlie called over her shoulder.

"I think he's a changed man. It's yet to be seen if he's learned his lesson."

"Oh, you can bet I've learned my lesson!" Jerry spoke with amusement in his tone. Angel spun around, realizing he'd let his guard down.

"I didn't hear you come in." Angel's tone conveyed his irritation for being caught off guard.

"I noticed," Jerry said grinning. "You were admiring the view." He gave Angel a nudge in the shoulder as he came to stand by him. "Can't say I blame you. I would have chased after her when I was your age."

Angel knew Charlie was in the bathroom again and couldn't hear what they were saying, so he looked at the man and shook his head.

"I'm not sure she's my type. She's a Bible thumper."

"Son, that's the best kind. You'll never go wrong by finding a woman who'll pray with you and for you. That's exactly what I'm looking for in a woman."

"You're in the market, too?"

"Yes. But this time, it'll be for love." Both men stopped talking as Charlie came out and spoke.

"I don't know if I can stay here or not. This place has to be expensive."

"Sure you can. You won't have to pay the bill." Jerry laughed, thinking he'd made a joke, so Angel laughed too.

"I know, but I can't imagine what rent would be on a place like this."

"You're right about the cost. We won't be staying here long. We'll downgrade as soon as we can. I won't have access to the kind of money I used to, so I must spend what I have wisely."

*****

Charlie looked at the man and nodded. It was strange hearing him say *we* like they were married, and she couldn't help but wonder how much he'd changed. She glanced at Angel, then around the room.

She wanted to bring up the subject, but didn't know how. She started to speak, but didn't. Instead she glanced over her shoulder to her bedroom. How could she tell Jerry she'd feel uncomfortable staying in this apartment with just the two of them?

"I think I've overlooked a few things," Jerry stated. He turned to Angel and hit him on the arm with the back of his hand. "I think you should stay here for a few nights, camp out on the couch. I don't know if anyone has anything against me, but I'll feel safer with you here. Does that suit you?"

Charlie knew the question was directed her way. She smiled and nodded. "I think it's a good idea." She didn't say the word *chaperon*, but it's what she was thinking.

"Then it's settled. Angel, for now you're my new bodyguard slash driver. For the next couple of weeks, I'll be working with, or against Rico, trying to see what I can do to turn the tables on what he's done. I'll need all the help I can get."

Jerry slipped his shoes off and continued, "Rico won't like the changes I'm going to make, but hopefully, he'll come around sooner or later."

"He might not be the only one who doesn't like the changes." Angel stated and Jerry nodded.

"You could be right. That's enough talk about business. I'm hungry. Angel, will you run out and get us something to eat? Charlie, after you change, see if you can find some flatware and napkins and then figure out what you're going to teach tonight in our first Bible study."

*****

After they'd eaten and cleared the table, Jerry and Charlie sat in the kitchen, Bibles open, having their study. Angel sat on the couch, but he could hear Charlie's lesson on faith. Her beauty and her smile kept him listening.

"I think you could learn more if you would join us, young man."

Angel didn't make Jerry ask twice. He crossed the room and sat down at the table. He didn't have a Bible, and since he was supposed to be this tough guy, he sat down, leaning back sipping on his bottle of beer.

He didn't like to drink on duty, and he hoped Jerry didn't notice it was taking him over two hours to drink one beer.

Charlie picked the subject of faith and Jerry seemed pleased. Angel went to church with his mother in his younger years, but he didn't know a thing about Bible study. They read a lot and jumped from verse to verse. It reminded him of being in class, kind of slow, but interesting at times.

*****

The Bible study lasted about an hour. Jerry said his goodnights after jotting down a few errands for Charlie to take care of the next morning. He then headed off to bed.

The next few minutes were awkward for Charlie. She closed her Bible after marking a couple of places for the next study.

"This is so strange and it happened so fast. Are you used to this kind of stuff?" Charlie asked, keeping her tone low.

"What do you mean? Bible study?" Angel replied. Charlie threw an empty soda can at him, which he caught and sat on the table. "I know what you mean. I'm used to all kinds of situations. It sort of goes with the job."

"I'm not used to people making decisions so quickly. I moved in with Allie because it was my only choice, but this seems odd."

Angel nodded and shrugged. "Take advantage of the situation. You love the apartment. Jerry seems harmless; enjoy yourself."

"I don't know if I can. What if I do something to tick him off and he throws me out as quickly as he invited me to move in?" Angel rose and came to stand beside her. He leaned down close enough to kiss her, but instead smiled.

"Trust me; he'd be an idiot to let you go."

Charlie put Jerry's Bibles in a nearby bookcase. She kept thinking about Angel and wondered why he hadn't tried to kiss her. They'd stood so close, but then he straightened and walked into the kitchen washroom.

She took this time to check for extra pillows and blankets and found all she needed in a hall closet. The apartment was stocked with every daily necessity. It seemed Rico wanted to impress his dad. He'd gone to a lot of trouble getting everything ready. *He must be disappointed to not have things going his way.*

Charlie got the pillows, sheets and a blanket for Angel and laid them on the couch. As she turned around, she almost ran into him. He was standing only inches from her, again.

93

"How did you do that?"

"I guess you were lost in your thoughts."

Slowly, she sighed and nodded, once again feeling let down when he moved away. Was he teasing her? Trying to see if she would make the first move?

Chapter 15
Change and Uncertainty

The morning sun came shining in on Charlie as the smell of bacon floated into her room. *Did Jerry know how to cook?* She glanced at her watch; it was ten till seven.

She showered, dressed in jeans and a green top and headed to the kitchen. Jerry stood at the stove frying bacon and sausage. Four toasts popped out of the toaster as she walked into the room.

Jerry turned, smiling. "Butter those, please."

"Sure." Charlie moved to get the butter. She noticed the blanket and pillows stacked on the end of the couch. "Where's Angel?"

"He stepped out a while ago."

"Funny, I didn't picture him as an early riser." Charlie turned, butter in hand, and Jerry handed her a knife.

"How long have you known Angel?"

"Not long; we run into each other here and there."

"Are you and Angel involved?"

Charlie considered this a personal question, but Jerry kept it straight and to the point so she answered, "Not really."

"What about you and Rico?"

This time she laughed, and shook her head. "Nooo, your son's . . . well, he's not my type."

"So you only work for him?"

Charlie thought for a moment, considering how she should answer. Jerry glanced her way, then back to the frying pan. "I'm not sure what to say. I don't want to upset you."

"Tell me the truth."

Charlie raised a brow and then nodded. "Alright, but it's not pretty, and you're not going to like it." Charlie paused as Jerry glanced her way; he shrugged and she went on.

"Rico found out my dad needed help. He managed some how to cut through the red tape and get my dad scheduled for back surgery. Rico said if I didn't go on a blind date with some up-and-coming senator, that he would cancel the surgery."

Jerry didn't speak. Charlie wondered if she could have told him in a better way. The truth would be hard to hear, no matter how she said it. She glanced over her shoulder, sending up a prayer, wishing he'd never asked. After a long moment Jerry spoke.

"He's only following in the footsteps that I made." Jerry took some of the sausage out of the pan and laid it on a plate. "It's hard looking at yourself in the mirror, through your children. I didn't know he would stoop that low, but I should have expected it."

"Well, maybe you can amend your patterns, show Rico a new way of life. Rico can change, too. Look at your life. Look at how much you've changed. He has to see that."

"You're right. I've changed a lot, but I was brought down low. I'm not sure Rico will change until that happens to him."

"Sometimes we have to see things for ourselves. In the meantime, we can do our best to help him."

Jerry turned, his brow furrowed as he glanced down, and then back, up. "You said *we?* You mean after what he's done to you, you're willing to help?"

"Yes. I have to, and I have to forgive him. Actually, I already did. It's not always easy, but we must try to be like Jesus. If we can't show people love, then we aren't doing something right."

Jerry smiled. "It seems I got out of jail at the right moment. God put you right in front of me and he used Rico to do it."

"I think you're right. A few days ago I felt lost I wondered; what am I doing here. Sometimes God puts us in places where

96

we're out of our element. He's there, waiting for us to turn to Him so He can help us move into the next part of His plan."

"So you think there's a plan for everyone?" Jerry asked as he began to mix up the eggs.

"That's a big question. I think there's something we all can do. The plan is to get as many souls saved as possible. So, yeah, I guess we all have a purpose. Maybe there's one person out there no one can reach but you, or me. We need to live close to God so He can lead us to that person, or to something we must do in order to get the plan moving in the right direction."

"I didn't know getting saved would be so hard." Jerry shook his head as he adjusted the heat under the eggs.

"Well, getting saved is the easy part. It's what comes next that sometimes bogs us down. It's the staying in the Word and knowing God's will. Those things aren't always so easy to do, or figure out."

"That's where I'm at now." Jerry turned to set the eggs on the table. As Charlie poured the juice, the front door opened and Angel walked in.

Angel wore a deep blue shirt that suited his hair and complexion. Charlie raised a brow as he sat down his load and slipped out of his leather jacket. There was something appealing about a man wearing a shoulder holster.

She turned her attention back to breakfast. She didn't want to be caught staring. Angel walked into the kitchen, a box of croissants in his left hand with a bag of decaf balanced on top of the box. Charlie gave Angel a quick smile as she placed the napkins on the table.

"I'm trying to become healthy." Jerry took the coffee from Angel as he moved to the counter to mix his brew.

"You should stop drinking coffee altogether and go to juice." Angel opened the refrigerator door and set a carton of apple juice on the table.

Jerry laughed. "I can't give up everything at once. I've given up lying, cheating and stealing. What can you expect from a mere man?"

"So you've really turned over a new leaf?" Angel also took the milk from the refrigerator setting it down by the juice.

"If that's what you want to call it. I'm born again, saved and washed by the blood of the Lamb."

"You remind me of my sister-in-law." Angel sat down in a chair to the right of Charlie.

"Is she a widow?" Jerry smiled.

"No, her husband is alive and well."

"Oh well, I'll find the right woman soon enough." Jerry sat down and placed the toast in the middle of the table. "Charlie, will you ask the blessing over the food?"

Chapter 16
Adjustments

Charlie found it amazing how things could change in a matter of hours. After breakfast, Jerry handed her a handful of cash and sent her shopping. After changing into a pair of dress slacks and a white pullover, she went to the market to buy some fruit and fresh vegetables.

She also bought a couple of church dresses, and, because Jerry would need some extra income, she picked up a few local papers so she could look over the want ads for her new employer.

She was now in a cab on her way to The Oasis to meet Jerry. She called her mother on her new cell phone, and gave her a few details about her new employer. When the cabby stopped, she paid him, got out and bid him a good day.

She paused at the entrance to the club wondering what kind of mood Rico would be in, since he now knew about Jerry's plans. Charlie doubted he would agree to dismantle the prostitution ring. Jerry's plans to build a center for women who needed help would go against Rico's way of earning money. She knew the two would clash.

Jerry wanted to provide job training for the women while giving them a place to live. She admired his passion for trying to make up for the way he used to live.

The money Jerry would receive from Rico would cover some of his new projects, but he would need a way to make money soon. Jerry said he wanted to work with Rico, not against him.

Charlie knew Jerry hoped Rico would come around to his new way of thinking. He wanted Rico to avoid the consequences of a life of crime.

When Charlie went inside the club, she found Angel and John playing pool. Angel looked toward the side office, but then shook his head, letting her know things weren't going well.

Charlie stepped behind the bar to get a bottle of water, and then joined Angel and John. Angel wasn't winning, but he didn't seem to mind. She felt like she'd known this young man a lot longer than a few days. She gave him a warm smile as she sat on a nearby barstool.

"Come to cheer me on?" Angel asked, and Charlie liked the flirtatious smile he gave her.

"Do you need cheering?"

"He sure does. It's a shame the way he plays." John took his turn and sank the five ball into a corner pocket.

Angel looked at Charlie for sympathy and smiled. "Pool just isn't my game." He then looked across the room and Charlie followed his gaze.

The office door opened and Sam came out. He went to the bar, got something out of the cooler, and then straightened, smiling when he saw Charlie. "Hey, glad to see a friendly face."

Charlie moved from the stool, walked over to Sam, and leaned on the bar. Today Sam wore jeans and a white dress shirt. He looked much better dressed like a man than he did a woman.

"What's going on in there?" Charlie glanced to the office and back to Sam.

"I'm sweating bullets, is what's going on! They asked me to oversee the signing of some papers. I'm a notary, and I've pasted my seal on a few things so far, but it isn't pretty.

"If I'm understanding it right, some of the property was taken by the feds, but most everything was signed over to Rico years ago. They're hashing it all out now. Jerry owns this club and two other places in town."

"So they've come to a few decisions. Are they agreeing on everything?" Charlie asked.

"No Way! Jerry declares he wants to close all the bars down. He wants to turn them into all kinds of things like restaurants, soup kitchens. Rico isn't having any of it, and he's fighting every step of the way.

100

They're going over the papers right now, deciding and declaring which of them gets ownership to what. I don't think Rico really has to relinquish anything to Jerry, if he didn't want to, but I guess some part of him still wants to please his dad. I kind of wish I'd called in sick. I better go. I don't want to get either one of them mad at me. Also, Jerry said no dancing here tonight and no liquor is to be sold. People can play pool and hang out, but that's it."

"I'll tell Angel and John." Charlie said as she watched Sam walk back into the office. She caught a glimpse of Rico leaning forward to sign some papers; his dad sat on the opposite side, behind the desk. Rico tossed down the pen, pushing his fingers into the thick curls of his hair. He didn't look happy.

*****

After hearing Charlie repeat Jerry's orders, Angel stepped outside to speak with Ron, the doorman. Ron snorted, saying he would pass along the word, but it would be devastating for business. Angel walked back to the pool table. He couldn't believe Jerry was going through with his plans. He couldn't help but wonder what this would do to the case.

How could he catch Rico in the act of anything if Jerry closed down all the clubs? Angel returned to the pool table to find John standing a little too close to Charlie to suit him.

A pang of jealousy ran through his being, and he realized he was starting to have feelings for Charlie. He would need to be careful and keep his mind on the case, not his new employer's assistant.

It would be good to find the right woman, settle down and maybe have a couple of kids. But with a wife came responsibilities, and with Charlie, he'd also get a Christian wife. Right now he didn't need the complications this would bring. She'd want him to go to church, be nagging him about this service or that.

He didn't see anything like that happening in the near future. What kind of cop would he be if he were going to church? It would take away his edge. How could you shoot someone if you were full of love and thinking all the time that your next bullet could send someone to meet their eternal maker?

Angel pushed these thoughts to the back of his mind as he always did when they tried to intrude on his daily life. There would be time for that when he grew older. Right now he had a case to work on, and a beautiful girl to flirt with.

"Looks like there'll be a lot of unhappy patrons showing up tonight." Angel picked up his cue stick and looked at the table. However you sliced it, pool was not one of his strong points.

"They'll just find some other place to hang out," John leaned on the cue stick, shaking his head. "I don't like a lot of things that go on around here, but if Jerry thinks he can save the whole world by closing down a few clubs, he's wrong."

"Well, he's trying to do his part." Charlie didn't seem to like John's comment but Angel liked the bit of irritation he heard in her tone. "We all have to follow our heart, and I think for a change, Jerry is listening to his heart instead of his wallet."

"Well, that's a good way to go broke," John's tenor showed irritation also. Angel took this opportunity to win a few points with Charlie. He laid his cue stick down and looked at her.

"I heard rumors about his changes, but I didn't believe it until I saw it. If he can be as productive at being good as he was at being a criminal, he'll have it made."

Even John gave a slight nod to this comment as he walked to the bar. Angel was glad to see him go and stepped in front of Charlie as she sat on the stool. "You look very business-like today."

"I went out and ran a few errands for Jerry."

"He's going to make you earn your money."

"I think so." Charlie glanced to the closed office door.

"I'm supposed to stay here until he's done. Do you want me to call a cab so you can head back to the apartment?"

"No, I think I'll wait a while. I'm kind of hungry. Do you think we can order a pizza?"

Angel nodded, smiling. "I know we can. Pick out a booth and I'll call one in. There's a phonebook behind the bar. What do you like?"

"Anything but anchovies."

Angel made a face. "No worries there. I won't be ordering any of those."

*****

Charlie climbed down from the bar stool and looked around the room. She found a booth in an out-of-the-way corner and sat down. As she watched Angel, she smiled. She liked this man, maybe too much.

He was *so* cute . . . no . . . not cute, a puppy was cute. Angel was extremely attractive. She kept her eyes on him. He went to the bar, picked up the phone and made the call.

A couple of times he glanced her way. She wondered what his intentions were. Would he be interested in anything more than a one-night stand? How did a girl go about finding a man who wanted to be serious, and date, instead of . . .

"Lunch is ordered. They said it wouldn't be long." Angel sat down and Charlie realized she didn't know what to say. Why did he make her so edgy? Did she have the same effect on him? As she raised her gaze to his dark eyes she decided . . . no . . . he wasn't the least on edge.

Charlie rested her hands on top of the table. Angel reached out and took her hand in his. He stayed quiet as he sat drawing a circle on the back of her hand. Finally he spoke.

"How about I ask you a few questions about your personal life? Are you dating anyone special? I don't see an engagement ring."

Charlie knew Angel wanted an excuse to touch her, but she didn't care. She moved her hand, looking at her ring finger, as if thinking. She didn't, however, take her hand from his.

"No one's asked, but I think I'd like married life."

"You think?" Angel met her gaze and laughed, "Don't most women have that part of their life mapped out in *great* detail?"

"I guess so. There is kind of a blueprint, but I see a lot of blank spaces. I'm not sure what to put in some of the slots."

"What kind of man do you see in your future?" Angel raised a brow, giving her a quick smile.

What was he asking? Was he fishing for something or making conversation? Charlie looked at his hands. He opened them, giving her an opportunity to move from his touch.

She bit her lip to keep a smile hidden and used the same move on him. She slipped her hand into his, looking at his ring finger. "I don't see a ring either," she sat drawing an imaginary line on the back of his hand.

"I don't date much, so it's not likely to happen soon." Angel's tone showed no emotion and Charlie wondered if he was stating a fact or giving her a warning.

She looked up and studied him for a brief moment, and then looked back at his hands. She wrapped her right hand around his for a moment before reluctantly pulling it back; she met his gaze when he spoke.

"What kind of man do you see in your future?"

Charlie hesitated and looked into his eyes. "I'm open for suggestions. Do you have someone in mind?"

This made him smile; he even laughed. "You may regret asking. I do have someone in mind. I may be prejudiced, but I think I've found you a good match." He once again moved his hand across the table, but this time instead of taking her hand, he laid his hand on the table palm up.

She looked at the gesture, and then looked into his eyes. He wasn't smiling this time. He was serious, or at least it seemed that way. Was she really thinking about dating someone who worked for Rico? As she began to reach out to him and she placed her hand in his, she realized . . . yes, she was.

*****

Angel could see the hesitation, but Charlie took his hand. He felt relief. She was willing to give him a chance. He mentally chided himself for breaking his own reserve; minutes ago he'd declared her 'off limits.' Still, this boosted his ego. Though he might not be the most reputable person, she was willing to give him a chance . . .

Chapter 17
Unexpected Path

Charlie felt some relief when Angel got up to get the pizza. Should she be thinking about dating him? She recalled seeing Angel slide his gun out of his holster with such ease. Was she being too judgmental? She also recalled how John treated her, following Rico's orders, even when he didn't think it was the right thing to do.

Angel paid for the pizza, picked up two cokes, carried them over to the booth and sat down. A picture of Angel with a beer in his hand flashed through Charlie's mind; another good reason not to date this man, and she spoke before thinking.

"You're drinking a coke, but the other night you drank a beer. Do you drink a lot?" Angel raised a brow and Charlie could see he was curious about her question. She went on with the reason for asking. "My dad drinks now and then. It can turn into a problem, if you let it."

Angel nodded, opening the pizza. "I'll share a secret with you if you promise not to tell Jerry or Rico."

"Sure," Charlie nodded. "You can trust me."

Angel leaned in and smiled. "I'm not a heavy drinker, but in this job people have preconceived notions. I find myself trying to be something I'm not just to impress or confirm something people think of me."

Charlie smiled. "You can be yourself around me. I'll try not to have any predetermined ideas about you."

"That'll be a nice change." Angel picked up her can of soda and opened it. "I don't want you to break a nail."

"Now, who's jumping to conclusions?" Charlie laughed.

Angel smiled and took a bite of pizza. At times that intense gaze intimidated Charlie, but in other ways she liked it. Charlie compared her past love life to Angel's, as best she could. Did he have more than one serious relationship in his past? She bet he did. She worked at the church and at school. She never found much time for the boys. Most young men she found attractive drank and didn't go to church, so she kept to herself.

Angel held her attention from the moment she looked into those dark eyes. His looks matched the kind of man she liked, and down deep she felt something.

She always hated it when people talked about being connected or feeling lightning strike, because she wanted to experience that kind of love. She liked Angel, but she couldn't say it was love at first sight. She felt a desire to know more, an intense attraction, and a basic need to be near him. Did love start with such simple emotions?

Charlie wanted answers. This time she was going to test the waters, step out and see what the possibilities were. She'd discovered in the last few weeks that things weren't always as they seemed. Some paths appeared out of nowhere, unfamiliar and daunting. As she began to walk forward, keeping her light bright within, she found things were changing for the good. If a person was willing to work hard and carry their light so others could see, the possibilities were endless.

Charlie closed the pizza box and looked up to see Sam walking in their direction. He sat down beside of Charlie with a sigh. "Finally, I'm done."

"How are things going?" Charlie asked turning to face Sam.

"Not good. Jerry looks like he wants to hit Rico, but he's trying to be nice. Whatever he's got, religion, born again . . . I can see the change."

"It does change you inside, if you allow it to," Charlie replied, stealing a glance at Angel. He raised a brow as if to say, 'was that directed at me?' She ignored it.

"I never went to church, none of my family did. I never saw any use for it. All they want to do is take your money." Sam shrugged and looked at Angel.

"You better watch." Angel looked at Charlie, "don't get her started. She'll have you repenting before you know it."

Sam laughed and shook his head. "It'll take some hard work to get me to change; Jerry's already trying to convince me to come work for him and quit dancing."

"He offered you a job? That's great!" Charlie smiled.

"Yeah, but I don't know if it can pay as good as dancing."

"It may not," Charlie mused, "but it would be a lot less degrading."

"I guess you got me there," Sam laughed. "I do hate wearing dresses. I don't have the legs for it." With this Sam rose and headed for the door, giving them a wave as he left.

Angel was shaking his head. "That one is *too* weird for me."

"I know." Charlie picked up her cola, but sat it down. "I came from a small town, and a lot of things I've seen in the last few months are just plain crazy."

"You'll find a lot of gays and bi's in this town." Angel added glancing once more at Sam as he walked away.

"He's not either, or at least he says he's not. It's the love of money that keeps him going in the wrong direction."

"Well, you know the old saying, 'The love of money is the root of all evil'."

Charlie leaned back and smiled. "I'm impressed; you got it right. Most people say money is the root of all evil."

"Hey, I'm not a total heathen. My mother quoted quite a few verses to me along the way."

"Good to hear it; maybe some of it soaked in."

"Are you trying to preach at me now?"

"No . . . not yet." Charlie moved out of the booth. "I think you'll know when I start preaching."

"I caught a few things you were tossing my way last night during Bible study." Angel pushed the pizza box to the edge of the table and glanced up.

"Did you now?" Charlie smiled at Angel as he scooted over to the edge of the booth and stood up. He was taller, but not much, and his eyes mocked her. Once again they stood close, but this time he wasn't teasing her. It was as if he was trying to decide what to do.

A part of her wished he would kiss her, but she didn't want him to think she was a pushover. "Will you be joining us tonight when we study?"

"If you ask, I'll think about it." Angel's voice was low and it filled Charlie with apprehension, but it was also making her look forward to the next few days.

"Then consider yourself invited." Charlie didn't give him time to respond as she walked past him, moving toward Jerry. A smile played on her lips. A few weeks ago she would never have thought about thanking God for the recent happenings in her life. But now, as she felt things moving in the right direction, she nodded and gave thanks for this unexpected path she was on.

Chapter 18
The View

Jerry wanted to beat some sense into his son, make him see what a mistake he was making by continuing to break the laws of God and man. He prayed Rico would open his eyes to the truth before it was too late. Jerry held some hope that Rico wanted to do the right thing. After all, he allowed Jerry to take over half of the business. Rico didn't legally have to relinquish any power to Jerry, but out of respect he had.

In time, Jerry wanted to take complete control, but legally he was at Rico's mercy. If he couldn't talk his son into turning everything over to him he was at a loss. The only way he could ever get control back was if Rico went to jail. He'd been sure, years ago, to add the clause if his son went to jail for any reason, all assets would be returned to his name.

The bickering and paperwork drained him. He looked outside at the empty parking lot. A voice in his mind told him he was crazy to close the doors of a club that took in loads of cash. He could do a lot with the income from the clubs.

Jerry knew he couldn't make money from unlawful pursuits, and then turn around and use it for good. He wanted to use his faith. He needed to believe God would help him find ways to help people. He'd ask Charlie to find more Bible verses on faith to help him know he was on the right path.

Jerry looked up as a couple came to the door, chatted with Ron and then turned to go. This gave him an idea. He could have a club, one with dancing and music, but he'd have to make some changes. He'd have to get rid of the poles and change the bar over. It'd be a risk, to have a club with no alcohol, but he'd be willing to try, on down the line.

The Oasis would be turned into a coffee/doughnut shop. He'd work with Charlie in the morning to find someone to do the renovations. He looked at his surroundings. There was enough room for two businesses, if he could find a crew to split the building in half. There was a lot of work to do and it was exciting. The changes he wanted to bring about would affect a lot of people.

The briefcase in his hand held the list of the businesses he now controlled. It took over five hours to hammer out what Rico would turn over to him. Jerry tried to pick the places that could be changed into respectable shops.

None of the buildings he now owned would be large enough for his big project. He always had a soft place in his heart for women. For once, he was going to use his love for the weaker sex to help them.

He wanted to give them a place to live if they were homeless, and to help them further their education so they could have a better life. There were so many young women on the streets, abused kids and runaways, who fell prey to pimps and drugs.

There needed to be more places that would take in young women. He wanted to build a safe haven where they could seek shelter. Jerry spoke to his son about his new escort service but Rico refused to stop his women from working the streets. He had this twisted belief he was helping them; Jerry tried to show him he wasn't, but he wouldn't listen.

Jerry walked over to stand by Charlie and laid the brief case on the bar and sighed. "Well, I've begun my work."

"Good. How did Rico take it?"

"I didn't take it well!" Rico snapped as he came out of his office. "My dad comes in, steals my body guard and my new best gal. He tries to dismantle everything I've accomplished in the past few years. How did you think I would react?"

Jerry looked at his son and was about to confront him about blackmailing Charlie, but she spoke before he could say anything. "Well, to be honest, I wasn't cut out for that kind of work. The kind of work your Dad will be doing suits me a lot better."

"And I pay better," Jerry tossed in, thinking if Charlie could take the high road, so could he. Rico crossed his arms and looked at his ex-bodyguard.

Angel shrugged and glanced from Jerry to Rico. "I just do what I'm told, and Jerry out-ranks you."

Jerry laughed at this comment. "Yeah, I still do."

"We'll see about that!" Rico turned, pushing the door open and almost knocking John down as he came in. "Are you jumping ship, too?" Rico snapped.

Everyone looked at John and he stood there, indecision showing on his face. Finally he shrugged, saying, "I guess I am."

Rico shook his head, and hurried out. It was easy for Jerry to see his son was angry, but still he hadn't put up much of a fight. His son took the changes, like a man. "It's a shock to him how I've changed," Jerry shook his head and sighed, "but he's going to have to get used to it because I'm not turning back."

Charlie patted Jerry on the arm and smiled. "That's the right attitude. Once Rico sees you're serious, it'll be easier for him to think about changing too."

"I hope you're right." Jerry shrugged his shoulders. "I'm ready to head back to the apartment. For now, we have use of the limo." Jerry tossed his driver the keys. "Angel, bring the car around."

"Yes sir."

John, you stay here tonight and watch the place. Since we're closed, there might be a few angry customers feeling the need to break out some windows."

"I'll see to it."

"Thanks for coming to work for me; you won't regret it." Jerry patted the young man on the shoulder as he and Charlie headed out the door.

"Goodnight, Miss Charlie" John smiled.

"Goodnight, John."

Jerry was tired, but filled with ideas of what to do. With all of the dreams he had, Charlie would be busy the next few weeks. She might even have to hire her own secretary. It was about that time he laughed out loud. "I'm acting like there's two of you. If you need any help ask Angel. I don't need a bodyguard and I'll be staying in most of tomorrow making phone calls.

"You don't mind do you, Angel?" Jerry smiled as he made the comment. He could see the young man was interested in Charlie. If he had his choice, he'd pick Charlie for Rico. What man wouldn't want a woman like Charlie to be his daughter-in-law?

*****

Charlie smiled at Jerry's sarcastic jab at Angel.

"I don't mind, sir," Angel answered as he pulled the limo into the garage and parked the car. Angel held the door open for Jerry and Charlie, then moved to the trunk and took out a suitcase. Charlie glanced back and did a double take when she saw the suitcase.

"I didn't think you'd mind if I brought over a few things." Angel called over his shoulder as he closed the trunk.

"No, that's fine," Charlie smiled. "After all, we don't want you wearing the same clothes all week, that's for sure." Her tone was playful.

"Okay, smarty pants," Angel bumped her lightly with the suitcase as they climbed into the elevator.

Charlie glanced at Angel and he winked at her, making her smile even more. She felt like a starry-eyed teenager when she was around this man. It was a good feeling and it made her forget some of her troubles.

After all, she was still wanted for stealing her sister's boyfriend's gun, for taking his money, and she didn't want to think about her ex-roommate. Allie was still hurt and angry the last time they'd spoken. She should try to call her, but what could she say? She doubted if Allie would even pick up.

When the doors opened, she pushed the thoughts out of her mind. Twenty minutes later she was giving Angel half her closet space and a couple of empty drawers for his personal items. She stayed close, watching him as he hung up his shirts. "I can hang those up if you want," Charlie offered.

"You might wrinkle them on purpose," Angel spoke, not looking at her.

"I wouldn't do that. Ruin your image?"

"You think I have an image?" Angel glanced at Charlie and then looked back at his shirts.

"Sure, you're Cool Hand Luke." Charlie liked the smile that came to Angel's lips, but he didn't look at her. Instead he kept working with his clothes. She moved around him and pushed back some of her dresses making more room.

"Does this mean we're roommates?" Angel gave Charlie a quick glance and a smile.

"In a way. But you still have to sleep on the couch." Charlie watched and waited; she knew that brow of his would shoot up while he was thinking of what to say.

"Oh, well, a man can't have everything . . . but he can dream," he added giving her a wicked smile. She tried to ignore his tone and asked him another question.

*****

"Did you think about going to work for Rico instead of Jerry?"

"It crossed my mind." Angel didn't want to seem too attached to Rico. He planned on watching Jerry for a while to see what he could learn, and then go back to Rico, if it became necessary.

"But you chose Jerry."

"Well, he chose me." Angel answered truthfully and then continued. "I wasn't sure what to do. I figure no matter what, we'll be around Rico and Jerry."

"Yes, I can see that coming. Jerry's going to want to try and spend a lot of time with Rico. He wants to erase some of the corrupt seeds he's sewn."

"Looks like he has his job cut out for him."

"Yes, and us, too. I've got some serious work ahead of me. I may not be qualified for this job, but I'm going to try."

"Well, I'm here. If you need anything, let me know. I'm no genius, but I've done a bit of everything."

"That means a lot. I appreciate it." Charlie smiled.

Angel hung up his last two pairs of pants and then stuffed his socks and shorts into a drawer while Charlie turned away. She was so shy. He smiled and pushed the items haphazardly into the drawer and closed it. He turned to find her picking up her Bible.

"When Jerry gets finished eating, I guess we'll start our study. Are you joining us?" Charlie turned to face Angel. He could see she was hoping he'd say yes.

"Well, I may not participate, but I'll sit in."

"Thanks," she smiled and crossed her arms as she stepped closer, keeping her tone low. "I hate to say it, but Jerry makes me nervous. I guess it's all the things he's done in his past." She laughed and shook her head "This is strange for me. I've never stayed in an apartment alone with a man. I don't care if he is older than me."

"Well, it's a good thing I'm here," Angel found himself placing his hands on her arms in a protective way. Thankfully, she didn't step back. As a matter of fact, he could tell she relaxed.

"It does make it easier, but I know my mother wouldn't approve."

"You do know you can trust me?" The officer in Angel came out. He looked into her eyes; he was not being romantic now; he was genuine. He wanted her to feel safe.

"I don't know why, but I do trust you. Is that a good thing?" She laughed, teasing him. He smiled, stepping out of cop mode.

"I think it is." Angel moved his right hand up her arm. He watched as his hand caressed her skin and thought that it felt right to be close to her.

He looked up and smiled, realizing he'd shown a part of himself to Charlie; his quiet side, the side of him that could sit and hold her for hours while they watched TV or talked.

Though he didn't want to, he moved his hands. "We'd better get out of here before Jerry wonders what we're up to. I don't want him getting jealous of me and giving me the boot."

Charlie looked at Angel, shaking her head, "Do you think that's why he brought me here?"

Angel knew the moment the words were out of his mouth, it was a mistake. He wasn't sure, so he shrugged. "One can never tell. I don't think so."

"I hope not," she whispered. "I don't want this to get complicated."

"Just be careful. Try not to give him any wrong signals."

"I don't want to. I hope he doesn't think I'm interested in him, because I'm not. I guess some younger women might want to chase after a man like Jerry."

"More than you think. Men with that kind of money and power seem to attract younger women."

"Not me," Charlie whispered.

"Are we back to the type of men you like? I never did get an exact answer on that."

Charlie shot him a look and tugged lightly on his tie. "I thought you had the perfect man picked out for me."

"I do. But I have many different sides. I'm not sure which one to show you first. I don't want to scare you off."

"I don't scare easily. After all, I did pull you out of the bushes. I could have left you there."

"I haven't forgotten. I'm grateful for what you did."

"You were busted up, but I couldn't help but be wary of you."

"I'd never hurt you." Angel crossed his arms studying the woman before him.

"I didn't know that."

"You know it now, don't you?" Angel stood to his full height and to satisfy his desire to touch her, he took her hand in his and kissed it.

"I'm well convinced of that fact, now."

"Good. If you need more convincing let me know." He forced himself to move away and went to the living room. She

115

followed and when Jerry got off the phone, they began their study on faith.

*****

Jerry kept nodding off so Charlie suggested they call it a night. She put away the Bibles and brought out the pillows for Angel while Jerry slipped off to his room.

Charlie knew Angel was busy out in the hall making a few phone calls, and she wondered who he was talking to. She couldn't help but think he was talking to some young lady even though he claimed he wasn't dating at the present time. Was he telling the truth?

She turned out the lights and walked over to gaze at the Chicago nightlife. She loved looking out over the city. She couldn't help but think of Allie as she watched Chicago sparkle in the moonlight. She would try to call her friend in a few days; hopefully her anger would be subsided by then.

Charlie sighed. She wanted to go out on the terrace but the weather wouldn't allow it. The night air would be cold; since they were up on the higher floors it would even be colder. She thought about calling home, but it was late and she didn't want to wake anyone.

She prayed silently that Rico wouldn't cancel her dad's surgery. Maybe she could talk to him; maybe Jerry already had. Hopefully he wouldn't be so angry with his dad that he'd take it out on her. She'd held to her end of the bargain; she was willing to go out on the date. Would he hold it against her that the man cancelled at the last minute?

Timing seemed to be working against her. Jerry came back a week too early; her dad needed this surgery and soon. She knew everything was in God's hands and forced herself to think positive, instead of focusing on the bad things that could happen.

The sound of the front door closing brought her out of her thoughts. She turned to see Angel walking to his makeshift bed. He laid his phone on the table and started taking off his shirt. She realized he had no idea she was there.

He stopped, took off his belt and sat down. She turned her back and looked out the window. She figured he'd lie down and go to sleep but a few seconds later, she felt his hand on her shoulder.

"Are you trying to become a peeping tom?" His tone was low and playful.

"No, I am not." She didn't want to turn and meet his gaze, so she spoke, not thinking how it would sound. "I'm just enjoying the view."

"That's what all peeping toms say," Angel whispered and Charlie had to laugh.

"I didn't mean *that* view, I meant this view," she gestured out the window.

"Then why won't you turn and look at me?" His tone mocked her and she could feel how close he was.

"I was thinking about speaking, but then you started . . . I never meant to . . .

"I know what you mean. I'm fully dressed. You can turn around."

Slowly she did as he said, not sure how far he would take his teasing games. Thankfully, all his clothes were on, but his shirt was unbuttoned. In the moonlight, she could see the beginning of a tattoo on his left shoulder.

It had her attention and she started to reach up and push his shirt back, but stopped. She realized she was beginning to feel way to comfortable with this young man. She caught herself and pointed, "How long have you had the tattoo?"

"Close to five years. I wasn't thinking clearly. I'd just bought my first Harley, and let's just say . . . I did a little too much celebrating."

"So you don't get a new tattoo every time you get a new bike?"

"No. One tattoo's enough."

"What about the bike? Did it fair as well as the tattoo?"

Angel raised a brow. "I guess. It's got some scratches, but I still have it, and it runs good."

117

"What kind of tattoo is it? A bike?" Charlie could see the amusement in his eyes as he moved into the moonlight and pulled the corner of his shirt back to reveal a sword.

Charlie stepped closer, bit her bottom lip, and then spoke, "Wow! I bet that hurt."

"It did. That's the reason I only have one." Angel turned loose of his shirt and smiled. "You can stay and watch *the view* as long as you like, but I need to get some sleep."

Charlie didn't want the moment to end, and when she spoke Angel turned, looking at her. "I've seen many things since I've came to this town. Some good some bad, but there's a few things I just can't forget."

Angel raised a brow, he would know she was flirting with him but she didn't care. She smiled and spoke, reaching out with both hands to tug lightly on his open shirt. "Some things in this city are just so incredible, you want to save the memory so you can look at in your mind, over and over again. I have a few favorites locked away," she closed her eyes for a second and smiled, then opened them and looked at him.

"Well?" he mused.

"Picture perfect." Charlie turned loose of the shirt and considered kissing Angel, then decided she was going to wait him out. "Good night, Angel."

*****

Angel fought the urge to reach out and take Charlie into his arms as she walked past him. He wanted to kiss her. Her little word game was cute, but the brief look of desire he saw when she looked at his tattoo was hard to take. The quick kiss he gave her that morning in the apartment was nothing compared to what he wanted.

He watched her walk into her room and close the door. He was tempted to follow but knew it wouldn't do any good. This young woman was a lady. Angel knew getting involved with Charlie would mean a commitment of some kind. He was attracted to her, but didn't know if he was ready or willing to do what it would take to win her affection.

Chapter 19
Oasis II

Angel sat in the limo across from the Independent Church of God; he'd dropped Jerry and Charlie off at the door less than an hour ago. He sat waiting, thinking. Would this week ever end?

The last few days had dragged by. Angel seemed to spend most of his time behind the wheel. He was taking Jerry all over town to meet with contractors so he could look at some new rental property. Jerry was keeping him busy and away from Charlie.

Angel frowned as he tapped the steering wheel. Every time he'd think he was going to have some alone time with Charlie, Jerry would send him on some errand. The only time he got to see her was when they ate breakfast or said goodnight.

Charlie was busy too, setting up appointments, typing out papers, surfing the net, and making phone calls, helping to bring Jerry's plans to life. She stayed in the apartment most of the time, and seemed too tired to talk, or flirt, as they said their goodnights.

Angel didn't know what Jerry was paying Charlie but it wasn't enough. She worked most days from eight till six, and some days later than that. Her work, and Jerry's contacts, were bringing it all together. By Wednesday, workers would be on site to start the renovations on The Oasis.

Angel took out his phone and dialed Joe. It rang three times and his brother answered.

"Hello?"

"It's Angel."

"Hey, what's up?"

"Another boring night following Jerry to church."

"Nothing going on?"

"I wouldn't say that. I've seen Rico twice this week and he's up to something. I just don't know what. He claims he's going to make things happen, with or without Jerry."

"Well, he kept things moving while Jerry spent his nights in prison finding Jesus." Joe paused, yelled at one of the kids, then went on with his thought, "Jerry's becoming a Mr. Goodie Two Shoes sure is messing up this case."

Angel laughed. "That sounds strange. You're complaining because someone's a law abiding citizen."

"Funny, but true. The only concrete thing we've got is Rico and his escort service."

"Is there any talk about pulling the plug?" Angel asked.

"Not yet. See if you can get a line on something soon."

"Will do."

"Later."

Angel didn't bother saying goodbye; Joe was gone. He flipped his phone closed and pushed it into his pocket looking at the church doors.

After the service, he'd be driving Jerry to a late dinner, then deliver some papers to Rico at his new club. He hoped to have time with Charlie somewhere in between.

*****

Charlie glanced at Jerry during the closing minutes of the service. Relief washed over her; thankfully, Jerry liked her church. Two nights ago she'd dreamed about running all over Chicago trying to find a church that suited her new employer. She could see a smile on his face; Jerry loved the little church as much as she did.

It was obvious the young pastor was Bible based. Tonight's sermon about the woman with the issue of blood kept Jerry's attention. She knew he would soon want to read Mark chapter 5, verses 25-34, and do a study on the woman, and what helped her to have such great faith.

120

As soon as Brother Jenkins dismissed the service, Jerry went to shake hands with Pastor Tracy Miner. Charlie thought Jerry wanted to tell the young pastor about his plans for Safe Haven, but he hadn't.

When they were walking toward the door, she leaned in and whispered, "Why didn't you tell Brother Tracy about your plans?"

Jerry shrugged. "What if they find out who I am? They may kick me out of the church and I like it here."

"More the reason to tell them about Safe Haven. You need to let these people get to know you so if they do hear something in the future, they'll have some good facts to balance against it."

"I see what you're saying, but not tonight. I'm ready to go when you are."

Charlie nodded, walked over and said goodnight to Nyssa, and a few minutes later she and Jerry headed out to the car.

*****

"I have some papers I want you to drop off to Rico," Jerry spoke, not sure he should be asking Charlie for help in this way.

"I know. You mentioned it earlier."

"There's more to it than the papers. I want you to talk to Rico. He thinks I've lost my mind and I want you to try and say a few words to him. I know you might not be able to work any miracles, but I'm hoping you may be able to reach him where I can't. He asks about you almost every time we talk."

"I don't mind speaking with him."

"Are you sure? I don't want you to feel uncomfortable."

"I don't mind. Now that I don't have to work with Rico, I can handle it."

"I sure do appreciate your help," Jerry paused, placing his hand on Charlie's arm before they reached the car. "I'd also like to apologize to you for making you stay in such close quarters with Angel. I'm going to work on that. I can see now it's not proper for you to stay with me, but it's not much better for you to be staying with two men."

Charlie knew he was right, but she didn't want to be separated from Angel. Although, since that night she'd looked at his tattoo, they'd hardly had time to speak to each other. In the end, she knew she'd do what Jerry suggested.

"You do what you think is best. I trust Angel, if you decide to leave things as they are."

They both grew quiet as they got in the car, and Charlie noticed Angel didn't have much to say either. He asked a few general questions about the service. 'Did they enjoy it?' 'Was there a big crowd?' But after this, nothing was said.

*****

When they pulled up to The Oasis II, Angel frowned. He didn't like this at all. What was Jerry up to, asking Charlie to come to the club? He knew she didn't like these places, and though there were no strippers, she still didn't like being around people who were drinking.

As they went into the building, Angel led the way to Rico's office. His anger was evident as he pushed a drunk out of the way that tried to ask Charlie to dance.

Once at the office, he stood to the side while Jerry held the door open for Charlie to enter. Angel noticed Jerry staying back. He leaned in so he could hear what the boss had to say.

"We won't be here long. I'll also be going out of town for a few days. I'll be arranging for Charlie to stay with some of her church friends while I'm gone. You can go back to your apartment. I'll be making new living arrangements soon."

With this Angel watched as Jerry went into the office and closed the door. There was anger rushing through Angel's veins. He didn't like the new changes. His feelings seemed to be right.

Jerry was beginning to separate him from Charlie, and he was starting to push Charlie towards Rico. Angel didn't like it one bit, but there wasn't a lot he could say, but he'd keep his eye on Charlie, that was for sure.

*****

Charlie didn't feel at ease with Rico, but he was being nicer than usual. He stood when she came into the room and offered her a seat. She sat and gave him a slight smile. She liked it better when she had no dealings with this man, but knew she should try to be a light to him, if at all possible. "I see you and your dad have settled a few things."

"A few. It's going to be a while till everything's done. Dad is being disagreeable; he's throwing away a lot of money."

"He's not doing this so he can throw away money. He's doing it because he doesn't think this is the way to earn money any more. It goes against what the Bible teaches, and since he's saved now, he's trying to follow the pattern Jesus left for us to follow."

"He never seemed to mind before."

"True, but he's changed now; he's *born again*," Charlie leaned forward and spoke candidly to Rico. "If you give your heart to God right now, there would be a change inside. You would see things differently; you would even have a new way of thinking. But, until you get saved, there's no way in the world you're going to be able to understand what's happened to your dad."

"So, you're saying if I get saved, I'd think like him."

"Yes. There might be some personal differences, but if you truly gave your heart to God, people would see a change in you. Let me give you another example. Have you ever eaten fried green tomatoes?"

Rico made a face and shook his head no.

"Good, then let's say I have a plate of them in front of me. I taste them. All you can do is see them; you can't taste them. Well, there's no way you will be able to enjoy them like I do. I won't be able to tell you what they taste like because you've never tasted anything like them."

Before he could say he didn't want to taste them, she went on. "Well, it's the same situation when you get saved. I can tell you all about it; how great it is, how it will change your life, how

123

it will give you a love for people you've never felt before. But, if you can't feel it, or taste it, you're not going to understand it."

Rico nodded and gave it some thought and when he spoke she knew, though he might not agree, he understood her premise.

"What if I don't want to eat your fried green tomatoes? What if I tell you I'm happy with my steak and potato? What then?"

"Then there's not much I can do. I can't make you get saved. I can't force you down on your knees and make you invite Jesus into your heart. All I can do is show you through my life how much better off you could be. That you would be happier and more peaceful if you were filled with the same love I have. There's nothing in this world like going to bed at night and having the assurance if you don't wake up, there's a better place waiting for you."

Charlie could tell by Rico's expression he was interested in what she had to say. He raised his brow once and even nodded his head. So she went on. "The first questions are, do you believe in God? Do you believe in heaven? If you believe in heaven, do you think you can live any way you want, and still go to heaven?" She surprised him by stopping and waiting for him to answer.

"Are you asking me that?" Rico gestured with his hand.

"Yes. Do you believe in God? If I'm going to help you, I have to know what I'm dealing with."

"You want to help me" Rico laughed and leaned forward, "after I tried to make you . . ."

Charlie interrupted him by holding up her hand. "I really do want to help you. I've forgiven you for what you tried to do to me. I have to forgive you even if I didn't want to. In order to keep my heart right with God, I have to forgive you."

"So you didn't want to forgive me?" Rico laughed.

"That's not what I said," Charlie leaned back, seeing for the first time that Rico could be a likable person when he wanted to be. "I did forgive you, and since I didn't have to go on the date, I'll admit, it wasn't hard.

*****

Rico was amazed at Charlie's comments. He leaned back, wondering if she was telling the truth. "You're trying to tell me you're not angry with me? I blackmailed you into going on that date. I threatened to call off your dad's surgery."

"But you didn't." Charlie smiled, and Rico nodded, he didn't want to admit he forgot all about it. The door opened and Rico was glad for the interruption.

Jerry stepped in and came over, placing his hands on Charlie's shoulders. "Is my son boring you?"

"No. He can be a charmer when he wants to be."

Rico smiled and glanced at his dad. "I was thinking of asking Charlie if she wanted to have a night cap." Rico knew Charlie didn't drink but he wanted to irritate his dad and much to his surprise, his dad smiled.

"She doesn't drink, son, but she might allow you a cup of coffee or a late supper." Jerry patted Charlie on the shoulder and stepped back to look her in the eye. "I've got a late supper to go to, but I'll leave Angel here to drive you two home. You can talk as long as you like. Let Angel know when you're ready to go."

"I'll take you up on that offer, considering I paid his salary last week," Rico said, forcing a smile at his Dad.

*****

Jerry laughed and stepped out, pulling the door closed. He walked over to where Angel was sitting at the end of the bar. The young man was nice, and though Angel liked Charlie, Jerry was going to do everything he could to keep them apart. He was going to do some matchmaking between Rico and Charlie. He put his hand on Angel's shoulder and the young man looked up. There was anger smoldering in those brown eyes and it wasn't going to get any better.

"Rico and Charlie aren't finished yet. I want you to wait here and drive Charlie home. Of course, if they want to go out, take them where ever they want to go."

"Yes sir."

Angel's tone was low and Jerry knew he should feel sorry for the young man, but all he could think of at the moment was his own flesh and blood. He stepped back and forced a smile as he spoke. "I'll see you in the morning." Jerry took out his cell phone, called a cab and five minutes later he was gone.

Chapter 20
Jealously

It was hard to not walk into that office, grab Rico by the collar, and rare back and hit him. Angel sat at the end of the bar glancing at his watch and sipping on a bottle of beer. His patience for this case was running out.

Ten minutes later a young woman carried a couple of drinks into the office, and about an hour later, the door opened and Charlie and Rico stepped out.

Angel looked away and wrapped his hand around the neck of the bottle after seeing Rico put his hand on Charlie's shoulder. He relaxed his grip and looked back to see Charlie standing alone.

He waited as she searched the crowd, and enjoyed seeing her face light up the moment she spotted him. He knew that old feeling of jealousy and he didn't like it. Angel tried to put his emotions in check as Charlie walked toward him.

Tapping the neck of the bottle, he turned facing her as she approached.

"Hey, sorry we kept you waiting. I never meant to stay that long." Charlie gave Angel a soft smile that dissuaded his anger somewhat.

"Don't worry about it. That's what I get paid for."

"Well, I'm ready to go to the apartment. Rico said he'd be out in a minute." Charlie glanced over her shoulder, and looked back when Angel spoke.

"Were you guys working on something for Jerry?" Angel started to lift the bottle to his lips, but when Charlie spoke he stopped, setting the bottle on the counter.

"No, just chatting. Jerry wanted me to talk to Rico, to see what he thought about his dad's new ideas."

"So this was Jerry's idea?" Angel felt somewhat relieved and a bit of his anger was transferred to Jerry. So the man wanted to do some matchmaking. Well, he needed to leave Charlie alone. Angel took a quick drink and then looked up.

"Of course, it wasn't my idea." Charlie wrinkled her nose as if she smelled something bad, but then laughed. "I know I'm supposed to love everyone, but I can barely tolerate that man."

Angel reached and gave a gentle tug on the gold cross hanging from a chain around Charlie's neck. "I recall you saying in Bible study that you were supposed to love your neighbor as yourself."

Charlie pulled the cross from his grasp and laughed. "I try, but some people are easier to love than others, but either way, I do my best to not show a partiality."

"That's obvious." Angel turned, leaning on the bar; his tone was short and his anger was returning.

Charlie reached out and placed her hand on Angel's shoulder. "Have you been sitting here thinking I'd rather be with Rico than with you?"

Angel shrugged, "The thought crossed my mind."

"It shouldn't have." Charlie moved to stand in front of Angel and he turned on the barstool to face her again. She moved closer, tracing a circle on the back of his hand.

"Then why were you with him?" Angel didn't try to hide his anger this time when he spoke.

"I didn't have a choice. Jerry asked me to speak to Rico."

Angel grumbled. "You've gone from taking orders from one DeLusa to the other?"

"If you didn't want me spending time with Rico, why didn't you say something?"

"It's not my place. I'm not your boyfriend. I'm just the driver." Angel gestured towards Rico, "Your escort's coming." He turned on the barstool, moving away from Charlie.

Charlie stepped back. He could see the confusion on her face. She had no idea why he was pushing her away. Anger made him say it, but it was for the best.

Rico's expression told Angel he'd made the right choice. The look was a look of ownership; a look that said 'you can't have her, she's mine.' Rico was power hungry, and taking Charlie would be a great triumph over Jerry.

Angel's thoughts were confirmed when Rico came up and placed his arm around Charlie's shoulder. Though her brows furrowed at the man's touch, and she even stepped away, Rico didn't give up. "What do you say we go out and get a late supper or a nightcap?"

"I think I'll pass, but thanks. Which way to the powder room?"

"Down the hall," Rico pointed, "you can't miss it."

Angel tried to seem disinterested. He turned, drinking down the rest of his beer. He knew why Rico had this sudden interest in Charlie. Rico wanted to steal the one thing that was driving his dad at the moment, and in Rico's eyes that was Charlie.

Rico would want to take away Jerry's motivation, if he could, he'd love to change the direction in which things were moving. Angel knew that removing Charlie from the picture wouldn't return Jerry to his old way of life, but did Rico know this?

Angel wanted to bring the man down a notch or two. He wanted to make it clear that if it weren't for Jerry, Charlie wouldn't be giving him the time of day.

This case, and Rico, was grating on his nerves. He wanted Rico in jail . . . now. When Rico stepped closer, Angel didn't bother to look up.

"Nothing's going to happen between you and Charlie." Rico's arrogance only irritated Angel further.

Angel wanted to say those same words to Rico, but instead he looked up with a question. "What did you say?"

"You heard me." Rico pursed his lips into a snarl.

"I'm just here to take her home."

129

"Right." Rico shook his head, "I'm not stupid. Charlie's off limits! You got that?"

It took all of Angel's self-control to shrug and turn away. Showing any interest in Charlie would only make this pit bull worse.

Angel shrugged, "She's a beauty, but she's looking for a ring and wedding vows, nothing less." Angel rose, tossed down some money on the counter, and then looked at Rico. "You can waste your time if you want to."

"I know what I'm getting into. She's a challenge. The old man thinks he can change me, but it's not going to happen. But . . .I may be able to change her."

Angel tried to keep his expression neutral as he spoke, "It's your dime, spend it as you see fit." Before Rico could answer, Angel picked up his jacket and swung it over his arm, heading out the door. "I'll have the car around front in five."

*****

Charlie stood in front of the mirror. She wasn't looking forward to the ride home. When Rico put his arm around her, she wanted to slap him. She'd not said anything that would suggest she wanted a relationship with the man.

Also, she didn't know what Angel's problem was. He seemed jealous and then detached. Rico wasn't helping matters either; he acted as if they were dating when they weren't.

Charlie turned and looked from the door to a small window and wondered if she could squeeze through it, escape, call a cab and go home.

Instead, she washed her hands and walked toward the front exit. Her heart sank when she didn't see Angel waiting. She moved toward Rico and forced a smile as he spoke.

"Are you sure you don't want to get something to eat? I know plenty of places that are open at this time of night."

"No, thank you. I'm tired. It's time I head back to the apartment.

Rico reached out a hand. "Would you like me to help you into your coat?"

"No thanks. Angel will be sure the car is warm."

"Yes, I told him to go out and get it ready." Rico smiled.

Charlie nodded. She wanted to get away from Rico. Would he take a cab home, or expect Angel to drop him off? She smiled stepped toward the door, hoping he'd call a cab.

"Goodnight." She wanted to say it was nice chatting, but it wasn't. She hoped her conversation helped in some way, but she didn't want to do this again any time soon.

"I'll see you to the apartment." Rico stepped toward the door, resting his hand on Charlie's shoulder.

"Oh, that's not necessary."

"I insist."

Charlie nodded and moved forward. As she walked to the car, Angel stepped out and opened the door. She wanted to tell him that having Rico tag along wasn't her idea, but there was no time. Rico was right on her heels, giving Angel orders as she climbed in.

"You'll need to drop Charlie off at the apartment, and then you can drive me to my place."

*****

"Yes sir," Angel said through clinched teeth as he closed the door behind Rico. He walked around the car, letting out a breath of frustration. He opened the door and as he pulled out of the parking lot, he heard the glass partition roll closed.

Angel didn't understand Charlie; she was a grown woman. Why didn't she tell Rico to find his own ride home?

Angel took the shortest route possible; although he was angry, he knew Charlie had to be uncomfortable riding alone with Rico. Jerry should be ashamed of himself, asking her to baby-sit his disreputable son.

There was no way he could have Charlie's best interest in mind. Born again or not, when this case ended, Angel was going to give Jerry DeLusa a piece of his mind.

*****

"Jerry usually doesn't do that," Charlie gestured, wishing she could get out of the car.

"I don't like the help listening in," Rico added.

Charlie didn't think of Angel as 'the help'. She nodded and did her best to keep up with the small talk. It might not be easy, but she wasn't going to let herself get into this situation again, even if she had to tell Jerry that Rico made her feel uncomfortable.

Rico's hand was way too close, and she hoped if she screamed Angel would be able to hear her. She prayed for some idea to keep Rico on his side of the car.

After a moment her prayer was answered. Grabbing her purse she looked for her phone, "Wow, I forgot to call mom. It won't take but a minute."

She gave him no time to respond. She took out the phone, opened it, dialed time and temperature, and then flashed Rico a smile. She knew about how long it would take them to get to the apartment, and if she could kill a few minutes, they would soon be there.

As the recording told her what time it was, she began to talk as if the machine had picked up, "Mom, so sorry I missed you..." The message she supposedly left was longer than a minute and she hoped Rico wouldn't notice. When she closed the phone and pushed it back into her purse she began talking, "Its late, I bet they're in bed already."

"I'm sure she'll be sorry she missed your call."

"Yes, I don't get to talk to her much. Your dad keeps me busy."

"Well, you could always come back and work for me. I'm sure I could find something for you to do." The smile on his face was not something Charlie wanted to see.

"I like working for him; he keeps me busy. I think his plan will do a lot to help the needy women of Chicago." She prayed as she glanced at her watch again. She inwardly sighed as she felt the jolt of the speed bumps that were at the entrance of the underground garage.

Charlie felt the car slowing and rather than thank Rico for a nice evening, she began to commend him for allowing Jerry to take over some of the businesses.

She waited for Angel to open the door, when in reality she wanted to jump out and hurry upstairs. Seconds after the car came to a stop, her door opened. She stepped out, glancing at Angel for a moment. He still looked angry.

"Good night." Charlie hoped Rico would stay in the car, but he didn't. He stepped out and she turned, finding herself between Angel and Rico.

The wrong man reached out for her hand. Rather than let him draw this out, she gave Rico a quick handshake, but he held her hand in his, as he spoke.

"I hope we can talk again soon. I can see you're a true believer. I don't know if it's because of Dad's past or what, but he doesn't seem as sincere."

"I think your dad is a changed man, and he's trying to prove that to you. Give him some time; give him a chance."

"I'll try. But there's so much I don't understand. Maybe you can help me find a better perspective."

"Maybe," Charlie pulled her hand from Rico's and he leaned towards her but she pulled back. "Good night."

*****

Angel hid his smile of satisfaction and closed the car door once Rico was in. He stood there a moment making sure Charlie stepped into the elevator alone. Once the doors were closed, he climbed behind the wheel and pulled out. As he did so, the window came down an inch and Rico called out his address.

Angel programmed the Garmin and took Rico home. This case was turning into a twist of knots and he didn't like where any of it was heading. The man tried to kiss Charlie and, thankfully, she didn't want anything to do with him.

Jerry might be a changed man, but he still had some things to learn. It wasn't right for him to put Charlie in a spot where she felt obligated to speak to his son.

It was obvious now to Angel how Charlie felt about Rico. He was sure she cared about his soul, but also was just as certain she could see through his phony sincerity.

Angel didn't know anyone as sweet and honest as Charlie, but even good people had their limits. He hoped tonight that she'd had her fill of being alone with Rico DeLusa.

Chapter 21
The Argument

Charlie felt relief when she stepped into the quiet apartment. She took off her shoes and poured a glass of water before she found the note from Jerry on the kitchen table. It said his late supper had cancelled and he'd retired early.

"Good thing. I've had my fill of men tonight." Charlie sat the glass in the drainer and went to her room. She took her jacket off and could easily tell she reeked of smoke. Feeling like she needed to get the smoke and smell of that club out of her hair, she stripped and took a quick shower. She washed her hair and felt the tears sting her eyes as she thought about the past few hours.

She knew it wasn't Angel's place to protect her from Rico, but still she felt disappointed and frustrated. They were starting to talk and flirt. He wasn't her boyfriend, as he said; he was just the driver. Still, she wished there'd been something he could have done to keep her from having to ride with Rico.

She should have insisted on riding home alone or up front with Angel. It wasn't going to happen again; she wouldn't allow it. Being alone with Rico in the back seat of that car was too much. Having him so close made her uneasy. She didn't trust him, and as she dried her hair, she prayed she'd be able to talk to Jerry about his son.

She wanted to help Rico, but she couldn't be alone with him. Sometimes you had to distance yourself from trouble.

An hour later, when she stepped out to get a cup of yogurt, she found Angel standing at the sink. He must have thought she had gone to bed, because he was standing there with his shirt off, drinking a glass of juice. She stood, looking at him, wondering if she should speak or slip back into her bedroom.

The sight of him standing there overwhelmed her somewhat. He was so attractive and in such great shape. When he raised the glass to finish the juice, she could see the muscles in his arms. Would he accuse her of being a peeping Tom again, or would he be too angry to talk to her?

While she was trying to make up her mind he spoke. "I thought you would be sleeping by now." He wasted no time in turning, and walking to the couch, he picked up his tan shirt, slipping it on. He buttoned two buttons before he looked at her.

She had plenty of time to look at the tattoo again and notice there was no chest hair. He was tanned and smooth. The fact he was modest either for himself, or her, pleased her. It wasn't common . . . in this day and age.

"I took a shower. I wanted to get the smell of smoke out of my hair."

"Yeah, it's hard to get rid of."

"I guess you took Rico home."

"I dropped him off." Angel kept his comments brief as he began to spread his sheet out on the couch. Charlie moved to help him and laid the pillows out. "We can switch if you want. I'll take a night on the couch."

*****

Angel looked at Charlie. It wasn't fair that he was angry with her, but he couldn't help it. He didn't want to talk, but he didn't want to be rude either. "Thanks, but no need. None of us will have these same sleeping arrangements much longer."

"What do you mean?"

"Didn't Jerry tell you?" Angel could see she didn't know what he was talking about.

"Tell me what?"

"I don't want him to hear us talking," Angel motioned for her to follow and he walked toward her bedroom. She came in closing the door, and stepped over to him.

"Jerry's planning on moving soon. He said he'd be leaving for a few days and that you'd be staying with someone from church. He said I should go back to my apartment."

"I didn't know. He didn't mention it."

Angel moved closer, supposedly so he could keep his voice low. "I think Jerry's working on putting some distance between us, so don't be surprised if he starts trying to push you on Rico."

"What? Do you think that's what tonight was about? Why would he do that?"

"I guess because he thinks you'd be good for Rico."

"Well, that's not happening!"

"Don't cross him Charlie. He may have you convinced he's a changed man, but I'm not sure. Try not to make him angry."

Charlie sighed. "Why didn't you tell me?"

"I didn't think it would change anything. You would have still tried to save his soul!" Angel's voice rose and he began to pace. "I hope you know you can't save everyone."

"I know. I was only doing what Jerry asked me to do. He wanted me to talk to Rico about the recent changes in his life."

"He wanted to push you two together." Angel stepped in front of Charlie. He was so angry, not with her, but with this whole situation. There wasn't a lot he could do. Things were closing in; he didn't want to blow his cover.

"Maybe he does want us to get close. I didn't see you doing anything about it. Why didn't you say something? I didn't want to be alone with Rico in the back of that limo."

"Did he hurt you?"

"No, but what if he had?"

"I could hear you. I was listening. At any moment I would have pulled that car over . . ."

"That would have been nice to know." Charlie sounded so soft and vulnerable at that moment. She started to turn, but Angel put his hands on her shoulders.

"Don't you know it was pure torture for me to allow him to be alone with you in the car, or at the office? I wanted to hit him when he tried to kiss you."

Angel looked into her eyes. She seemed to soften, and her eyes told him she believed him, but she still wanted to blame him.

"All I know is, you didn't do anything."

"How could I?" Angel turned loose of her and stepped back. He ran his fingers through his hair and closed his eyes, breathing in deeply before looking at her. It would be so easy to tell her the whole truth right now. To let her know he'd been working undercover for six weeks, and explain why he couldn't protect her, as he wanted to.

Instead he looked at her and shook his head. "I'm working. This is my job. We're not dating or married. I don't have any right to say anything. You, on the other hand, could have said something. You could have told Jerry you didn't want to talk to Rico, or mentioned to Rico when he tried to kiss you, that you're not interested."

Angel knew this wasn't getting them anywhere. He knew down deep she was hurt and as frustrated as he was. But still, her words stung him.

"I know we're not dating. I know you're an employee. Still, some part of me thought there was something you could have done. I guess I was wrong. Go to bed. I don't want to talk about this anymore. I'm tired and I've got a lot to do tomorrow."

Angel wanted to tell her he was sorry, wanted to take her in his arms and kiss her. Instead he turned and left, closing the door behind him. This wasn't working. The case was falling apart because Jerry had come back and closed down so many of the businesses.

Rico seemed to be distancing himself from guns and drugs. Then, there was Charlie. She kept edging her way into his feelings and causing him to not think straight. Jerry was in the way. Angel wanted this to be over, and the sooner the better.

Chapter 22
You're Fired

When Charlie woke the next morning, she found Jerry at the kitchen table reading the morning paper. Angel's blankets lay folded on the couch with his pillow on top.

"I've got some good news and bad news." Jerry took a sip of coffee. "The good news is I've subleased this apartment and it's going to make us quite a bit of money. The bad news is, we need to be out in a few days.

"Also, I'm going out of town, but I won't be gone long. You'll need to find another place to live for about a week. I'll find better living arrangements for us when I return."

"I see." Charlie didn't mention she'd already heard this news from Angel. She fixed a cup of tea and sat down to have some bagels with cream cheese.

It would mean some adjusting, but Jerry's plan would save them money, and in the long-run things would be better. It did leave her in a pinch. With Allie still angry, and her Aunt Verla still away, she had no place to go.

She'd found out through her mother that Verla had decided to stay in Florida. Eventually her aunt would be moving into a new apartment there. So for now, Charlie didn't have a place to stay.

Charlie looked at Jerry. "I talked to Rico last night. I hope he didn't get the idea I was interested in him. He tried to steal a kiss when he dropped me off."

Jerry laughed, folding the paper and putting it aside. "He's just testing you. He's had a rough life and hasn't been around many women that have any self-respect. I'm sure there are times he doesn't know how to act around you."

"Maybe so, but it did make me feel uncomfortable."

"I'll speak to him about it if you want."

"No, not yet."

Charlie was going to wait to see if Jerry wanted her to be alone with Rico again before she mentioned anything further. After eating her bagel, she looked up at Jerry. "As far as finding a place to stay, I'll ask some of the people from church, see if they have a room they might want to rent.

"That's great, just let me know. Sometime next week I hope to have us a less expensive place to live. I have plenty of money right now but there won't be any more coming in for a while, so I want to be very frugal."

"That's wise. I'll keep working on finding a building that suits your requirements."

"Yes, do that. I'll be sure and give you some money before I go. We'll sit down soon and figure out your salary."

"Thanks, that'll be good."

Jerry stood up and walked to the sink, washed his hands and turned to Charlie, "If you ever see me wasting money, be sure and point it out. It's kind of hard to learn a new lifestyle."

"I'll make you a list." Charlie looked up when Jerry broke out laughing.

"Is it that bad?"

"I'll give you the list and leave that up to you to decide." Charlie smiled and reached for the morning paper.

Jerry walked past her and patted her on the shoulder, "I'm so thankful I found you." He then turned and went toward his bedroom. Before he closed the door, he called over his shoulder.

"If you need to go anywhere, call a cab. One of the expenses I've gotten rid of is Angel. I sent him back to Rico."

Jerry was out the door before Charlie could say anything, but her heart sank. Did that mean Angel would be out of her life? That wasn't going to be easy to get used to.

He should have left her a note or something. Maybe he'd call her later in the day. It really didn't matter; somehow she'd see to it that their paths crossed again.

*****

If Angel wanted a day off, he had one; Jerry informed him minutes after he woke that he was fired. He needed to report back to Rico the next morning.

When Jerry went to shower, Angel slipped into Charlie's room to get his clothes. She never even knew he was there. He wanted to bend down and kiss her or touch her, but he kept his distance.

Almost twelve hours had passed since he'd slipped out of the apartment. Angel sat behind his desk at the station, hating the last few days. He looked up as Joe sat down. His brother handed him a cup of coffee.

"So tell me, did Jerry really find God?" Joe began.

"I guess, but I find it hard to believe."

"Me too. I don't trust him . . . or Rico."

"You don't have to worry about me. I'll never trust either of them."

"Good." Joe seemed preoccupied; he sat looking at his watch and glancing out the door.

"What's up? Something on your mind?" Angel asked.

"Yeah, Vanessa wants me home early."

"I see. Does she want you there before the kids get home?" Angel smiled.

"No, I wish it was something like that. She called and said to come home early. It seems we need to move some furniture around. She's invited that girl from the church to stay with us for a week."

Angel nodded. It had to be Charlie. She was supposed to find someone to stay with. "You say that girl? What girl?"

"The one you want to meet," Joe leaned back, rocking in the chair, a smile on his face.

Angel nodded. He sat forward; relieved somewhat Charlie wouldn't be staying with Rico or Jerry. "So, will she be helping to take care of the kids?"

"I hope so."

141

"A built in baby sitter could come in handy." Angel raised his brows up and down in a joking manner.

"Hmm, you could be right." Joe rose from his chair. "I better get back to work and get home as early as I can."

"Sure. I'll be just a phone call away," Angel said with a smirk.

"Yeah, right. You're just hoping I'll invite you over so you can meet Charlie."

"Hey, that's a good idea."

"Like you hadn't already thought about that."

Angel shrugged, playing dumb. Joe shook his head and called over his shoulder as he left the room. "That's not going to happen anytime soon."

"If you won't invite me over, I'll get Nyssa to do it." Joe waved his hand as if to dismiss his brother, and walked back to his office.

Angel watched as Joe left. He wondered if he should tell his brother that his soon-to-be houseguest was the young woman who was working for Jerry DeLusa.

*****

Around five, Jerry and Charlie shared a cab; he dropped her off at the church where she was going to meet Nyssa. Jerry gave Charlie a check, and gave her a kiss on the cheek when he hugged her.

When she climbed in the car, what Nyssa asked surprised her, "I don't mean to pry, but before we pick up the kids, I have a question."

"Sure. What's that?"

"That man who dropped you off, did he kiss you?" Nyssa started the mini van and waited.

"Yes, on the cheek."

"Are you dating him?"

"Nooo," Charlie laughed making a face as she glanced at Nyssa. "Jerry's my boss. He recently got saved and he's a hugger, but that's the first time he kissed me."

142

"He looked too old for you, but I thought I'd ask. You never can tell these days."

"You're right, and Jerry's nice, but older is not my type. I think he'd like it if I went on a date with his son, but he's not my type either."

Nyssa pulled up to the red light and smiled. "Since we're on the subject of men. Are you dating anyone? I've not heard you mention any names."

"No. I had dinner with this guy the other night, but nothing you could call dating."

"But you like him, don't you?"

Charlie laughed, "I guess. Why do you ask?"

Nyssa pulled into the driveway of the school and parked. She glanced at her watch and then turned to Charlie, "We've got a few minutes until the kids come out so let me give you a test."

"What kind of a test?"

"It's simple. It's something the kids made me do the other night after supper. You close your eyes, think of something blank, like snow, and then you think of the guy."

"What? Are you kidding?"

"No, come on, do it." Nyssa laughed.

Charlie shook her head, put a straight face on and took a breath, doing as Nyssa said. She pictured a white, bright, snowy scene, and then brought to mind the image of Angel, standing at the sink with his shirt off.

"There it is. I can see it. You're smiling."

Charlie laughed and shook her head, "You should have seen him with his shirt off! You'd be smiling too!"

"What? You're not dating him but you've seen him shirtless? What's going on here?"

"It was nothing like that, but he's so cute and he has this tattoo right here," she said drawing a finger across the left side of her chest.

"Joe has a tattoo on his back. I love it. It's so sexy. I wouldn't want him to have them all over, but I like that one."

"I know what you mean." Charlie smiled, and then glanced back to Nyssa. "Well, did you pass the test?"

143

Nyssa nodded as she saw the kids come running out. She smiled and turned to Charlie. "I guess so. After all these years I still smile when I think of Joe. But don't think you're getting out of this so easy. Young lady . . . sometime soon you'll have to tell me how you got this guy that you're not dating to take his shirt off?"

Charlie blushed and giggled, "We've barely kissed, and it was nothing like that."

"You'd better behave," Nyssa said with a knowing smile.

Chapter 23
Detective Work

The next few days Angel didn't see Rico often. He'd either left town or had gone into hiding. This gave Angel some free time, so he spent most of it spying on Charlie. He wanted to drop by and see her, but he couldn't. He didn't want her to connect him with Joe. She might start putting it all together and figure out he was a cop.

Angel used the break in the case and the weather to his advantage. He took his bike out of storage for a few days and followed Charlie and Nyssa around town. He didn't think they were in any danger, but he wanted to do some on the job training and keep his tracking skills up to par.

Twice he followed them to church, and once he trailed behind as they went out for pizza. A few times he camped out in a rental car, watching the house, until the sun come up.

The following day, Angel cut his snooping short and went back to his apartment to get a bite to eat. He found a message on his machine from Juan saying Rico would be back soon, but no word about where he'd been or what he'd been up to.

He would go to the club later to see if Juan knew anything about Rico's trip. It might end up being a late night, so he thought he'd catch a few zzz's. He sat down and picked up the remote. He was about to kick back when he heard a knock at the door.

Angel tossed the remote on the couch, and as he got up, pulled the Glock from his holster. He racked the slide to chamber a round and stepped toward the door. He wasn't expecting company and only a handful of people knew where he lived.

He leaned against the frame staying clear of any shots that might come through the thin door and called out, "Yeah, what do you want?"

"It's Joe! Open up."

Angel took the chain off the door, opened it, and stepped into the kitchen. When Joe slammed the front door shut, Angel looked up. He knew something was wrong; Joe looked furious. As he reached into the refrigerator to take out a cola he slowly asked, "You want something to drink?"

Joe shook his head no, "I didn't come to socialize."

Angel could see his brother was ticked. He reached in, took out a bottle of cola and pushed the door closed. He walked over and sat down, opening his drink.

"What's up?"

"Good question." Joe paced a few steps, and turned to face Angel, crossed his arms and spoke; "I want to know why you're casing my house."

Angel sighed deeply and ran his fingers through his hair, "Man! I didn't want you to see me."

"No kidding! Now tell me, what are you up to? *Why* are you watching my house?"

"It's not what you think."

"I don't know what *to think*. I've been going over this in my head. I keep asking . . . why is my little brother watching my house?"

Joe moved from one side of the apartment to the other. Though they were raised in different homes and states, Angel knew Joe had a temper.

He might as well face up to what he'd done. "You're not going to like this." Angel tightened the lid on the cola, sat the bottle on the table and stood, facing Joe.

"Angel, what are you up to?"

"Well, the reason I'm watching your house is of a personal nature."

146

"Personal?" Joe nodded in a slow and deliberate manner. "Go on."

"Well, it's because of the girl that's staying with you."

"Charlie?" Joe gestured with his hands in the air, "What's she got to do with any of this?"

"A lot," Angel exhaled a deep breath, ready for the punch when it came. "How's your temper lately?"

"Angel!" Joe growled.

"Okay," Angel held both hands up in surrender, "Do you remember the night I went missing?"

"Of course."

"Well, that night I was knocked out and left in the bushes. Charlie found me."

By the time Angel got out the last few words, Joe had him by the collar; the lamp was lying in a heap, and the bottle of coke was rolling in the floor. He hoped his brother's temper was abating. Otherwise, the slam against the wall might be followed by a hard punch.

After a moment Joe spoke. "Have you lost *all* of your good senses? You should have told me she was involved with Rico. Did you even consider my family's safety?"

"Of course. That's why I was watching the house."

Joe moved back, releasing Angel from where he'd pinned him to the wall. "Ok, ok. But I still don't like any of this."

Angel rubbed the back of his head and kept his distance. Joe had that angry expression again, and Angel readied himself for another trip to the wall.

"Does she know you're a cop?" Joe spat out.

"No." Angel picked up the lamp, looked at it and dropped it back onto the floor. "She doesn't know. She thinks I'm a body guard."

"This is a mess! If the brass finds out she's in my house, it could ruin everything." Joe shot Angel an angry look. "You sure have your head in the wrong place."

"I didn't think it would put anyone in danger. Charlie's just a secretary. I'm sorry. I guess I didn't look at it from all angles."

"Sorry?" Joe stepped closer to Angel.

"If you're going to hit me, go ahead."

"Is that an invitation?"

"Not really. But I'll allow you one good punch."

Joe moved closer to Angel, looked him eye to eye and spoke in a low tone. "Don't ever dare do anything even close to this again."

"Yes sir," Angel said, acknowledging Joe's rank as his superior and his older brother. This got him a nod and then Joe paused. He seemed to be thinking things over in his mind and after a moment turned and spoke, still sounding rather angry.

"There's two things I need you to do. The first thing is, you have to stop hanging around my house! We don't need Charlie tying this all together.

"The next thing is to get Charlie out. I don't care where she goes, Angel . . . but I want her out. . . of . . .my . . .house!" Joe pushed his finger into Angel's chest for emphasis, and then walked toward the door.

Joe left the door on its hinges and for that Angel was grateful. He stood in the doorway; also thankful Joe hadn't punched him. Joe was still shaking his head and grumbling as he walked down the hall to the elevator.

Angel knew his brother wouldn't kick Charlie out on the street, but he also knew he'd have to work on getting her out of there soon.

*****

The next morning Angel got a call from Nyssa. She explained that Charlie could stay with them as long as she needed, regardless of what Joe said.

He thanked her and apologized again. She assured him it wasn't necessary, but there was something in her tone that told him she wasn't done with him yet. After a few minutes of talking about the kids and the weather, she got to the heart of the conversation.

"I need to say something. Charlie isn't here, so I can speak freely."

148

"Yes Ma'am, I'm listening."

"I know you've been in and out of Joe's life for some time now, and I don't feel as if I have the right to tell you what to do. But I'd like to give you some good advice. I hope you don't mind."

"I don't mind." Angel knew he was getting ready to get a lecture, but he liked Nyssa and knew she meant well. She'd always been like the older sister he never had.

"I know you're working undercover, but I have to say I don't like it that you're part of our family and Charlie doesn't know."

"I don't like it either, but for now, there's not a lot I can do about it. Undercover work is never easy."

"I understand." Nyssa paused for a few seconds, "I'm not even suggesting that you put yourself in danger. I'm just venting."

"Trust me, no one wants Charlie to know the truth more than me. I want to tell her. She thinks I'm a thug, and I hate it."

"That brings me around to my other point. There's no easy way to broach this subject, so I'll just jump in. Charlie isn't the kind of girl you usually date."

Angel sat down in his recliner. "I don't know what she's told you, but we're not dating."

"Maybe not, but I have an idea you're closer to Charlie than you're ready to admit. I care for you, Angel, but I know you've never had a long-lasting relationship, so be sure you think this through."

"I will." Angel paused, thinking out loud, "did she say much about me?"

Nyssa laughed. "Now do you really think I'm going to tell you that?"

"You can't blame a guy for trying." Angel put his ear close to the phone and after a few seconds wondered if Nyssa had hung up on him, but after a moment she spoke.

"Angel, I will *not* be happy if Charlie ends up getting hurt."

"I'll be careful."

"She'll make some man a fine life partner some day."

"I know. I can see that."

"If you break her heart, I'll let Joe beat you up."

Angel laughed, "I'll keep that in mind." He wondered if Joe mentioned he'd considered doing just that.

"One more thing . . . Angel, if you're as smart as I think you are, you won't let this one slip away."

Angel looked at his phone; Nyssa didn't say bye or anything, she immediately hung up. He pushed the phone into his pocket, letting her words sink in.

Chapter 24
Changes and Choices

Joe didn't like being kept out of the loop, so for the next few days he kept a close eye on Charlie, Jerry, Rico and Angel. None of them seemed to be doing anything very interesting, but still he followed them as closely as possible.

He kept thinking that since Jerry had gotten out of jail and was in the middle of things, that this whole case was going to be a washout. Jerry's arrival was untimely to say the least. Maybe now that he was trying to get his life on track, Rico would be free to get back to business as usual.

Keeping an eye on four people wasn't easy, but most of the time Jerry and Charlie traveled together. The two of them were bouncing all over town looking for rental properties; they'd finally settled on one at Fifth and Main. They'd been back to it twice in a week's time.

At first, Joe thought the old man had inappropriate feelings toward Charlie, but after seeing them interact he changed his mind.

Rico's activities had been a little more interesting. He'd just come back from a quick trip to El Paso. Since his return, he'd been using Angel strictly as a bodyguard. It was as if Rico knew something was coming his way.

Angel hadn't been by the precinct in days, but he'd checked in now and then, letting Joe know things were going well, but something was definitely up.

Friday morning when Joe checked his voice mail, there was a message from Nyssa. She said she had some news about Charlie. He wanted to know the details, so he called her. Across the street, Angel and Rico entered a coffee shop as he dialed Nyssa.

"Hi, honey." Vanessa's voice was cheerful.

"I hate Caller ID," Joe complained.

"Why?"

"It takes away the element of surprise." Joe leaned back taking a sip of coffee.

"Well, I have a surprise for you. Charlie's going to be out of the house by tonight, and I'm sending the kids to see your mother for the weekend."

"Is that so? That sounds like fun." Joe smiled.

"It will be, if you can manage to get home before I fall asleep."

"I'll do my best. So is Charlie moving out?"

"Yes. She's going to move into an apartment in the building Jerry's buying. She said Jerry's going to make rooms available and see how many women he can get off the street. He's going to get Brother Tracy to help with the outreach. He asked me if you could help."

"Me?" Joe laughed.

"Yes. He wanted to know if fliers advertising the new shelter could be given to women who are picked up and brought to the station for prostitution, shoplifting and other things like that."

"I think I can swing that. Tell me, does Charlie think Jerry's really changed?"

"Yes, she does. They have a Bible study every night. She even had Angel sitting in when he was staying at the apartment."

"She managed that? Wow! He must have it bad."

"Sound familiar?" She teased.

"Yeah, it does. I recall some young pup following you around. I think he even joined choir to be near you."

Nyssa laughed and Joe smiled. Even now, after fifteen years and four kids, he was still crazy in love. She'd not managed to get him to give his heart to God yet, but he knew some day he would. The timing wasn't right.

"So, will you be home before midnight?"

"Honey, since the kids are gone and Charlie's out of the house, I may be there before five." Joe held the phone close to his ear listening to his wife. He smiled and laughed when she was done speaking, "You better hope your pastor doesn't hear you talk like that."

"Hey, we're married. It's *all* legal!" Joe smiled, told his wife he loved her, and looked at his watch. He pushed his flip phone into his pocket and tried to get his mind back on Rico and Angel, instead of thinking about his plans for a romantic evening with his Nyssa.

*****

It didn't take Charlie long to pack and be on her way to her new apartment. She looked down at the twin bed with a smile. Jerry was downsizing and so was she.

She prayed as she unpacked. Tomorrow her dad was going to have surgery. She wanted to be there, but it wasn't going to happen. She couldn't afford to put her new job at risk, even if she could afford the bus fare now. There were so many things to do, and for now, she was Jerry's only employee.

Jerry kept her busy making phone calls and taking applications for the office spaces they were going to lease. He hoped this would provide jobs for some of the women who would be living in the complex.

The plans were rough at the present time, but they would tweak them to fit their needs as they went along. Charlie recalled back to when she first moved in with Allie and some of the conversations they had. She knew it would be hard to get some of the women to change their lifestyle.

Even though their circumstances were less than desirable, some of them made a lot of money, and for them that was what it was all about!

When her cell rang, she dropped her clothes on the bed and grabbed the phone, hoping it would be Angel. He hadn't called in days and she missed talking to him. She didn't recognize the number. She answered, wanting to hear his voice. "Hello?"

"Charlie, I need to talk to you."

It was a woman and she was crying. "Allie? Is that you?"

"Yes," the crying continued, "I need to talk to you. I've got a big problem. I don't know what to do."

"Where are you? I'll come and meet you."

"I'm at the clinic, but I can meet you at Jim's Diner."

"I'll be there in twenty minutes." Charlie dropped what she was doing and headed over to Jim's. Allie sounded upset. Charlie hoped and prayed her friend didn't have Aids. It was something Allie wouldn't talk about, though now and then, she would get tested.

When Charlie walked into the diner, Jim shot her a look of worry. She ignored him and went back to the booth where Allie was sitting.

She dropped down beside of Allie and took her hand. Her soft bronze skin was covered in tears and though they'd not talked in weeks, Allie wrapped her arms around Charlie and held on tight.

"I don't know what I'm going to do."

"What's wrong, Allie? What happened?"

Allie moved her arms from her friend's neck, shook her head, and grabbed another tissue from her pocket. "So many things have changed since you left that day."

"Good or bad?"

"Good, great; until now. Do you remember that guy I was telling you about?"

"William?" Charlie questioned.

"Yeah, Will. We've been datin' and we still haven't . . . you know." Allie paused, took a deep breath, and then went on. "Several nights ago, I was coming home and one of my old John's crept up behind me.

154

He pulled me into the alley and offered me money. I told him no." Once again Allie burst into tears and for a few moments she cried on Charlie's shoulder. Finally she was able to speak again.

"He raped me . . . Charlie, I'm pregnant with that pig's baby. I'm afraid William is going to leave me. I don't know what to do. I had this feeling something was wrong so I went down to be tested. They told me I'm pregnant."

"I'm so sorry." Charlie wiped a few tears away from her friend's face. "I wish there was something I could do."

"There is. You can go with me tomorrow to the clinic."

"Sure, I can do that. What time?"

"I don't know, but it won't take that long. It's still early."

Charlie grew quiet when she realized what her friend was saying. "Allie . . . are you talking about having an abortion?"

"Un huh."

"But you can't! The baby's a part of you."

"What? . . . You want me to keep this thing."

"Its not a thing, Allie. It's a baby. It's *your* baby."

"I don't want it. I won't do anything that might come between William and me. I'm trying to go straight. That's what you wanted me to do. Now you have to help me."

"I'm sorry, Allie. I can't help you do that. You need to think about this. You can't just kill your baby."

"Why not? I didn't ask for it. It's not William's and I only want to have his child. Not this man's."

"I know it would be hard. But you should talk to him about it. See what he says. If he loves you maybe he. . . "

"You don't know men very well! They don't want anything to do with their own children most of the time, they sure ain't gonna want to raise someone else's!"

"You should at least ask him." Charlie could tell her friend was getting angry and she started pushing to get out of the booth.

"Let me out. I'll get one of the other girls to take me. I can see you won't help."

"Allie, I can't help you. I wish I could, but I can't. Think about this, in the future every time the day passes that your baby would have been born, you'll be wondering what he, or she, would be like. Who would this child have turned out to be? And, wishing you had kept it. Please, Allie, think about this before you do it."

"I already have and I can't have this b a . . ."

"You can't even say the word can you?" Charlie stood looking down at Allie for a moment. "You know it's wrong, down deep in your heart. Say it. Say it out loud. Tell me you want to kill this baby?"

Allie didn't speak; she only looked at Charlie and shook her head no. Her dark eyes rimmed with tears again as she headed toward the door, not turning around to face Charlie or the truth.

Chapter 25
Chance Meeting

Angel knew Rico well by now, and the way he was acting said it all. Angel no longer did the driving; he was a fulltime bodyguard. Rico wanted the protection Angel could provide, but didn't seem to trust him with all his secrets.

Something was going on. Rico looked over his shoulder way too often, and for the third time since he returned from Texas; Rico was going to a private meeting.

The new driver, David, sat behind the wheel, and once again Angel waited in the car. Something was brewing, and Angel could smell it.

Rico had spent three days near the border, without Angel, and since his return, he'd been meeting with different buyers. Drugs or guns? Angel needed to find out; maybe they'd get *that* bust after all.

It was close to six p.m. by the time the meeting ended. Rico and his two cohorts walked out, shook hands and headed to their cars. As Rico climbed in and sat down Angel looked at him and spoke.

"I don't know why you're paying me to be your bodyguard. What good am I here, sitting in the back of this car? How can I protect you like this?"

Rico didn't answer but looked up at David. "Back to the club," he ordered. After a few minutes he turned to Angel and spoke. "I'm not afraid of those guys!"

"Then who are you afraid of? Don't you think it would do me some good to know what I'm supposed to be protecting you from? You didn't even take me to Texas!"

"That may have been a mistake. I didn't plan well. If I go again, I'll be taking you."

"Good. I like to earn my money."

"Don't worry. It could get messy soon. I've got two different buyers nipping at my heels. When I sell to one, and not to the other . . . well one of them isn't going to be happy."

Finally, something to go on. Rico looked on edge. What was he getting them into? Angel let the silence fall for a moment, and then spoke. "You do know if you start selling drugs here you'll be stepping on toes?"

"I know," Rico looked out the window. "It's not drugs."

At that moment the phone rang, and Rico started speaking in Spanish.

Angel only knew a smattering of words but he heard munitions, which meant ammunition, dinero, which meant money and Estados, which meant states. He was guessing Rico was bringing guns over the border but he didn't have a clue when it was going to happen.

When the car came to a stop at The Oasis II, Rico stepped out, phone to his ear, arguing with his dad. "I know I've been unavailable, but you could leave them at my office. I need those papers!"

Angel moved around to the other side of the car and waited. Rico agreed to something, hung up and took another call. In between calls, Rico pushed the mute button, and looked at Angel.

"Wait in my office. I'm expecting some important papers and I don't want them lost. Dad claims he sent them once already, so be sure you get them this time. I'll be back in about an hour."

Angel didn't argue, because it would mean an opportunity to snoop in Rico's office. He nodded and went inside. The club wasn't busy so he made his way back to the office. He dialed Joe as soon as he closed the door. The minute his brother picked up, he started talking.

"I got something. Get ready, this could be our chance to squeeze our bird and learn something."

"I'll put it together. Is he there now?" Joe asked.

"No, but we can bring him in; he owns this place. Have the guys look behind the bar. I'm sure they'll find something and they won't have to look very hard."

"I'll get on it. We'll be there in about thirty minutes."

Angel closed his phone and put it away. He knew Rico kept a small stash of marijuana behind the bar, enough so they could take him in. They needed to get Rico to the station to question him. Maybe then they could figure out when and where the guns would be coming across the border.

*****

Charlie got the call about ten minutes after she left the diner. It didn't take her long to figure out Jerry's problems. He needed some papers delivered to Rico, ASAP, but due to a meeting with their new renters, he didn't have time. Charlie agreed to run the errand for him.

It didn't take her long to pick up the papers, get another cab and head to the club. She'd been to The Oasis II before, and she couldn't help but wonder if she would run into Angel. It'd been almost two weeks since she'd seen him; she hoped their paths would cross soon.

Charlie paid the cabby. Walking toward the entrance, she felt out of place. She suppressed the urge to turn and go and was relieved to see a friendly face at the door. John smiled and waved at her. "Let me guess, you're here to see Rico."

"You're right."

"He's not here. Would you like to wait?"

"I guess so. I need to make sure he gets these papers."

"His office is down the hall. Third door on the right."

"Thanks," Charlie started to go but turned and asked, "Is Angel here?" She could see irritation on John's face, but he answered.

"He's here somewhere." Charlie noticed John could care less if she found Angel. Was he jealous? John was nice looking, but she couldn't help it if she wasn't interested in him.

Sometimes it was best to not be overly friendly; you didn't want a person getting the wrong idea. John seemed like he could be one of those people, taking any bit of friendship to be more than it was. He also seemed the type to want more than a goodnight kiss on the first date.

The way he looked at her made her feel uneasy. Angel, on the other hand, had some of these same traits but there was something about him that drew her to him. Maybe it was her own stupidity to think he was different, but she hoped he was. She remembered how he teased her about what kind of man she wanted and how he'd seemed jealous of Rico.

It wasn't fair to be angry with him. It should have been enough to know he didn't want her alone with Rico. She hoped to get the chance to apologize, like she should have done that night. It's never a good thing to let the sun go down on your anger. The Bible plainly taught against it.

Charlie walked down the hall to Rico's office, grateful the music had faded to a dull roar. She slipped into the bathroom before heading into the office to wait. She checked her hair and makeup. Since she'd been in a rush all day, she brushed her teeth. Her mother taught her years ago to carry a toothbrush and small tube of toothpaste for such an emergency.

Once done, she double checked everything and placed the items in her purse, stepping back out into the dim hallway. Bon Jovi's, 'You Give Love A Bad Name' was playing on the jukebox. Charlie paused at the office door. With Rico gone she didn't see any reason to knock so she put her hand on the doorknob and went in.

160

Chapter 26
Caught Red Handed

When Angel saw the door opening he knew there was no way he could put the papers away in time. He'd tried to lock the door, but couldn't. He started to jump to his feet, but instead, pulled out his Glock. He readied for the first shot.

When he saw Charlie's shocked expression, he exhaled, and put his gun away. He was trying to figure out what to say, but she spoke first.

"Who did you expect?"

"No one in particular. Rico's got me jumping at shadows," Angel stood, walked over and closed the door. He then walked back and closed the files. He stacked several files on the edge of the desk and placed some back inside the top drawer. He wasn't sure he'd placed them in the right order and wondered if Rico would notice. Placing two files into another drawer, Angel looked up at Charlie. She was watching him too closely.

"Were you snooping?"

Angel wondered should he play dumb, go on the defense, or ask her a question. He decided to try a small combination of all three. He pushed the drawer closed and crossed his arms. "Me snooping? You're the one that came sneaking into Rico's office. I'm supposed to be here. Besides, do I look guilty of something?"

"You were doing good until you got to that last part. Yes. You look guilty."

"But of what?" Angel moved closer, positioning himself so the next time he moved, the file he'd placed on the edge of the desk, would fall. He held out his hand to Charlie. "I believe that file's for me."

161

"Can you be trusted with it?" Charlie took the file out from under her arm, reaching it to Angel.

"Maybe. Maybe not." His comment made her smile, but she handed him the file and he took it. "I see you're still running errands for Jerry."

"Yes, I like my job."

Angel laid the file on the desk. Charlie followed his movements, and he knew she suspected something, but what?

When Charlie turned, looking toward the door, Angel knew it was time. There were voices in the hall; one of them was Rico. He couldn't have planned it better. Angel took one step forward and papers went everywhere; he bent down and began to pick them up. When Charlie knelt beside him, she was playing right into his plan.

Angel moved closer to Charlie and bent on one knee. He held most of the papers in one hand. He could hear Rico getting closer; hear the man's deep laughter. Angel knew this would look staged to Charlie. He only hoped she wouldn't say anything to Rico. He looked at Charlie when she spoke his name.

"Angel . . . what's going on? Did you knock those papers off on purpose?"

Mistake or not, Angel thought it best to be honest with Charlie. "Yes."

"I thought so." Charlie spoke so softly he barely heard her.

Angel ignored Joe's voice in his head saying, '*what are you doing?*' If Charlie mentioned anything to Rico, it could blow his cover, or worse. He spoke, hoping he could trust her. "I don't want Rico to know I've been snooping. I need to throw him off guard."

Charlie nodded as Angel moved closer. He held the files in his right hand while he moved his left hand, pushing his fingers into Charlie's hair. Soon Rico would step in.

"I've been wanting to do this for a *long* time. I'm sorry it's going to be like this . . . rushed, and for the wrong reason." Angel then moved in to kiss Charlie just as the door came open.

Angel knew the minute Rico walked in, though his eyes were closed as he kissed Charlie. He hoped Charlie wouldn't slap him, or push him away, and she didn't. She even tentatively kissed him back. When Rico cursed, they pulled apart and Angel moved his hand from those red curls and helped Charlie to her feet.

"Sorry about that," Charlie whispered, to no one in particular as she took the file from Angel and began to place the papers inside that she'd picked up. "I guess it got knocked off."

"Wonder how?" The bearded man with Rico called out. He elbowed his partner, a smirk on his face. Charlie was blushing now. Angel felt sorry for her. She looked at him briefly, and then placed the file back on the desk.

"Sorry. I'm afraid they aren't in order anymore," she directed this comment to Rico and picked up the file that she'd brought with her. She held it out to Rico. "Jerry said to place this in your hands."

"Good thing," Rico spat out as he took the file. Rico looked angry enough to hit Charlie, but he didn't.

"I should go. It looks like you have business to take care of." Charlie wasted no time stepping toward the door that was still standing open. The bearded man stepped back to allow her to pass.

Angel moved toward the door calling out as he left, "I'll see to it she gets home safe."

The bearded man who made the last clever remark laughed, and slapped Angel on the back as he walked by. "I'll bet you will."

"They're not an item," Rico's anger flared again as he turned to follow Angel.

"They look like they are." The bearded man put a hand on Rico's shoulder and shook his head no. "We have business to discuss. I don't have time for you to be chasing after women. Let's look over this paperwork."

Angel knew Rico would be furious, but he had to speak to Charlie. He didn't know what to think. She'd covered for him perfectly, even after he all but lied to her. As Rico slammed the door shut, Angel hurried to catch Charlie as she walked down the hall.

It took him only a few paces before he was beside her. He placed his hands on her shoulders and was about to speak when he heard a voice call out. "This is the police. Everyone stop, put your hands over your head and lock your wrists together."

"Great!" Angel sighed. He wanted to speak to Charlie, but now he couldn't. He moved her out of the line of fire in case Rico came out, guns blazing. When they stepped around the corner, two officers came to them.

"Come with me," a tall officer grabbed Angel and pushed him out the door. Once outside and around the corner, Joe appeared. Angel began pacing and yelling at the same time. "Get Charlie out of there now!"

"What's she doing here? I don't want her to see me!" Joe yelled.

"She was delivering some papers. Get her out of there!"

Joe nodded, found a lady officer and explained what he wanted. Angel described Charlie to the officer. A few seconds later, Charlie was in a patrol car. She would be taken to the station and put in one of the holding rooms.

Chapter 27
Arrested

Charlie kept glancing at her watch; it was almost eight. She wondered where they'd taken Angel. She'd seen Rico being escorted to a back room, watched a couple of young men fighting with three officers, and shook her head at their actions. She guessed they'd be spending the night in jail. When Charlie saw Jerry come in, she looked up and shrugged.

"I'll have you out of here soon. I'm sorry this happened." Jerry walked over to where Charlie was sitting and pulled out a chair. He reached out and took her hand as she spoke.

"It's not your fault. I'm sure they'll let me go soon."

"It shouldn't be taking so long. This is ridiculous."

"Are you here to bail out Rico?"

Jerry shook his head and let go of Charlie's hand. "No, but I did talk to him. I offered to bail him out if he'd agree to try and change. They found drugs in his office and behind the bar. He says he knew nothing about it."

"Do you believe him? I've never seen him do drugs."

"I haven't either, but I know he hangs out with people who do. I'm sure he's involved in some way."

"I'm afraid so," Charlie said, shaking her head in disappointment.

"Me too. But I'm not bailing him out; he can spend the night in jail. Maybe it'll help him to see he needs to change."

"We can only hope."

"Yes, we can." Jerry rose to his feet. "They told me not to stay long, but I'll do my best to see they release you."

"Do you know if they're keeping Angel?"

"No, I don't know. I haven't seen him," Jerry added.

"Well, thanks for the help. I'm sure they'll let me go soon."

"I'll see to it," Jerry kissed Charlie on the forehead. "I'll be back in a few minutes. The renters won't be here until tomorrow, so you can stay at the apartment tonight."

"That's okay. I can get a cab."

"I won't hear of it. After tonight, you'll need a good night's rest. Don't worry about anything. I'll take care of you."

*****

Angel glanced over his shoulder as Joe came into the screening room. He quickly turned his attention back to Jerry as he bent down and kissed Charlie on the forehead, and then he scowled as the man walked out of the room. Angel stood with his arms crossed, looking on. "I can't wait to be done with this case. I don't trust that old man."

"Don't you mean you're jealous of him?" Joe laughed.

"Jealous? What makes you say that?"

"Well, he seems to spend more time with Charlie than you do. I've seen him kiss her twice, and after all he kicked you out of the apartment. That had to burn."

"Is there any way we can keep her here?" Angel tried to ignore the things Joe said.

"We could book her. I don't think you want to do that."

Angel grumbled under his breath and shook his head no. "I don't want her to go home with that old man."

"Do you want to talk to her before I send her home?"

Angel blew out a breath. "I don't think it'd be a good idea. Right now, I'm not in the right frame of mind."

"What do you mean?" Joe's brow furrowed.

"I want to tell her I'm working undercover."

"You're kidding . . . right?" Joe walked over and looked at Angel.

"No. I'm not."

"Are you so caught up with her that it's messing with your head?"

166

"Not like you mean. Not to the point where I'm making mistakes. It's more like, I want to. That old man thinks I'm not good enough for Charlie. He's pushing her and Rico together."

"I don't like the way you're talking."

"I know what I'm doing. I'm just venting."

"Well, be sure you're venting where she can't hear you. We can't have her messing things up when we're so close. If we can get Rico to cooperate we might be able to get these guns off the street and shut him down."

"Doesn't it bother you to put so much of yourself into a case just to see some punk get off scott free, when they should be going to jail?"

"Yeah, it does. If there was something I could do about it, I would. Am I going to let the bigger fish go because I'm too worried I'll lose my bait? No!"

Angel and Joe worked well together, but sometimes they didn't see eye to eye. It kept things interesting, and when they did butt heads they respected each other. Angel looked at Charlie. He wanted to talk to her, but he was frustrated with the whole situation.

The two-way glass was spotless and Angel could see Charlie's every expression. What was she thinking? His ego told him she was thinking about him. After all, he was thinking about her. He didn't have *any* trouble recalling the kiss, though it was brief. Did she have any idea he was a cop? Would she care if he was trying to double cross Rico?

He wanted to talk to her, but not here. Joe would pull him off the case if he knew how involved he was becoming with Charlie.

*****

Lloyd knew the bathroom was off limits since Rico was in there, but it was the best chance he'd have to speak to the man. He whispered a few words to the guard at the door, smiled and shrugged. The man nodded, stepped back letting him in.

When Lloyd stepped in, Rico stood at the sink washing his hands. "They're really hammering me about some gun shipment

167

coming in to the states. They think I have something do to with it."

Lloyd stepped closer to Rico keeping his voice low. "I'm not wearing a wire. I came in to let you know something. That girl, Charlie, the one who went home with your dad, I think she's a plant. I saw Joe work all around getting her booked this evening. There's no need for him to do that."

"You think she's a cop?"

"No, I don't think she's a cop. But something's up or Joe would have booked her. I found this for you. It's a way to take care of her if you want."

"I don't want to have any part in doing something to a cop," Rico grabbed a hand towel shaking his head.

"It's nothing like that. The guy I saw in Indiana is in town. Something about Charlie really got to him. He's so angry that he filed a report at the station. I got one of the girls to get me his name and number. I think he'd be more than happy to take Charlie off your hands."

"I'll take that." Rico looked at the name and phone number. "I saw Charlie in my office, she was snooping through some of the papers. She might have seen something, but tell me, why would the police be using her? She's from out of state."

"They could be having her help in order to get some of these charges dropped. I don't know for sure. I do know it's strange she wasn't booked, and that Joe was keeping her out of the limelight."

"I thought it was strange that Dad took up with her so fast. I'm wondering if he's up to something. I don't think he could change that much, but he might turn on me to keep from going back to jail."

"Could be, I don't know," Lloyd shrugged. "She might be working with the cops. I can't say for sure. But I thought you might find this newsworthy of a bonus."

"I'll see what I can do."

Lloyd nodded and walking out the door, made his way back to his post. He spoke to the guard that was watching the door. "Thanks man; never eat a burrito on a work night."

168

Chapter 28
Reflections

After running through the drive-thru for an early breakfast, Angel dropped by the apartment to see Charlie. He was surprised when Jerry answered the door. Rather than invite Angel in, Jerry stepped out into the hallway. The two men looked at each other for a moment.

"I need to speak with Charlie."

"That's not going to happen." Jerry snapped.

"What?" Angel said with a slight laugh. "Since when did you become her guardian? Charlie's old enough to decided who she talks to."

"Since last night. I apologized to her. I realize I've done her a disservice by asking her to be around my son when he's not living right. She'll be working for me, but only handling and dealing with things I deem safe and reputable. You, young man, along with my son, are neither of those things."

Angel's temper slid up a notch. Clinching his fist, he tried to control it, and then thought, why should he? Jerry didn't know his true identity. The man thought he was a thug . . . a thug that wasn't getting his way.

"I know that I work for your son, but let me tell you, old man, you don't have any right telling Charlie who she can, or can't, see. I want you to tell her I'm here. Then let her decide what she wants to do."

Jerry shook his head; "I'll call the cops if I need to."

"Go ahead, I don't care. I want to talk to Charlie."

Jerry shook his head no. "If you like this cushy job you have with Rico, you better think twice before you cross me. I may not be young anymore but I still can get things done in a pinch. You need to go."

"You're a Bible thumper now. What are you going to do to me?" Angel was taller than Jerry and he took a step closer, but the man didn't scare easily, maybe not at all.

"Son, I don't want to hurt you. I don't even want to fight with you. I'm a Christian now and that means, even though I don't always like it, I have to act different. I'm supposed to turn the other cheek and show love, even when I don't want to. But it doesn't mean I'm perfect, either.

"If you know what's good for you, you'll buy yourself a Bible and start reading it. Start going to church, and then maybe some day you'll be worthy of that young woman in there."

Angel wasn't sure what to say, but he couldn't walk away without getting in a few jabs. He stepped back and smiled at Jerry. "I think maybe you're saving Charlie for yourself. Maybe you like younger women, and you've decided she'll make a good wife." He thought this would make Jerry mad, but the man laughed.

"Son, you've got a lot to learn. Go on and be about your business. Charlie is off limits to you, and to Rico, and she's not on my short list for wives. So go on and try to make something of yourself before you try to impress someone like her." Jerry turned, closing the door in Angels face.

This old man kept surprising and irritating Angel. There wasn't much he could do for now, so he turned and walked away. A part of him wanted to push the man aside and go on into the apartment, but he decided against it.

As he rode down in the elevator, he thought about Charlie and the things Jerry said. The man was right about one thing. Angel was surprised Charlie had given him a second look while he was working for Rico.

Though he'd not done anything terrible, he knew she went to church, and it confused him even more to think about it. Why did she have anything to do with him at all? Why hadn't she slapped him when he'd kissed her?

Was she starting to have feelings for him? Was Nyssa right? Would he regret it if he let Charlie slip through his fingers? If he did want to date her, how did you date someone who went to church?

Angel ran his fingers through his long hair, thinking about his brother. Would Charlie ask him to cut his hair short, just like Joe's? He tried to picture himself dating someone who went to church. There were so many rules; you can't do this and you can't do that. Would he even want to be married to someone who went to church?

His dad talked a lot about the rules and regulations of the church, and how they had come between him and his first wife. Lila wanted him to go to church three times a week. She wanted him to stop going to the movies, and he couldn't drink anymore. She even quit wearing makeup and jewelry.

Maybe he was better off if he didn't date Charlie. He didn't want to start seeing her, just to end up hurting her because he couldn't live as she did.

Angel's thoughts drifted to his brother and how he and his wife got along. Nyssa went to church a couple of times a week and she wore light make-up. Joe drank now and then, but he didn't drink at home.

Joe did have short hair and no facial hair. Maybe some things weren't an issue with his brother, but he did seem happy. Angel let out a deep breath when he hit the cool air and headed to his car. He was young and good-looking; why was he even thinking about settling down?

There was lots of time to think about the woman he wanted to spend the rest of his life with, and there were plenty of women to pick from. Besides, he had a good job that kept him way too busy to think about getting married.

Angel put the key in the switch and started his car. He put his hands on the wheel, shook his head and laughed. He'd listed a lot of reasons he shouldn't date Charlie, but as he sat there, the only thing he could think about was how soft her eyes had looked that second before he kissed her.

Chapter 29
Transformation

"I'm not sure Rico's going to want me there," Charlie glanced out the window; they were on their way to the park to meet Rico.

"He may not." Jerry sighed and shook his head. "I don't know what to do about that boy. The sad part is, I led him here. I've got to change things, show Rico that all those years we were both going down the wrong path."

"Keep trying, don't give up. Staying in the Word will keep your faith strong. Faith is the key to getting things done."

"I'm learning. I've started reading one chapter in the Bible every morning. Did you know if you read only three chapters a day, you could read the Bible through in a year and a month? I'm reading Acts, but I need to read the whole Bible; there's so much I don't know."

"You could read the Bible all the way through ten times and still not know it all, but we should keep trying."

Jerry leaned forward and spoke to the driver, "Pull in, over there, to the right of that limo."

Charlie noticed Angel and the driver standing by the door of Rico's car. None of them paid any attention as they drove by. She couldn't help but notice how handsome Angel looked; he wore a dark suit, a white shirt and deep blue tie. As they passed, she noticed his hands were on his hips and he'd pushed his jacket back, revealing his gun. Her brow furrowed. Most of the time he kept his gun hidden; now it was out in the open for all to see.

The cab came to a stop and Jerry handed the driver a fifty. "Wait here. If I need to pay more, I will."

The driver took the money, shook his head no, and leaned back, pulling his cap over his eyes. Jerry and Charlie got out of the cab, walking in the direction of the limo. When Rico came closer, Charlie could see from his expression he was angry. When he spoke, she knew for sure what he was thinking.

"I don't know why you brought her; she's not family. I thought you wanted to have a *family* meeting."

"I understand. Charlie please wait in the car."

"Certainly." Charlie started back to the car, turned and looked at Angel. He looked right at her and then turned away. He didn't smile or acknowledge her in anyway, and she turned and went back to the cab. She'd deal with Angel and his shifting attitude later.

Charlie waited outside the cab, trying to ignore Angel, and prayed for Jerry. He and Rico were arguing. It didn't look like Rico would change anytime soon. Ten minutes later, Jerry came walking to the cab. They both got in and Jerry told the driver to take them to Fifth and Main.

Even the cabby could sense something didn't go well. Charlie noticed him stealing glances at his male passenger. When Jerry started speaking, Charlie knew the cabby was taking it all in.

"I asked Rico to give up his part of the business again and he said no. He isn't ready to give up his sinful life. I should have known this wouldn't be easy."

"We all want to see our loved one's saved and going to church."

"True, but I don't know about Rico. I told him he needed to understand I'm not the same person; that I've turned my life over to the Lord. He laughed at me when I told him it was time for me to start disciplining him. But that's what your pastor advised me to do."

"When did you talk to Brother Tracy?"

"I called him the other day and he gave me some of the verses I quoted to Rico. 'Discipline your children; you'll be glad you did, they'll turn out delightful to live with.' Proverbs 29:17. He said it would be easier to understand in the Message version."

"I can see how that wouldn't go over well."

"No, Rico told me I couldn't make him do anything. He's my son, and if I can make a difference in his life, I'm going to."

"You can. It may not be easy, but you can do it with God's help."

Jerry nodded. "I begged him to let me help. I even tried to hug him; he pushed me away saying I could go hug my new child."

"I'm sorry," Charlie rested her hand on Jerry's arm. "I think he's angry because I didn't want to see him socially."

"I never should have asked you to talk to him. I'm sorry I put you in that place."

"No hard feelings; I understand."

"Thanks," Jerry looked out the window at the new building he'd rented and shook his head. "I've done all I can do. The only way I can discipline him now is to take away his power and money. I'm going to talk to a lawyer and see where I stand. Until then, I've put him in God's hands and asked the Lord to help him to realize a need for a Savior. It took going to jail for me to see the truth. I hope he doesn't have to sink as low as I did to learn the true lesson of life."

*****

Rico's anger kept rising as he walked to his car. He wanted to go out and do every mean and despicable thing he could to spite his dad. He'd done so many of these same things! How could he think he was so much better now because he got down on his knees and said a few prayers? Did he really think he could change his life so easily?

Slamming the door fed Rico's anger. He looked at Angel after barking at the driver to head back to the club. "I didn't see you paying any attention to Charlie. What's wrong? Did she leave a bad taste in your mouth?"

"In a way. Some things happen on impulse. It can't go anywhere with her. I'm not putting up with all of her sermons for a couple of kisses. It's not worth it."

"Well, maybe you do have some sense after all." The two of them sat in silence until Rico's anger once again boiled over. Rico spat out a few more words before taking out his phone and making a call. "I'll show him. He says he's turned me over to God, and that he'll be praying for me. Well, I'll give him something to pray about."

Rico made three phone calls and finally found the right man. If his dad was angry now . . . just wait until he discovered his son's next venture would be into human trafficking.

Chapter 30
Too Little, Too Late

Benny stood leaning against the doorframe, waiting to speak to an officer about Charlie. It was Monday, and his head was throbbing from staying out all weekend. Since he was running low on cash, he needed to find out where Tammy's pesky sister had gone. He wasn't going to let her get away with stealing his money and gun.

Being at the police station wasn't his idea of a fun time, and he was thinking about turning and leaving when someone spoke.

"May I help you?"

Benny smiled and straightened, giving the girl his best smile. "Hey, if I'd known they had pretty girls like you down here, I would have gotten arrested a long time ago."

The young woman smiled, and seemed unsure of what to say. Benny knew he was nice looking, and since he and Tammy had broken up he'd dropped about ten pounds. He smiled at the girl, holding out his hand. When she took it, he bent over, kissing her fingers lightly as he spoke. "Benny's the name; lovin's the game."

The young woman laughed, pulling her hand back. "My names Rachel. How can I help you?"

"For starters, you can give me your number, or at the least take mine."

"Maybe the latter." She smiled stepping back.

"I can deal with that." Benny walked over to *Rachel's* desk, grabbed up a pen and paper and jotted down his phone number. He straightened and stepped back. "Call me sometime."

"I'll think about it. Now, can I help you?"

"Yeah, I'm here to see if you guys found my girlfriend's sister. She's been missing."

The woman frowned. "That's terrible. Why don't you go over and have a seat at the back desk. I'm sure Joe can help you. He should be back in a few minutes."

"Thanks."

Benny sat down, stealing glances at Rachel until she rose and walked down a nearby hall. Bored, he moved his attention elsewhere. Leaning forward, Benny studied a frame on the officer's desk; he looked at the picture-perfect family. The man stood behind his wife and four kids.

Benny's lip snarled; he knew their sort. He'd bet they went to church every Sunday and were the type to be on one of those perfect family sitcoms.

He sat back, tapping his finger, keeping an eye out for Rachel. Minutes later he spotted the man in the picture down a back hall. He was walking with what looked to be an informant. The second man had long hair and was wearing a long leather jacket.

The two men spoke for a moment and then walked down the hall, out of sight. Benny sighed, tilted in his chair, and thought about leaving. He turned back facing the desk as the officer approached. Benny stood and shook hands with the man, hoping *finally* someone would get him some satisfaction.

*****

Joe sat down, looking at the man sitting at his desk. He wanted to start on his paperwork, but he'd have to take care of this first. He took out a sheet of paper, a pen and then forced a smile. Joe started taking down general information . . . name, address and complaint.

"Now what's your reason for coming in?"

"I want to know if there's any news on my finance's sister. She's been missing for a while. She stole my gun and took some money, but I'm more worried about how she is."

"What's her name? We have so many missing people; I'm sure someone's working on her case."

"I came in once, but thought I'd check back and see if there was any news. Her name's Charlie Anderson."

Joe looked up, trying to hide his surprise. He'd seen the report, and Charlie had never been reported missing. Nyssa questioned her about the flyer, but refused to ask her if she'd stolen anything.

Charlie assured them her family knew she was safe and staying in Chicago. Joe found it hard to believe Charlie would steal anything, but he'd be sure and ask her about it. "So you're looking to get your gun back?"

"Sure, but I want to know if she's okay. The last time I talked to her sister, Charlie was still missing."

"Well, you know I'm not supposed to give out any information to someone who isn't family."

"Really? But she took my gun and money. You should have to tell me where she is."

Joe could see the guy had real anger issues with Charlie. "Was the gun registered?" Joe tried not to smile as he watched the punk start to fidget.

"I'm not sure . . . it was a gift. I can check with my ex and see."

"You do that," Joe nodded trying to seem as if he really cared. "If you can't bring in proof of registration, I'm sure the gun is lost. Now, about the money, how much did she take?"

"Close to eighty dollars."

"That's a lot of money."

"It sure is."

Joe made a note and then stood, holding out his hand. This guy looked kind of dumb. He'd really like to get a copy of his fingerprints. He was more than likely guilty of something.

"Would you like to register with the state for free? We can take your prints, an official address and phone number. It might help in getting your money back." The man thought about it for a moment, and then a bell went off in his head, and he spoke.

"No, thanks. I'll check in now and then. If you find my gun, let me know."

"I sure will. But I'll need that registration before I can give it to you."

"I'll see if I can find it."

The punk turned and left. Joe folded the paper up and placed it in his desk. He'd try to talk to Charlie about this Benny person and see what she did with his gun.

Benny could still file a complaint, but Joe doubted if he'd be back again. He looked pretty worried when Joe asked him if he wanted to register for free.

Chapter 31
Dangerous Secrets

Angel drove home, wondering about Rico. What would his anger make him do? They might get a lead on some flesh traders, if Rico followed through with his plan. Later, he'd call Joe and let him know they needed to keep the leash loose on Rico for a few more days. Let him get in deep, get some names and maybe the whereabouts of some girls.

Angel loved his job, when he was able to put scum away and help those in need. It kept him going, even on days when he began to hate the world.

He pulled up to the light and sat waiting. His thoughts, as usual, had moved to Charlie. Instead of turning right, he made a hard left, making a U-turn. He wanted to catch Charlie before she went upstairs to join Jerry. Since Rico was on the warpath, Angel wanted to warn her to keep her distance.

He knew he shouldn't tell her the whole story, but he wasn't taking any chances when it came to Rico. The anger Rico was carrying around made him more dangerous. Angel didn't want Charlie getting in the crosshairs of what Rico was feeling.

The excitement was building in his heart and mind; he so wanted to tell her he was a cop. He'd been spinning it around in his mind; was he going to kiss her again? Charlie was beautiful; he could easily imagine all kinds of things about her. A smile came to his lips as he turned right onto Lake Park. It pleased him no end that she was willing to take up for him when it came to Rico.

He'd wondered why she'd gone along with his charade. Did she know, somehow, he was working undercover, or did she like him so much she didn't care? He couldn't wait to find out.

When he got to the building, it was five p.m. He knew she wouldn't be home, so he waited. The building became busy around six, with many tenants coming and going. Angel frowned when Jerry stepped out of a cab, and he ducked down so he wouldn't be noticed.

He sat in the shadows, tapping his thumb against the steering wheel, listening to an old tape of the Eagles. A cab pulled close to the elevator. Angel turned off the tape player and climbed out as soon as the cabby left.

Angel knew the doors would close before he had time to speak to Charlie. He darted to the steps, ran as fast as he could to the second floor, hit the up button, and had about fifteen seconds to catch his breath. When the doors opened, Charlie's gaze met his, and for a fleeting moment he saw worry on her face.

When she saw who it was she smiled, and made his day. "Angel. What are you doing here?"

"I need to talk with you. Can you step off for a minute?"

"Sure," Charlie didn't hesitate to take his hand as she stepped off the elevator.

Angel wasted no time in speaking. "I wanted to talk, but Jerry won't let me see you."

"What?" Charlie followed Angel a few steps away from the elevator. He turned to face her and leaned against the wall. "When did you talk to Jerry?"

"Yesterday." Angel paused and held up a hand as a gesture. "I'm not here to complain; he thinks he's doing what's best. But we need to talk. Would you join me for dinner, or is Jerry expecting you?"

"I can go, but I've already eaten . . . we can go sit and talk." Her comment made Angel smile; he held out his hand and they walked to the elevator.

Angel unlocked the car and held the door open for Charlie. He then walked around to the driver's side, climbed in and buckled up. "Do you have some place in mind?"

"No, but I'd prefer anything else over one of Rico's clubs." Charlie added.

"Don't worry; I see that place enough as it is." Angel started the car, shifted into drive and pulled out. He glanced at Charlie as they turned onto the street. "I take it you didn't know Jerry was trying to keep us apart."

"No, I had no idea. He did say he wasn't going to ask me to see Rico anymore and apologized for placing me in any uncomfortable situations."

"I think he's lumping me in with Rico." Angel glanced at Charlie, but in the fading light he couldn't see her expression. She didn't jump in with what he wanted to hear, but after a moment she spoke.

"I guess he might think you two are alike. After all, you do work for Rico."

"But what about you. Do you think I'm like Rico?"

"In some ways."

"Do I make you uncomfortable?"

"You can be intimidating."

"Then why did you come with me?"

"I'm not sure." Charlie sighed.

This time when he glanced her way, he could see she was turned in her seat, looking at him. Angel hit the turn signal, made a hard right into a parking lot and looked for an empty spot. He pulled into a well-lit area, parked the car and shut off the engine. Taking off his seat belt, he turned toward Charlie.

"Are you eating here?" Charlie glanced out the window.

"No, I want to talk. I need to understand something."

"What's that?" Charlie turned toward Angel.

"You and me." Charlie nodded, averting her gaze. "Are you afraid of me?" Angel's tone showed he hoped not.

"No," Charlie looked up and then shrugged. "Am I afraid of what being involved with you would mean? . . . Yes."

Angel moved, leaning forward to stress the importance of his question. "Then why did you let me kiss you?"

Charlie didn't take her eyes from his as she tried to answer. "I could say it was because I knew you were trying to distract Rico."

"You could. But is that the real reason?"

"It's part of it. I wanted Rico to see I wasn't interested in him."

"Was there another reason?"

"Do I have to say it out loud?" Charlie laughed.

"I'd like to hear it . . . out loud." Angel smiled and waited.

"If you insist." Charlie sighed and shrugged, "I *really* wanted to kiss you."

"Ahhh, music to my ears." Angel leaned in to try and steal another kiss, but Charlie stopped him by placing her finger gently on his lips.

*****

"I'm having second thoughts."

"That's not good."

Charlie lowered her hand, letting it slide down Angel's soft leather coat. She slipped her fingers inside the palm of his hand as she moved in the seat to get comfortable. Angel rested his elbow on his knee and waited for her to speak.

"I like you, Angel. You've got a good sense of humor. I enjoy spending time with you, but I can't see this going anywhere. We're different; I don't see us coming to any common ground. I go to church, you don't. I think most of what Rico does is repulsive and against God's laws, but you work for him."

"But I'm not Rico."

"True, but you live in his world. I don't. I landed in his playground by accident. You chose to be here." Charlie became quiet then went on with her thought, "I have to be honest; we could date, but I don't want to *just* date, if it's not going somewhere. Angel, you're not the kind of man I see myself having a future with."

184

"That sounds final. If that's the way you feel, why did you accept my invitation tonight?"

"Several reasons. One being I want to know what's going on with you and Rico."

*****

Angel could feel Charlie slipping through his fingers, and he didn't like it. How did he handle this? He sat rubbing his thumb across the back of her hand, trying to think of what to say.

Charlie spoke, not giving him much time. "Angel, why were you snooping in Rico's papers? What were you looking for?"

Angel looked up quickly. "Who do you trust more, me or Rico?"

"You, of course. I don't trust Rico at all."

"Smart girl. Keep it that way."

"I'll try, but if there's something going on, I need to know what it is."

Angel nodded. "It's complicated."

"I'm sure it is, but I don't want to say the wrong thing and get you in trouble. I've never seen Rico get angry, but I have a feeling he's got an extreme temper."

"He does, and I don't want it directed at you."

"Then tell me what's going on." Charlie pleaded.

Angel shook his head at the predicament in which he found himself. "You don't know what you're asking."

"You may be right, but I don't want to get in front of Rico *or* Jerry and say something I shouldn't."

Angel sighed. What should he do? Tell Charlie the truth so she would know exactly what she was dealing with, or should he leave her wondering and take a chance that she wouldn't say the wrong thing?

"We don't know each other well, but you *can* trust me." Charlie's tone was low, and Angel knew she wouldn't lie.

"What would you do if I told you I was stealing from Rico, or spying on him for a competitor?" Angel noticed Charlie didn't pull her hand away; instead she rested her hand over his.

185

"I would let you know I don't approve, and that you should consider the danger you're putting yourself in."

"You wouldn't tell Jerry so he could protect his son?"

"No. Rico's a big boy. He knows what he's doing. Besides, Jerry's facing some issues of his own. He's thinking about taking the businesses back from Rico to take away some of his power."

"When?" Angel straightened in the seat knowing this could cause him problems.

"I don't know."

"Great, that's all I need, another roadblock." Angel looked at Charlie, an idea coming to him. "Hey, Jerry listens to you. Do you think you could talk him out of doing anything to Rico for a couple of weeks?"

"Maybe. I'm not sure."

"I don't want you to say anything that would make him ask questions, but I need things to stay as they are."

"Why? How can it hurt things if Rico loses some of his clubs or his money? Are you afraid you'll lose your job?"

"No." Angel sighed placing two fingers on his temple and then he nodded, thinking this was his only way out. Angel took Charlie's hand in his, kissed it, then looked her straight in the eye, "You *can not* repeat what I'm about to say . . . to anyone. Not Jerry, not Rico, no one can know. This will be our secret."

"I understand."

"I'm not sure you do. We can only talk about this in private. If I ever shake my head no, or change the subject, you must do as I say."

"I will."

"Good, because if you don't, my life could be in danger."

"Angel?" Charlie closed her eyes but quickly opened them when he spoke.

"If the information I'm about to tell you gets to anyone, especially Rico, it could cost me my life."

"I had no idea." Charlie straightened and looked at Angel. "Then don't tell me. I don't want anything to happen to you."

Angel studied Charlie's expression. She did care, and he went on with his thought, "If you don't tell anyone, I'll be fine."

"You trust me with your life?" Charlie's tone was apprehensive.

Angel gave her question some consideration and decided he did. He took a deep breath and then spoke. "I don't work for Rico."

"Do you work for Jerry?"

"I don't work for either of them."

"Then who do you work for?"

Angel took a deep breath, letting it out slowly, and then he spoke. "The Chicago Police Department."

"What? You're a cop?" Charlie spoke these last few words in a whisper, "Are you serious?"

"Yes."

"This doesn't make any sense. Are you crazy? If Rico finds out . . ." Charlie shook her head. "But I found you on the street in the bushes, and they arrested you."

"They had to arrest me. It would have looked strange if they hadn't. The night you found me, Joe had just dropped me off. Then, some thugs mugged me and beat me up." Angel knew he had to bring up Joe sooner or later, so why not now.

"Joe . . . Vanessa's Joe?"

"Yeah, he's my half-brother. I know Nyssa didn't like keeping the truth from you. Don't hold it against them; they were just protecting me."

"This is all so strange." Charlie paused and looked at Angel. "I won't mention it to anyone, not Jerry, Joe or Vanessa."

"Good." Joe might not agree this was a good thing, but if Jerry changed anything, the whole case could go up in smoke. After putting Joe out of his thoughts, Angel spoke, "I'm sure this will explain why I've been on and off, talking to you, ignoring you." Angel paused, leaned in, placed his left hand under her chin and looked from her eyes to her lips as he spoke. "At least now I can do this with a clear conscious."

Angel moved slowly, unsure of Charlie's reaction, until his lips touched hers. She tilted her head to ease into his kiss; *this* is what he wanted. He kept it gentle, soft, and brief and then pulled back, trying not to overwhelm her with the passion he felt.

Charlie smiled, and lowered her gaze as Angel pulled back from the kiss. "So, you're an officer? That's good news."

"How so?" Angel pushed down the desire to lean forward and kiss her again.

"It changes things . . . between us."

"Are you saying you can see yourself having a future with Angelo Morganson but not the thug, Angel Blackwell?"

"That's exactly what I'm saying." Charlie smiled.

"I can handle that." Angel leaned in for another kiss, but Charlie pressed her hand against his chest and shook her head no.

"What do we do now, as far as Rico and Jerry are concerned?"

Angel let out an audible sigh, knowing his kissing session was over. He relaxed and spoke. "I'll keep trying to find something concrete while you think of a reason for Jerry to leave things as they are with Rico."

"I'll think of something."

"Run it by me first," Angel said quickly.

"I will, but do you think it's safe for you to do this?"

"No," Angel laughed. "But it's my job."

"I wish I could have known all along. I would have been praying harder." Charlie reached over and took Angel's hand in hers. "I prayed, but I should have prayed more."

"You were praying for me?" Angel looked at her hands wrapped around his. When she spoke, he looked up.

"Yes, I prayed for your safety, that you'd get a better job and find the Lord."

"My stepmother and Gram have been praying for my soul for a long time." Angel added.

"Sometimes it takes years to get a prayer answered. Like poor Abraham, he waited a long time to get the children God promised him."

"Those praying for my soul will be waiting a while, too. I'm not ready for that kind of a commitment." Angel could tell Charlie didn't like this answer, but she didn't say anything.

"It's good you're at least open to the idea. I know some people, like Rico, who can't even see themselves serving God. I don't even think Rico believes in God."

"It's hard to tell. I didn't think Jerry would be the kind of person to turn to God, but it looks like he has."

"I didn't know him before, but he seems to be trying to dig into the Bible and learn as much as he can. Catch up on all those years he missed out on."

Angel looked at Charlie, tugging on one red curl. "I'm not saying I trust Jerry, so be careful. I hate the fact that you're staying with him, but it's better than being in that old building."

"The furnace is broken so for now we're in the apartment."

Angel nodded. "I don't guess you would consider leaving town until this is over? I'm concerned Rico's anger will be directed at you because you're staying with his dad."

"Leave? I don't have anywhere to go."

"You could stay with me, I wouldn't even charge you rent." Angel smiled and waited, knowing what the answer would be.

"I don't think so; that would be too tempting." Charlie lowered her gaze. Angel was intrigued. He put his free hand under her chin and made her look at him.

"So, even you Bible thumpers get tempted?" He knew she'd understand he was teasing. She smiled, looking him the eye.

"We can be, when the right man comes along, or would that be the wrong man?"

"I think the right man sounds more appealing." Angel smiled.

*****

Charlie grew quiet and considered what Angel said. Could he be the right man; the one she'd spend the rest of her life with? Could it be she'd met her true love?

She hoped so. She'd not dated much, but she felt a pull towards Angel. Would she find out later it was only a physical attraction, and not love? It seemed like more. She hoped it was more. Charlie couldn't help but smile as she glanced at her watch. No matter where it led, it would be interesting. "It's getting late. I think I should head back."

*****

Angel looked at his watch and smiled. "Am I cutting into Bible study?"

"I wasn't thinking of anything particular. I have a long day ahead and I need to bathe and study some myself."

"That's fine. I'll take you back." Angel moved, buckled his seat belt, started the car, and then headed back to Jerry's apartment. "I think it would be best if you don't tell Jerry we met."

"I won't. He wasn't expecting me at any particular time. I doubt if he'll ask anything except how did my day go? I'll be sure and not mention this to anyone. I don't want to say anything that would put you in danger."

"I appreciate that."

For the rest of the ride, Angel and Charlie were both quiet. Neither of them spoke much, but as they were walking to the elevator, they held hands.

"It's going to be hard to stop smiling."

"Why?" Angel laughed.

"Because I'm so relieved you're not like Rico."

"Oh well, I thought it was because of my kissing skills."

"Those aren't bad either."

"That's good to know." Angel stepped forward and placed his hand on Charlie's side. "One for the road." It was more of a statement than a question. He leaned in, and Charlie tilted her head to meet him.

Once again he kept the kiss light and reserved. He didn't want to scare her off, but a part of him wanted more. If she was smiling from these little moments of affection, he'd sweep her off her feet when he unleashed what he was really feeling.

190

Chapter 32
Double Crossed

"Come in," Rico called when he heard the tap on the door.

David peered in around the doorframe, "That punk kid's here to see you."

Rico nodded. "Tell Angel to go get me a steak dinner. Once he's gone, send the kid in."

"Sure thing, boss."

Rico leaned back with a smile on his face. He'd taken Lloyd's advice and soon Benny would be taking that troublesome girl off his hands. He couldn't be sure Angel's feelings for Charlie were gone, so he wanted him out of the way while he talked with Benny.

Five minutes later, his door opened and the kid walked in. He closed the door, sat down in the seat opposite Rico, and leaned back.

"So, let's get down to it. I don't have all day. You say you want me to take Charlie off your hands? I can do that."

"That's what I want." Rico didn't like this punk's attitude, but he wanted his help, so he was willing to put up with some of his smart mouth. "I know where she's staying, but I need to know if you'll be taking her out of town, maybe even out of state."

"That could happen if you give me the funds to get us out of town."

"I think I can take care of that," Rico said, smiling. "How long before she's out of my hair?"

"You give me some cash and I'll take her away tomorrow."

Rico nodded, took out his wallet, and placed five one-hundred dollar bills on the table."

Benny coughed and rubbed his chin. "Have you seen the price of gas lately."

Rico's brow rose; he paused and then laid down some more cash. "A thousand should cover it."

"That's more like it." Benny reached out and took the money. "That'll cover Charlie, but I have something for sale, information I think you'll want to hear."

"I'm not in the market for gossip."

"I think you might want to hear this."

"Don't be so sure. Now go on, or I'll find someone else to get Charlie out of my hair."

Benny didn't move and he shook his head no. "That would be a mistake. I know how to handle Charlie. Give me five minutes of your time. You won't regret it."

Rico glanced at his watch, and then leaned back. "You've got two minutes."

Benny nodded. "Fair enough. My bit of news has to do with that man that just walked out the door."

Rico looked up quick. Could Benny be talking about Angel? "The guy in the black leather coat?"

"Yeah, that one . . . the guy that you sent out to get you a steak. Does he work for you?"

"Yes, he does."

"I bet he's your right hand man?"

"He's close to that." Rico leaned back; he didn't like the smug look on the kids face.

Benny nodded and moved to the edge of his seat, smiling. "If you can lay down some serious cash, I'll tell you a bit of news that you never would have guessed."

Rico looked at Benny, called David on the phone and a few minutes later, there was a total of twenty-five hundred dollars on the table between Rico and Benny.

"It's up to you; that's as high as I'm going." Rico took out a cigar and lit it.

Benny shrugged. "I think it's worth at least five, but I'll take this." He started to reach out and take the money, but Rico slammed his hand down on the table.

"Not until you talk, and it better be good."

"Oh, it's good."

"Then lets hear it." Rico took a puff on his cigar and waited.

Benny nodded, pulled his hand back, and spoke. "Fine. The man that walked out; yesterday I saw him at the police station. He was in the back of the building talking to this guy who took my statement about Charlie."

Rico's brow furrowed and he sat up straight pulling his hand back from the money. "Are you sure? The man that just left here? You got a good look at him?"

"I got a great look. I was sittin' only yards away. I looked down the hall and saw the cop I was supposed to talk to. He was walking along side with your guy. I was hoping he would hurry up and take my statement.

I figured the guy with the long coat and dark hair was an informant, but when I saw him today it hit me. I thought, why would a guy who works for a big shot like you be hanging out at the police department? It all makes sense," Benny laughed. "He's a cop."

Rico shook his head. "No."

"Yes." Benny smiled. "I saw him. There's no doubt in my mind."

Rico cursed, smashing his cigar into the ashtray. What good did it do to have a cop on the payroll when he couldn't catch something like this? Lloyd had sent him on a wild goose chase telling him Charlie was the leak. He'd deal with Lloyd later.

Rico leaned forward and pushed the money over to Benny, but when the kid put his hand on the money, Rico shook his head no.

"If I find out you're lying to me, I'll get every dime of this back, with interest."

"I may not be the smartest person in the world, but I wouldn't dare lie to someone like you. Check him out, you'll see. Your right hand man is nothin' but an undercover cop."

*****

When Charlie's cell phone started ringing during breakfast, she kept the smile from her lips as she rose from the table to answer. Hopefully, it would be Angel calling to wish her good morning.

A frown came to her pretty face and she bit on her bottom lip, saying little as she listened to the man on the other end. When she hung up, she looked at Jerry and explained her best friend had been taken to the ER.

Thirty-five minutes later Charlie sat in the emergency room with William for the doctor's report. Allie had been beaten and left on the street. She'd managed to dial William and he'd called 911 and headed to the hospital where he knew they'd take her.

"I don't understand why this happened," William's brows furrowed as he spoke. "We both know Allie's past lifestyle; maybe someone got angry with her."

"I don't know, could be," Charlie all but whispered.

"The last few weeks she promised me she's not been seeing anyone." William seemed embarrassed about the subject and Charlie wondered if Allie had told him about the baby.

Charlie tried several times to check in with Allie, but she wouldn't return any of her calls. She couldn't help but wonder if Allie was telling the truth.

Had she stopped seeing other men? Had she told William about the rape? This man cared for Allie; she'd be an idiot to let him slip away.

They sat in silence waiting. An hour later the doctor came out. They both stood and walked to meet him.

"How is she?" They said in unison.

"She's going to be okay. She has a few stitches. She looks a lot worse than she is; don't be shocked by the cuts and bruises on her face and arms. Someone took out their anger on that young lady."

"When can we see her?"

194

"They're going to do an ultrasound on the baby and then you can go in. It's more than likely fine, but we have to be sure there was no trauma. She's not awake enough to tell us if she was hit in the stomach or not."

Charlie wondered if the doctor noticed the look of surprise on William's face. He didn't seem to.

"I'll have someone come out and get you when we're done with the ultrasound."

William made his way back to a seat and sat down, looking out into space. Charlie moved to sit beside of him and wasn't quite sure what to say.

"Did he say baby?" William leaned over, staring at nothing.

"Yes he did," Charlie answered.

"She didn't tell me." William looked at Charlie. "She's closer to you than anyone. Did she tell you?"

Charlie didn't want to lie; the truth was out now so she nodded. "Yes, a few days ago. I've been trying to reach her, but she wouldn't take my calls."

"A baby?"

Charlie watched in awe as the man leaned back and smiled. "We're going to have a baby!"

"Hopefully, if all goes well."

"Oh, yes. Let's pray." William didn't ask Charlie if she prayed or not, he leaned over and took her hand and began speaking. Tears came to Charlie's eyes as she heard the love in the man's voice.

It was obvious he didn't care who the baby's daddy was. He was praying and talking to God as if it was his own child. Charlie was sure it wasn't his, and that Allie was telling her the truth when she'd said she'd not slept with William.

"Amen." William said, and when he rose there were tears brimming in his eyes.

"I can see you care deeply for Allie. I'm so thankful you came into her life."

195

"I'm thankful she came into mine. I don't know why the Lord led me to that girl, but He did. I'm more than happy to receive the blessings He has for us. She's just so hard-headed."

Charlie laughed and nodded. "That she is. Don't give up, she'll come around."

"I know. I'm one of those people who want things right now. I want to jump right in with both feet. The Lord's helping me to have some patience. Now that there's a baby in the picture, maybe things will speed along."

Charlie wanted to tell William he needed to let Allie know how he felt, but she didn't know how. She prayed God would work it out and thanked Him that so far, Allie had kept the baby.

Chapter 33
God's Perfect Timing

Rico sat fuming. Should he continue his dealings with Marcus Moon? Would Angel be one step behind, interfering? He paused before making the phone call. A smile came over his lips. He'd take care of Charlie and Angel in one fell swoop, then he'd be free to show his dad what kind of man he'd become.

Rico studied a picture Moon's assistant faxed over. The women were beautiful. Moon promised only the best for his first shipment. Rico couldn't wait to see them. Some of the women thought they were coming to the States to find work. Others, however, knew their own families had sold them into slavery.

Moon's go-between was full of advice. He told Rico the beautiful women should be married off to the highest bidder, while others would be placed into prostitution.

As Rico viewed the pictures of the women, his thoughts turned to Charlie. It would be easy to smuggle her out of the country, to find a man overseas willing to pay good money for a white woman.

A smile came to his lips, thinking how this would infuriate his dad. The smile left as Angel came walking through the door carrying his steak dinner.

Rico kept the scowl from appearing and smiled at Angel. He couldn't believe a cop had managed to infiltrate his organization. A picture flashed before his mind of Angel and Charlie holding one of the files from his desk.

Were the two of them working together, or was Angel using the girl in some way?

Rico didn't care. All he knew was this cop wouldn't be in his way much longer!

"Here's your dinner." Angel slid into the booth and sat the huge bag on the table.

"Thanks," Rico said coolly. "I'll be needing you tomorrow around three for an important meeting, but for now you can take off."

Angel nodded, rose from the table, and then walked out the door. Rico looked at the food, shaking his head in disgust. There was no way he was going to eat anything that good-for-nothing cop brought in.

*****

Charlie and William were waiting in Allie's room. Charlie stood, praying and looking out the window, stealing glances at William as he sat, then paced and then sat again. A young mother who was being released had captured Charlie's attention.

The nurse stood waiting with the woman while a lone car pulled up. She watched as the young husband drove to the curb, got out and helped his wife and babe into the waiting car. Could that someday be Allie and William? She hoped so.

When she heard William speak, she turned and walked closer to the bed.

"Allie, I knew you'd be okay."

"I'm not so sure," Allie gave a weak smile glancing from Charlie to William. "I feel terrible and I hurt all over, not to mention I feel gritty and dirty."

"You're fine." William smiled, stole a glace at Charlie and then spoke. "Also the baby's fine."

"What? Who told you?" Allie scowled and looked to Charlie.

"She didn't tell me." William glanced up to Charlie, and then patted Allie on the hand. "It was the doctor. Don't be angry; it's a good thing. The baby's fine, but they want to keep you here for observation."

"Why? What's wrong?" Allie tried to sit up but winced, lying back down.

"Nothing honey, but you took some hard hits. They want to make sure everything's as it should be. The tests are coming back great, so don't worry . . . relax. Everything is going to be just fine."

"I didn't want to tell you," Allie said, the tears beginning to fall down her bruised cheeks.

"Why? You should know me by now."

"I was afraid you wouldn't want me," Allie sobbed.

"There's nothing that could cause that to happen." William placed his hand on Allie's face.

Charlie quietly moved out of the room, walking down the hall. Maybe this would finally make Allie realize how much this man loved her. She leaned her head against the wall, thanking God that Allie hadn't gone through with her plans.

Charlie smiled and took a few steps, also praying for Angel. It was still hard for her to fathom he and Joe were brothers, and that he was a cop.

What would Jerry say if he knew? Was Angel going to be part of a plan to get Rico on the right path? Jerry placed his son in God's hands only a few days ago. If Angel had his way, Rico would be going to jail, just like Jerry.

Sometimes answered prayers could take you down a rough road. Charlie had no clue that being on the streets and staying with Allie would bring her to this point in her life. She was sure glad it had. Still, it was hard to be thankful about the beating she'd taken from Benny's hands.

But if things hadn't happened just as they had, Allie might not have met William, or even thought about keeping the baby. Being a light in someone's life for a while could change them drastically. You could only pray you would stay on the right path and that, when it came time, you'd have enough faith to let God use you.

Charlie turned as William stepped into the hall. He smiled and leaned against the wall alongside Charlie. "I think she's going to be just fine. She's going to need a lot of rest, but she's okay. She wants to see you. Go on in."

"Thanks." She nodded, and then walking into the room, she could see Allie wiping away tears. "Is something wrong?" Charlie asked, walking over and taking her friend by the hand. She wasn't crying; she was all but sobbing.

Tubes and wires kept Allie tied to the bed, but Charlie held her arms open and let her friend cry on her shoulder. Why was Allie crying? No nurse or doctor had been in or out of the room to deliver bad news.

After a few moments, Charlie straightened and Allie leaned back, once again wiping her eyes. "Tell me, honey, what's wrong. You need to try to stop crying."

"I don't know if I can." There was the slightest bit of a smile coming to Allie's lips, but the tears were still flowing down her face. "I'm sorry I didn't wait for you, but I couldn't hold off."

"That's okay." Charlie still wasn't sure what was going on.

"William helped me to do it, he knew what to say. Oh Charlie, I finally know what it's like. I know why you always seem so happy."

Charlie looked at Allie and took her hand. Was she talking about being in love? Maybe she was on some kind of medication. Charlie forced a smile, and the look on her face must have said it all.

Allie laughed. "Do you know what I'm saying?"

"Not really."

"I got Jesus!" Allie cried out, the tears beginning to fall again.

"That's wonderful. I'm so happy for you." This time Charlie was crying too.

"William told me he wants to marry me and raise this baby as his. He's so good. I told him I didn't have a clue how he could have so much love. He told me if I wanted to know that kind of love, all I had to do was pray for Jesus to come and live in my heart."

"He's right, and I'm so glad you asked him in and finding William is great, but finding God is life changing."

"It is." Allie smiled and then gave a playful scowl. "Shame on you for not telling me about this sooner. I feel so new and happy."

"I tried." Charlie said, laughing as Allie smiled.

"I know you did. It worked. I'm hardheaded. I guess God had to knock me down to get my attention. Maybe this will teach me to listen to my good friends from now on."

"I'm just glad He did."

"Me too. I feel so free and light. I can't wait to start my life again with William." Allie reached out and grabbed her friend, hugging her.

"Thank you, God, for my friend Charlie. She helped save my life."

"It was my pleasure. Keep praying and trusting in Jesus. He'll take care of you."

"With Jesus and William, I'll be fine."

"That you will be." Charlie smiled.

The girls cried and hugged some more; they had so much to talk about. Allie was filled with questions about praying and God. Charlie promised her that there would be plenty of time to talk later.

"You need to rest now."

"Yes, she does." The doctor said as he walked into the room, with William right behind him. There was a smile on his face as he pointed toward the door. "You need to go find something to eat so this lady and her little one can get some rest."

"Little one." Allie smiled and she leaned up and hugged Charlie again.

They both began to cry. The doctor shook his head and pointed at the door again with his finger. Charlie laughed and walked out, giving William some private time with Allie.

Minutes later William also stepped out of the room as a nurse went in to check Allie's vitals. "I think he wants us to stay out a while," William laughed as he stepped closer to Charlie. "Allie does need the rest."

201

"She's so full of questions right now, it's going to be hard for her to get any sleep." Charlie laughed.

"I know, but it's good to see her so bubbly, and wanting to know more about God. She just couldn't wait to tell you, she all but ran me out of there to find you."

"We'll, she's all yours for now. I need to go and get some work done. Tell Allie I'll be back later, when I can."

"I will, and thanks for coming."

Charlie smiled." I'm glad I could help, and thank you for being there for Allie. You're a Godsend."

"I don't think I would go that far."

Charlie smiled and patted William on the shoulder. "I would. You came into the picture at exactly the right moment. With God's perfect timing."

*****

The rest of the day went fast for Charlie. She and Jerry worked overtime to get all the paperwork done for the building. The workmen installed a new water heater, some carpet, and things were coming along nicely.

Charlie worked on getting the beds prepared and the welcome packets ready to go. They'd be handing out the essentials to the women that stayed in the complex; toothpaste and brushes, deodorant and powders, body soap and hair gels, sprays and colognes.

There were so many items to purchase and so much to pull together in a short amount of time, and Jerry wanted the place to be open before Thanksgiving.

They would have an Open House, inviting as many people as they could to the dinner. Jerry was already planning the menu. He'd even bought some decorations for the women to use during the Christmas holidays.

Brother Tracy, Charlie's pastor, came by to help with some of the physical labor like setting up and moving beds and they were grateful for his help. He also wanted to start a small Bible study for the women who planned on staying in the building, and Jerry thought this was a grand idea.

Later that evening, they all sat down and shared the first home cooked meal in the kitchen; grilled cheese sandwiches and potato chips.

Charlie sat listening to the things that caused Jerry to have such a transformation. As he ate his sandwich, he talked about the food he had to eat and the treatment he received in prison.

"It was such a drastic change from the way I lived. It made me re-evaluate everything. I sat for days thinking about how I had lived, the money I'd wasted and how my lifestyle could have affected the people around me.

"I knew once I got out, if God blessed me, I wanted to help people, to make their lives better and show them what God did for me."

"I can see how losing so many of your privileges could bring you to a new realization," Brother Tracy looked from Jerry to Charlie as he spoke.

"Yes it did. I've always had a soft spot for the fairer sex, but living as I did . . . with such bare essentials . . .well, it made me come to see that I could do something to make women's lives better."

"I never would take a hand in the prostitution rings because of my beliefs. But I also couldn't see that the kind of businesses I ran contributed to the way these women lived. I wasn't doing anything directly against them, but I wasn't doing anything to help them, either."

The conversation went on for two hours. Charlie could see that these two men agreed on a lot of things. A few days ago, at Jerry's request, she told Brother Tracy about her boss. He was shocked. He thought seriously of asking the man *not* to join their congregation.

Charlie asked him to sit down and have a serious one-on-one with Jerry and, thankfully, Brother Tracy agreed. The two men left, sharing the same cab on their way to check out an abandoned house the church wanted to buy.

Charlie smiled, hoping that these two men would become great friends, and that together they would accomplish many wonderful deeds in the name of Christ.

Chapter 34
Revenge

With thoughts of Angel infiltrating into his organization, Rico didn't sleep well. When he did rise a little before nine, he began his day by calling Lloyd. He had a plan, and by the end of the day, he hoped to be rid of his latest problems.

He called David, his driver, to come pick him up. He then called Lloyd, asking him for confirmation on Angel. Rico listened as Lloyd made excuses about how large the department was, and how there was no way he could know what every person there was doing.

Rico gave Lloyd a description of Angel and the name he was using. Lloyd promised to do what he could to confirm the information and they hung up.

Rico showered, dressed in a winter white Armani suit and was waiting on the corner when his driver pulled up. He headed to a coffee shop to grab some breakfast. While he ate, he jotted down notes for his plan later on that day.

First, he would need to get Charlie and Benny to an out-of-the way spot. Then he'd get a couple of guys out there to beat up Angel. He didn't plan on killing him; killing a cop would bring down too much heat. But beating one up, well that wouldn't do too much.

Charlie was the key to getting Angel in place. She would come running *if* she thought Angel was in trouble. And, Benny . . . well, Benny would do whatever he wanted him to, *if* the price was right.

Rico still wasn't sure what role Charlie was playing, but he was tired of having her in his way. Once she was gone, he could sway his dad into coming back to his senses.

Rico smiled as he finished breakfast. It was a good feeling to know before long he'd be working side by side again with his dad. With both of them back behind the helm, no one could stop them.

*****

Joe sat looking at his desk. If he ever quit the force, it would be because of the paperwork. He could use his own secretary and keep her busy. He would much rather be out working the street and keeping an eye on Angel.

It was hard letting someone you cared for go out there alone. Joe leaned back in his chair thinking about getting a cup of coffee when he noticed something strange.

From where he was sitting, he could see into the file room. The door was open a crack and someone was in there. The lights were out but he saw movement and it caught his attention.

His brow furrowed. He sat up straight but couldn't see into the office anymore. When the person came out he'd be able to see who it was.

Ten minutes later, Joe heard the familiar squeak of the file room door. An officer stepped out and Joe raised a brow. He didn't know the man, but then again, with over ten thousand officers working for the CPD, it was no wonder.

Joe knew he'd recognize the man if he saw him again, so he went into the file room, and turned on the light. He studied the room and tried to discern if anything looked out of place. He cracked the door open and turned out the light.

The officer had to be looking at something in the file cabinet in the corner or else Joe would not have been able to catch the movement of the man.

Joe turned the light on and went over to the cabinet and began to look it over. From the outside, he couldn't see anything strange. This was one of the many file rooms and it held payroll information.

Slowly he looked through the files, picking through them one by one. About halfway back he stopped and wrinkled his brow.

One of the files was askew. He took it out and shook his head, glancing toward the door. Someone was up to no good. His prowler seemed to be interested in the new hires.

The list consisted of four pages, each page held about twenty names. None of the pages were missing; more than likely that meant the man was looking for someone in particular. He'd not been in the room long enough to copy all the names.

He could have taken a picture of the pages, but Joe hadn't noticed a flash. He replaced the files. He'd do some snooping of his own and try to get in touch with his brother. After all, Angel's name was included on the list of new hires.

*****

Rico sat in his driver's personal car. It was an older model, a beat up Pontiac. He scowled as he saw Jerry step out of the building with Charlie close behind. The two of them spoke for a minute and then his dad stepped into a waiting cab and left. Charlie went back inside.

David looked in the rearview mirror and Rico nodded. "It's time, boys." Rico smiled at the brute to his left, "I don't want her hurt; just get her in the car as quickly as possible."

Leo nodded and Rico smiled. David put the car into drive, went down the street, did a u-turn and came back.

As soon as the car came to a stop, David and Leo climbed out. Rico looked up and down the street. This was an older part of town and it was quiet this time of day. A young man walked down the street, his MP3 player kept him from hearing the shrieks Charlie made as Leo and David dragged her to the car.

Charlie kicked and screamed until she got in the car and saw Rico. He turned and smiled; she scowled back. "What do you want?"

"You. I need you to attend a meeting." Rico turned to David and said one word, "GO!" *It's hard to get good help these days.* Rico turned his attention back to the young woman in the back seat. She didn't look scared, only irritated. He didn't want her to know what he was up to yet; he wanted her to stay calm.

Her cell phone was taken, and she crossed her arms and sat as far away as she could from the man beside her. "Your dad will be furious with you for doing this."

"I don't care what he thinks. I'm tired of listening to him. It's time he paid some attention to me."

"What do you want with me, Rico?"

"You'll see soon enough."

It didn't take them long to get to the abandoned apartment building he'd chosen. Now, Charlie looked worried. "Rico, I want you to let me go." Charlie reached for the door, but Leo pulled her back.

"I can't do that." Rico turned in the seat as the car came to a stop. "I need you to help me do something and then you'll be taking a trip. Take her inside boys."

Rico stepped out of the car as Leo and David took Charlie into the building. She was screaming and fighting again.

"You might as well give up, Charlie, I'm holding all the cards now."

"Let me go, Rico."

It was obvious she was scared, now. Rico ignored the small pang of guilt he felt. "Tie her up! No need to gag her; she can yell all day and no one's going to hear her out here."

"Yes sir," David called over his shoulder, as he pushed Charlie into the building.

Rico paced, made a few phone calls and then went inside. Benny was on his way, now all he needed was Angel. Rico knew how to get him there in a snap.

When he went inside he found Charlie tied to a chair. She wasn't screaming but sitting there with her head bowed. It angered Rico that she might be praying.

"Go ahead! Your praying won't help." Charlie didn't look up, but kept on praying. Rico reached down, took hold of the golden cross around her neck and gave it a hard yank. This got her attention and she looked up, surprise showing in her eyes.

"Maybe now you will see that I mean business." Rico tossed the chain aside and smiled. "I know my dad's treated you like some kind of adopted child, but your easy ride is over. I'm removing you from the family tree." Rico laughed.

"I never meant to come between you and your dad. All you had to do was listen to him, and try to understand."

"Shut up! I need you to make a phone call. There's someone I need to teach a lesson."

"You won't get any help from me." Charlie shook her head.

"I wouldn't be so quick to say that. You'll be surprised what people will do when push comes to shove."

"I won't help you hurt . . ."

"Who? You won't help me hurt who . . . Angel. Go ahead say it. I know all about your precious Angel. He's a dirty cop, and he's been sticking his nose where it doesn't belong."

"Angel's a cop? But he works for you?"

"That might be convincing if I didn't already know the truth. You don't have to try and cover for your little boyfriend. The secret is out. Now, all I need is to get Angel to come here. Why don't you call him and invite him over."

"I won't do it."

"We'll see about that. I may not need you. I'm getting ready to call him and tell him I need to speak with him. He doesn't suspect anything, but if he's a no show I'll just let you give him a call."

"I told you I won't help you hurt Angel."

Rico smiled and reached into his pocket, pulling out a recorder. He rewound it, and pushed play. After he let Charlie hear her own voice screaming, he laughed, turned, and walked out of the room.

"Don't do it, Rico. You'll regret it if you hurt anyone."

This was the last thing Rico heard as he went to make his phone call. Angel didn't have any reason to suspect anything, but if for some reason he hesitated, Rico knew he could hit the play button and Angel would come running.

Chapter 35
Deception

Angel was at the club when he got the call from Rico. It didn't take him long to get in his car and head out to Grand & Calhoun. It wasn't a good part of town and something told him to be careful.

Angel could sense something in Rico's tone he didn't like. Arrogance, distaste . . . he'd not noticed it before and it worried him. Something was up; he could feel it. But what was it?

Since he would be untraceable if something happened, he called Joe. When he got voice mail, he shook his head. Of all the times for him not to answer! When he heard the beep he left a message.

"I've got a gut feeling something isn't right. See if you can reach me in about fifteen minutes. I'm arriving at 6985 Calhoun Drive. I'm meeting Rico in an abandoned apartment."

Angel closed the phone and put it in his pocket. He looked at his surroundings. He saw two homeless people going through a dumpster and a drunk sleeping it off.

He got out of the car and had that feeling again. Things were too quiet; it didn't look like a place where Rico would go for anything good. Pausing, he looked back at his car, then to the doorway. He was thinking about going back to his car when he heard Rico's voice. "I'm in here."

Against his better judgment Angel walked toward the empty apartment. He pushed the door back and could see Rico talking on the phone in what used to be the kitchen. He stepped in and immediately felt the impact of what more than likely was another 2x4. He sank to his knees holding the back of his head. "Not again." He shook his head and pulled his hand back, seeing blood.

As he tried to get to his feet, Leo and David searched him for weapons. "What's the deal?" Angel tried to get loose, but the men held him in place and Leo now had his gun.

Rico shook his head; his expression showed anger and disgust. "I know you're a cop, Angel! Save us some time. Where's your back-up piece?"

The first thing that went through Angel's mind was Charlie. She'd let something slip or he had misjudged her and she'd betrayed him. He knew there was no use in trying to deny the facts. He pulled up his right pants leg, showing them a small revolver. One of the men took it and shoved him to the ground.

Angel tried to work it out in his head what might happen if he took out a second back-up and began shooting. While debating with himself whether he should get up or not, he heard Rico speak.

"I have a surprise!" Rico took out a mini-recorder and pushed play. As the tape began, Angel's stomach dropped.

"Where is she, you pig?" Angel forced down the urge to charge at Rico.

"I think you're the pig here," Rico laughed. "You should have known better than to double-cross me."

"Well, you've got me now. Let Charlie go!"

"I don't think so. I have plans for her, too. She's leaving town with an old friend."

"What are you up to, Rico?" Angel wanted to ask Rico if he was jealous of Charlie; if he thought his dad would turn to him if she was out of the picture. But since he didn't want to anger him further, he said, "Leave Charlie out of this. She didn't do anything to you."

"I can't do that," Rico smirked.

It was at that moment the door opened and Benny walked in. Angel started to get up, but Leo shook his head, and pointed a gun at him.

Benny looked around, shrugged and stepped over Angel. "Where's Charlie?"

"She's in the back room. Can you handle her?"

"I *sure* can."

Rico smiled at Angel. "I never was one for violence. I think I'll head back to The Oasis. Leo, where did you park my car?"

"It's out back," the man motioned with his head.

Rico then looked at Leo and David with a smile. "You two know what to do."

Rico strode out the back door and a few minutes later Benny came out with Charlie. When Angel locked eyes with her, she tried to come to him, but Benny was stronger and her hands were tied.

"Angel, I'm sorry. I wish I could have warned you. I didn't tell Rico; he already knew. . . I'm praying for you!" Charlie called, as Benny pulled her out the front door.

Angel thought, *praying* . . . he hoped it worked cause he was gonna need it.

*****

Charlie fought Benny every step, turning to look back into the house as he dragged her down the sidewalk. She winced as she saw the big guy kick Angel. She had to get away from Benny. Rico was gone, and the two men were busy with Angel so they wouldn't try to help Benny catch her, if she managed to get away.

She'd escaped from Benny once; she could do it again. True, he wasn't drunk this time, but she had faith and she repeated in her mind, *"I can do all things through Christ who strengthens me."*

As she walked along a thought came floating into her mind, *"If he had to carry me it'd be harder".* Charlie began to tug and fight as Benny dragged her to the car.

"You can't take me home, I won't go. I'll never . . ." Charlie knew it would hurt, and since her hands were tied in front of her she couldn't brace her fall. She let her eyes flutter, turned loose of Benny's shirt, and fell to the ground.

It was hard to lie there when he slapped her, but she managed to be limp as a rag doll, and it worked. At first he tried to drag her and he managed to get her close to the car but then he dropped her to the ground, she guessed to open the car door.

It might be her only chance. She opened her eyes as she heard him curse and heard the crunch of leaves. As Benny walked toward the car, she made her move. As she rolled to her side, and rose to her feet, she prayed harder for Angel. She could hear glass breaking. She knew he was tough, but there were two of them, and one of them was a brute.

She was on her feet and moving before Benny turned. He'd reached inside the car for something, and it gave her more time to get a head start. She ran down the street. When she heard Benny yell at her to stop, she began screaming, "Help me! Someone stop that man."

Getting to a business that had a phone was what she needed, but most of this part of town was dead. She looked at a street sign as she ran, putting it to memory so she could tell the 911 operator how to find Angel.

Though it seemed forever to Charlie, she'd only run one block. She came sliding around a corner and ran into a homeless man and his cart. She pulled her hands back in pain and felt the blood flow.

"Please, stop the man behind me!" Charlie hoped the man could speak English and that he was sober enough to understand what she said.

Chapter 36
Old Joe

Old Joe, as most of the street people called him, knew something was up. He turned and ran when two men pulled a young woman out of a car and dragged her into a run down apartment building. He went down the street looking for help.

His appearance, and the fact that he was a drunk, caused most people to avoid him. Today was no different. No one would listen to his cry for help; no one would let him use their phone to call the police.

Since he couldn't call the police, he turned around and went back, pushing his buggy as fast as he could. He wasn't sure if he'd be any help, but he had to try.

Several times he'd been going through the trash behind the big complex on Main Street and the pretty red head spotted him, giving him money or food. He wanted to help her so much; he couldn't remember the last time he felt this powerless.

As he went hurrying back up the street, she came around the corner too fast. He was shocked to find the lady looking at him; she ran into his buggy and cut her hand. She called to him for help, and he nodded.

She ran on, hoping he'd slow down whoever was chasing her. He pushed his buggy out and started around the corner. A smile came to his face as a young man fell over his buggy.

He hadn't gathered much that day, so only a few things went rolling out. He picked up an umbrella he had found earlier and began to hit the man on the back, yelling at him.

"Leave her alone! Go away!"

"Stop it, you nut!"

215

"You have to leave. I called the police!"

"Quit it. Are you crazy?"

"I'm not crazy! You better go before the police get here."

The man straightened, but seemed in no hurry to leave. Old Joe stepped back shaking his head. "I saw you drag that girl into the car. You were going to kidnap her."

"I didn't do anything."

"Why don't you hang around and tell the cops how innocent you are."

The man weighed his options and then went back the other way. Old Joe picked up a few cans from his buggy and tossed them at the man.

A can of dented peas hit him in the back of the head and he picked up his pace. Joe kept throwing cans to make sure the man left. As he watched the man climb into the car and leave, two other men came out of the apartment.

Joe approached the building and the two men gave him a dirty look. One of them had a bloody nose. He picked up his pace, wondering what they'd done.

Maybe they'd left something good in the house. He grabbed up his buggy and the few things that had rolled out, and soon was walking up the sidewalk to the condemned apartment.

The men in the car drove off, and Joe looked around. No one seemed to be watching, so he pushed the door back and walked in. It was easy to see there'd been a fight.

There was blood on one of the walls, and several things were knocked over. He picked up a trashcan that was sitting in the entryway, and then began to put things into the can as he went through the house.

There was some tape, two cell phones and a pack of cigarettes lying on the floor. He wanted to hit the kid with another can of peas as he passed the chair where the young woman had been tied down.

He picked up a gold necklace with a cross and dropped it into his pocket. He noticed more blood on the floor and followed the trail around the corner. "My goodness." Old Joe hurried to the young man lying on the floor. He knelt down, evaluating the situation.

He knew if the boys found him at the scene of a crime, that they'd take him down town, but he couldn't just leave. This man needed help.

Old Joe looked up, and shook his head. On the wall written in blood were the words . . . dirty cop. He rose, ran to the trashcan, took out the best looking cell-phone and dialed 911. When the operator answered, Old Joe gave her directions and informed her about the young man.

"Officer down, he's a mess. There's blood on his hands and face. I don't see any gun shot wounds, but he took a beating. You better hurry; those two guys didn't show him any mercy. Joe rattled off the address and ignored the operator's questions. "I gotta go; you send this young man some help. Now!"

He knew if he went down town, he'd be hours answering useless questions. He didn't know anything that would help. He laid the phone down leaving the line open. He could hear the operator talking to him, but he ignored her.

Old Joe looked the young man over, shaking his head. He was breathing, and had a good pulse. There were nicks and cuts, here and there.

Only one cut looked worthy of concern. Old Joe looked around the room and found a cleaning rag. He tied the rag around the man's arm, just tight enough to slow the bleeding. Help would be there soon.

He rose, glancing over his shoulder as he went to the kitchen. Here he found an old can of pears and some shoe polish. As he left he took a few more items, including an ashtray and an expensive looking lighter that must have fallen out of someone's pocket.

Old Joe took one more look at the young man and sighed. It'd been a long time since he talked to the man upstairs. As he went out the door, he sent up a prayer for that poor man in the house and the pretty lady he last saw running down the street.

*****

Charlie found a phone at a liquor store, one block south of where she ran into the homeless man. The bartender took out a knife and cut her hands loose. She then borrowed a phone from a patron and made the 911 call. The lady washing dishes came out from the back and brought her a clean towel.

Charlie wrapped the towel around her hand. The cut wasn't deep, but it was bleeding. She reported an officer down on Calhoun just east of Maple. She described what the building looked like and mentioned Angel's car sitting on the street. What the operator said next gave her some relief, and she sat down on a stool while she answered the woman's questions.

"We got a call from someone at the scene. The information was sketchy. We were told an officer is down. Is that true? What went on? Were there gunshots?"

"There's an officer there, he'll more than likely need an ambulance. I don't know much. There were three men, one of them tried to abduct me." Charlie gave the lady a brief description of the two men who had beaten up Angel.

She gave their names, her name, her address and phone number, and then hung up. She headed down the street, hoping Benny was gone. Charlie prayed that Angel would be ok. Before she made it to the corner, she heard the sounds of an ambulance.

She turned and looked down the street, seeing a police car coming north on Calhoun. She turned to walk back to the apartment. Angel would have help soon. Who could have called before her? Would Rico have done that?

Charlie picked up her pace, running to the end of the block. By the time she got there, two cruisers sat, doors open. The ambulance sat, back doors open; the EMT's already inside. She started to move forward when she heard something. Her phone was ringing, but it was behind her.

She turned, following the sound of Allie's call coming in. As she approached the alley she peeked around, wondering how her phone had gotten from inside the building to here.

As she peeped down the space between the buildings, she caught a glimpse of the homeless man. She called out to him, but he was gone. She walked to her phone, bent down and picked it up.

As she explained to Allie where she was, and told her what happened, she scanned through the re-dials. She looked down the way to where the man had slipped around the corner. He'd made the call; the first 911 call the operator told her about.

Charlie mouthed a silent *'thank you'* and walked around to where a crowd was gathering. She took Allie off speakerphone, shaking her head at the people.

Where did they all come from? None of them came when they could have been useful. Did people care so little about their fellow man that they only came out to see the remnants of what was left when their help was no longer needed?

A few of them gave her strange looks. She had an idea some of them knew exactly who she was. It was a shame that there weren't more people who wanted to get involved when someone was in need. Most of them had a roof over their head and phones within reach. The one who had helped her most had been the one who needed help himself.

Charlie put her mind back on the conversation with Allie, mentally asking the Lord to forgive her for being so judgmental. Maybe some of them had a good excuse for not helping, but it wasn't her place to judge them; it was her place to pray for them to change.

She wrapped up her call with Allie and made arrangements to have William pick her up. He'd never heard of the Green Cricket but assured her he could find it. She pushed the phone into her pocket and stood behind a tall man with his hat on backwards.

She stayed in the background, hoping no one would notice her. She couldn't help but wonder about Benny. Would he leave town, or would he come back and try to kidnap her again. She pushed Benny from her mind and peeped through the crowd toward the building.

There were people on each side of the apartment now, and she spotted Joe coming out of the building. She stayed back;

feeling like this was her fault. Did she say something to bring this on?

She put her hand over her mouth as she saw the EMT coming out, holding the IV over Angel's head. There was blood on his face and hands.

Tears came to her eyes. She wanted to run to him and get in the ambulance and go with him, but it would only slow down the progress. She stepped back away from the crowd, watching while an officer closed the ambulance doors. As she watched them drive away she knew for certain she was beginning to fall in love with a young man named Angelo Morganson.

Chapter 37
No Greater Love

Joe rode in the ambulance with Angel. He sat off to the side as the paramedics worked on his little brother. He was first on the scene after finding Angel's message on his voice mail. All of his safety training went out the window when he found Angel. He'd forgotten about wearing gloves as he began to look his brother over for gunshot or stab wounds.

He looked down at Angel's blood on his hands, sighed and shook his head. The words 'Dirty Cop' flashed before his mind. Rico did this. He would see Angel to the hospital and then go looking for Jerry or Rico. One of them was going to jail and, at that moment, he didn't really care if both of them went.

The first thing Joe did once at the hospital was to give blood. Angel would need at least one pint and once the blood was collected, Joe sat waiting. Angel looked bad when Joe first saw him. Now that he was in the hospital, cleaned up and stitched up, Joe felt some relief.

There were stitches above his left eye, a cut on his right temple and a large scrape on the back of his head. He had three cracked ribs and the CT scan showed he had a bruised liver. One large bandage covered his left arm where Joe had found a homemade tourniquet.

The doctors gave Angel one pint of blood. If needed, Joe could give more. His brother would need plenty of rest, an IV for at least twenty-four hours and later on, another CT scan. Joe leaned back; it was going to be hard to keep Angel in bed. The man didn't seem to know what rest meant.

He was sleeping now but he was going to be in some pain later. Joe knew he needed to find Charlie. If he didn't know where she was by the time Angel opened his eyes, he'd have to sit on him to keep him in the hospital.

Angel's youth would help his healing process, but he was stubborn, and that wouldn't help anything. Joe rose, stood at the foot of the bed for a moment, and then headed out to see if he could find Charlie. He called Nyssa, but she didn't have a clue where she might be. She promised she'd make some calls and see what she could learn.

While Nyssa found him some leads for Charlie's whereabouts, Joe took time out to focus on Rico and that punk from Indiana. The 911 operator mentioned three men; Benny, David and Leo, but Joe knew Rico was the mastermind; so he headed to the man's favorite hang out, The Oasis.

By the time Joe got to the bar, Jerry was already there. He was pacing back and forth while his son sat in a booth trying to act as if he didn't care what was going on around him. Jerry turned and spoke as Joe walked toward them.

"We're not open yet," Jerry turned, dismissing Joe, but looked back when he spoke.

"I'm here to find some answers." Joe pulled back his jacket, revealing his badge and gun. "I may arrest your good-for-nothing son before I leave."

"I haven't done anything," Rico snarled and went back to his dinner.

"I know what you've been up to!" Joe crossed his arms to keep from pulling the jerk out of the booth and giving him a taste of his own medicine.

"I've been here all morning. Ask Randy, behind the bar."

"He's been here all day," Randy piped up and Rico shrugged and went back to eating.

Joe was so angry; here this pig sat eating like nothing was wrong. He bent down and looked the man in the eye. "If you don't tell me right now where Benny took Charlie, I may give you a taste of what you gave Angel.

"Charlie's fine," Jerry interrupted.

Joe turned around quick and came to stand before Jerry. "Were you in on this too, old man?"

"No, I was not! Charlie called me a little while ago, to let me know what my idiot son had done."

Joe stepped even closer, lowering his tone. "If you're telling me you know your son kidnapped Charlie, I'll take him in right now." Joe knew he was putting Jerry on the spot, and he didn't care; either he was a changed man or he wasn't.

"He doesn't know anything," Rico mused, a smile playing on his lips as he looked from his dad to Joe.

*****

Jerry turned and walked over to the bar and stood with his back to Joe and Rico, thinking and praying on what he should do.

Kidnapping? Rico kept going further in the wrong direction. If they could prove he did it, Rico would go to jail. Could he really be thinking about sending his only child to prison? He'd been there; he knew what a terrible place it was.

You lost every right; people told you what to do *and* when to do it. Even with his money it was hard to get the small things to make life easier. Now and then he could bribe himself a good cup of coffee, a few soft blankets and sheets. Jerry couldn't name how many daily conveniences he missed and longed for while in prison.

That didn't include having to protect yourself from those who wanted to hurt you. Jerry's time in jail was a wake-up call to more things than he could count. It was where he was brought to his lowest point, where he found out he did need Christ.

Would that happen for his son, too? Was this God's answer to his prayer? *How in the world did God give His only son for us miserable wretches when I don't know if I can give my son up to save his own soul.* Jerry kept his back turned on Joe and Rico while he prayed for strength to do the right thing.

223

"You might as well get out of here. He doesn't have anything to tell you."

Joe turned to Rico and pointed his finger at the man. "I'll get you soon enough, with or without him. You're going down, one way or the other. You're getting in deep, getting into moving guns and Angel said he heard you talking about dealing in human trafficking."

Rico smiled and took a bite of steak. "Who's Angel?"

"You know good and well who he is. You had him beaten and left laying in his own blood like a piece of trash." Joe took a few steps toward Jerry and spoke in an even tone. He wanted to make the man turn and look him in the eye, but he didn't. "Well Jerry, what will it be?"

"I told you to leave him alone," Rico's voice rose as he spoke.

Jerry turned and looked at Joe. He seemed to be unsure of what to do. The man nodded, then after a few silent seconds, spoke. "What kind of deal will you offer my son?"

Joe felt some relief, and he answered the best he could. "I'm not the DA, but I'd say if your son's willing to give us names and some solid information, they could work out some kind of a deal that would bring his jail time to a minimum."

Jerry looked at his son and walked over to the table, turning his back on Joe. "Will you make the deal, Rico?"

"What? I'm not making any deals. I don't need to. I'm not guilty of anything."

Jerry nodded, and while looking at his son, spoke to the officer. "Charlie told me Rico abducted her from the apartment building and took her to the place where you found the officer named Angel. My son kidnapped Charlie. I think you should arrest him."

224

Chapter 38
Pride Goeth Before a Fall

When Joe walked into the hospital to tell Angel the news, he found a male nurse and another woman talking to his brother. They were threatening to tie him to the bed if he didn't behave himself.

"I'll take it from here," Joe noticed from the looks he got that they would be happy for him to do just that.

"Where's Charlie?" Angel tried to sit up.

"Take it easy. She's fine. I don't know where she is, but she's okay."

"That doesn't make any sense. How can you know she's okay?"

"She checked in with Jerry, but she didn't tell him where she was staying."

"That pig, you can't trust him. I'm going to go find her."

"No, you're not. You have to rest. I'll find her and bring her here. I came by to tell you, at this moment, Rico should be in booking."

Angel stopped trying to get out of the bed and looked at Joe. "How did you do that?"

"I didn't. Jerry did."

Angel shook his head and Joe explained the story, but in the end he was sounding like a broken record. "That still doesn't tell me where Charlie is!"

"I think she's hiding from Benny. If you promise me you'll stay in that bed at least twenty-four hours, I'll head out and see if I can find her."

"I'll agree, but you've got to give me updates."

"I will and I'll get her here ASAP!" Joe turned to go but stopped when Angel spoke.

"I don't want her here."

Joe shrugged and then smiled shaking his head, "You little punk. You're worried about her seeing your ugly legs in that gown."

"I want to be standing on my own two feet when I see her."

"Sheesh," Joe muttered, waving a hand as he turned to go. "Whatever you say. I'll let you know when I find her."

Joe walked to the nurses' station and smiled at the lady behind the counter. "If he tries to get out of that bed again, knock him out with something."

"I'll be glad to." The young woman smiled, and the gleam in her eye told Joe that she just might do it.

Twenty minutes later, after stopping by the apartment, Joe's search for Charlie continued. Another thirty minutes passed and he received a call from the station. It seemed Jerry and his brother was trying to talk some sense into Rico.

Sitting at a light on his way back to the station, Joe's phone began to ring. He pulled the phone out, glanced at the caller ID and spoke. "What did you find out?"

"I got a call from one of the girls at the station. Charlie's been trying to reach you."

"Where is she?"

"She's staying with her friend's aunt in Oakwood." Nyssa gave Joe the address. He punched it into his Garmin and headed to find Charlie. He promised to invite her back to their home and hung up.

Following 'Ms. Garmin', Joe arrived on Linden Avenue in a matter of minutes. When he knocked on the door, a man with a scowl answered. "I'm here to talk to Charlie." Joe forced a quick smile and before the man could say anything, Joe showed his badge and the man nodded.

"Come in."

226

Joe smelled fresh coffee as he entered and couldn't help but notice the place looked spotless. He stood in the living room waiting on Charlie. He heard her coming before he saw her.

"Thank God you found my message," Charlie called as she came running to his side. "Have you seen Angel? Is he okay?"

Joe nodded as he reached out and put his hands on Charlie's shoulders. "He's in rough shape, but stubborn as ever. You can see him in a few days."

"A few days?"

Joe didn't want to tell Charlie why she couldn't see Angel, so he made something up. "We haven't found Benny. It would be best if you stayed out of sight."

"I see." Charlie dropped her eyes and sighed, but she looked back up with some hope when Joe spoke.

"We arrested Rico for kidnapping. Jerry told us his son took you against your will."

"*He did?*"

"Yeah, he did."

"Wow! I don't guess anyone can doubt his sincerity after this." Charlie tilted her head and her voice cracked when she spoke. "You know I hated to leave Angel with those men, but I didn't know what else to do. I called as soon as I got away from Benny. Some homeless man made a call too; he must have found my phone. I saw where he made the call."

Joe tilted his head. "That explains the home-made tourniquet I found on Angel's arm. You did the right thing by going for help."

"Tourniquet? How bad did they hurt him?"

"He's fine, don't worry. He's bruised, cut and beaten, but he'll survive."

"Are you sure? Don't lie to me."

"I'm not. He's stubborn and needs to rest, but he'll be fine."

Charlie sighed. "Tell Angel I'm sorry I couldn't help him more."

"I will," Joe forced a smile and spoke in a low tone. "Are you staying here?"

227

"For now. It's kind of small, but Allie and William are going to Florida tomorrow. That'll leave just me and Aunt Nettie."

"I'll send a patrol car by to keep an eye on this place for a few days, and I'll be sure to let you know when we find Benny. That way you can see Angel."

"Thanks, I appreciate that. Benny's kind of a punk most of the time. He's more than likely on his way back to South Bend. He would have never tried anything like this on his own. I know Rico was behind the kidnapping plan."

"I'm sure you're right. Still, we have a warrant out for his arrest, and we're waiting on a fax from South Bend with a picture."

"I've got a small picture of Benny and my sister." Charlie went into the other room and soon came out with the picture and handed it to Joe.

"Thanks, this will help."

"He's a few pounds lighter, and his hair's shorter now."

"What did he have on?"

"A red T-shirt and jeans, and I wouldn't be surprised if he didn't end up with a few cuts and bruises. The homeless man pushed his buggy out in front of him and he fell over it."

"I'll have them run this picture through the emergency rooms."

"I hope it helps."

"It will." Joe glanced toward the door. "I better go. If I don't get back and tell Angel you're okay, he'll climb out of that bed and come looking for you himself."

Charlie smiled in a shy way that made Joe realize how innocent she was. "I hope you know you're welcome to come stay with me and Nyssa." A smile came to Charlie's lips and she nodded.

"I appreciate the offer. If Allie and William find a suitable place for rent, I won't have anywhere to stay. Aunt Nettie can't wait to get to a warmer climate."

"Well, that settles it," Joe said as he stepped back. "I'll be here tomorrow evening to pick you up. Be packed and ready."

"I will be." Charlie's tone and smile said it all. She walked Joe to the door and called to him as he turned to go. "Tell Angel I'm praying for him, and I can't wait to see him."

*****

This time when Joe walked into Angel's room he found him sitting up and eating. He looked up when Joe walked in.

"Well? Did you find her?" Angel put down his fork and looked at his brother.

"Yeah, she's safe and sound. She's also coming to stay with us for a few days."

"You've seen her?"

Joe moved closer to the bed and nodded, "She's fine. I noticed a few scratches on her hand." Joe began to tell Angel how Charlie escaped from Benny.

A slow smile came to his brother's face and he nodded. "She's gotten away from him twice now. Do you have any leads on him?"

"Not yet, but we'll get him."

Angel nodded and sighed, looking at the hospital lunch. He made a face looking at Joe. "When do you think they'll let me out of here?"

"I don't know, but don't expect anything but desk duty for a while."

"How long?"

"The last time I saw something like this it kept Bill Johnson out for two weeks. Then he sat behind a desk for close to six months."

"Ah man, don't tell me that. I hate sitting behind a desk."

"Well, they might move you to another town, try to get you established if you still want to work undercover."

"I like it, but I don't want to get burnt out. Maybe I'll take a break."

"Don't you mean maybe you'll be seeing someone?" Angel tried to look as if he didn't understand. Joe laughed, shaking his head. "Don't play dumb with me. Besides, Nyssa is itching to play Cupid between you and Charlie."

229

"I kind of got that idea."

"You two make a nice looking couple. But she's a lot better looking than you."

"She is something!" Angel mused.

"I can bring her over tomorrow if you want."

"No, I'm serious. I don't want her to see me in here."

"Whatever you say, man," Joe shrugged. "Whatever you say."

Chapter 39
No Place to Go

Angel stayed true to his word. He didn't allow Joe to bring Charlie to the hospital. When he next saw Charlie he wanted to be standing under his own power, not laying in a bed wearing a dress.

The day he checked out of the hospital, Angel learned the investigation had officially closed. He didn't have a roof over his head anymore, and he didn't like the fact that he was homeless. Since most of his things were in storage and he didn't have a place to hang out, he called a cab and went to the station. He could check his mail and catch up on paperwork.

When Joe stepped into the office, Angel was tossing back some pain pills and wishing he'd stayed a few more days in the hospital.

"What in the world are you doing sitting at that desk?" Joe crossed his arms, shaking his head.

"Regretting it," Angel grimaced as he shifted in the chair.

"You need to be in a bed or kicked back on the couch."

"I don't have either at the moment. I guess I could get a hotel room."

"I don't think so. I have two good couches and one of them makes into a bed. Even better, I have two women who have been driving me nuts wanting to see you."

Angel smiled and nodded. "I'll take you up on that offer. I'm not feeling up to par. I could use some women fussing over me and waiting on me hand and foot."

Joe laughed and sat down nodding. "Well, if you come in my house wearing those bandages and that puppy dog look, that's what you'll get."

"It's a plan," Angel smiled, moved around and felt a bolt of pain. He grimaced and looked back toward his brother. "Tell me what's going on with Rico?"

Joe rocked back in the chair and smiled. "Surprisingly, Jerry and his brother, Alfredo, talked Rico into turning over his contacts. He'll be making a deal with the DA. Not sure what the specifics will be."

"Great. Then he won't be seeing any real jail time?"

"I don't know. We think he may deal his way out of some of the charges, but you know how it goes. If they can catch some of the bigger fish, they'll let Rico go without a hitch."

"That doesn't make it right."

"No, it doesn't." Joe sighed.

"What about Benny?"

"He's more than likely on his way back to South Bend. We've contacted the local authorities to keep an eye out for him. We could get him for accomplice to kidnapping, or maybe aggravated kidnapping. He didn't hurt Charlie; he didn't even get her in the car, so it would all depend on the judge and if he's committed a felony before."

"Great!" Angel shook his head. "I did all that work and got the crap beat out of me, *twice*, and nobody's going to jail?"

"We'll get a couple of gun runners out of this. If we're lucky, we'll show real freedom to a group of women who were headed for a life of suffering and abuse."

"I hope so. I'd hate to think I wasted all my time."

"It's never a waste of time. Sometimes it takes longer for all the pieces to fall into place."

"I guess you're right."

"I am this time," Joe smiled and rose from the chair. "I need to get some things done. When you get ready to go to the house let me know, and I'll run you home."

"Will do." Angel nodded as Joe headed back to his desk. He looked at the clock; two hours till quitting time. He wasn't about to tell Joe how bad the pain was. He'd kill the time pacing, paying a few bills and maybe head back to the break room to see if lying down for a while would help get rid of this pain.

Around five Angel rose from the cot, tried not to stretch and headed to gather his arsenal of medicine. After letting Joe know he was ready; he headed out to try to get in the car. It wasn't an easy task. When Joe came out five minutes later, Angel sat with his head leaned back, trying to will the medicine into his system faster.

Joe glanced his way, started the car and headed home. "I know you can't wait to see Charlie," Joe smiled, "but she won't be there when we get home. She's working late with Jerry. She might not be home until after church. They're having a three night service."

"Is she still working for that man?"

"Yes she is. It pays well, and the job suits her."

"I can't stand that old man."

"I still say you're jealous of him."

"That old man! Why would I be jealous of him?"

"We've been down this road once . . . because he spends more time with Charlie than you do."

Angel didn't say anything but looked straight ahead. He couldn't wait to get out of this car; his side ached. Every time Joe hit a pothole, Angel gave him a dirty look.

*****

"We're here," Joe glanced over at Angel. "Are you okay?"

"No, but I'll live." Angel grimaced.

"The nurse warned you to take it easy."

"I know. I never listen."

"Well, you can take it easy from here." Joe climbed out, scowling as he walked around to see if he could help Angel from the car. The look of pain on his brother's face caused him to reach out to steady him as he bent around trying to get out of the car. Angel let out a breath, a soft one, as he straightened.

233

"Cracked ribs, *and* a bruised liver, *do not* make for a fun time."

Joe nodded. "I cracked my ribs once, and you're right. That alone would be enough to deal with. Come on; let's get you in the house."

After hurrying to unlock the door, Joe walked in and found no one home. He laid Angel's bag on the coffee table and moved to close the door behind his brother as he came in. "We're working on moving the boys around and fixing you up a temporary room."

"The couch is fine."

"You won't say that after the kids come running in here on Saturday morning."

"You may be right there."

"Well, no worries about that; tomorrow the kids are staying with grandma. So if you hear anything upstairs, it won't be the kids."

"Man, don't go there." Angel moved and sat down.

"Why do you think we send the kids away?"

"Hey, I said don't go there." Angel smiled, "We single guys don't like to hear what we're missing."

Joe went to the hall closet and took out two pillows and brought them to Angel. "You may not have to worry about that much longer if Nyssa gets her way."

*****

Around six that evening, Angel laid down. By eight, he wandered into the kitchen to get a drink of water. He had the house to himself so he went back to the couch meaning only to rest until Charlie came home, but he fell asleep.

The next time Angel woke it was ten past eleven. The house was dark. Realizing he'd not taken his pain pills, he made his way to the kitchen to find a cool drink. When he came back to the living room, he found Nyssa spreading out a sheet and blanket on the couch. "You didn't have to do that."

"You looked cold. Besides, this'll make that old couch feel better."

"Thanks." Angel sat his bottle of water on a coaster, and then looked to his sister-in-law. "I didn't hear you guys come in."

"We were quiet; you looked like you were resting so well."

"I was. I need to catch up on about a week's sleep. You don't get any rest when you're in the hospital."

"No, you don't," Nyssa moved to Angel and patted him on the shoulder. "Get all the sleep you need. With no kids in the house, I think we'll all be sleeping in." Nyssa started to go but then paused. "Charlie's got the full sized bed. I'm sure if you ask, she'll switch with you."

"I'm fine, but thanks."

"If you change your mind, she's in the first room, upstairs on the left."

Angel smiled; he knew what Nyssa was up to. He wanted to see Charlie, but he didn't want to run her out of her room. Angel told Nyssa goodnight and she slipped up the stairs. He sat down and took his medicine.

Since he'd missed the last dose of his pain pills, the pain had raised to a level of eight. Angel stood, then began to pace, holding to his side. Now and then he'd glance at the stairs. The need to see Charlie was great; he argued with himself if he should go find her.

Walking back and forth Angel wondered what it would be like to be married, to have someone to come home to everyday. Joe seemed to be happy. A lot of the married people Angel knew didn't have good marriages; but those that did, at least one of them went to church.

Charlie was a Christian and this worried him. Would she become a nagging wife; always wanting him to go to church, asking him about his soul as his dad's first wife had done.

Angel experienced as much inner pain and turmoil with his mind and heart as he did with his body. He ran his fingers through his hair and took a deep breath, and regretted it.

The pain went deep and he pressed his hand to his side. He looked at the couch and wanted to kick the doctor for releasing him too soon. He was missing the pain shots and drip he received in the hospital.

Angel turned when he heard the creak of the steps. He expected to see Nyssa with some pillow or blanket, but instead he found Charlie. He wondered how long she'd been standing there watching him. She wore those blue pajamas. He'd seen her in them once at Jerry's apartment. He moved his hand from his side and waited, as she started moving toward him.

Chapter 40
Unwilling Patient

Charlie couldn't relax. The thought of Angel sleeping on that hard couch had kept her out of the soft bed. She'd wanted to talk to him when she came in from church, but knew he needed the rest. She'd stood watching him sleep for a few moments, wanting to touch him, but she hadn't.

She stood on the steps now; the lamp in the corner let her see the pain on his face. She'd not been praying hard enough, she could see that now.

He stopped pacing and suddenly grabbed for his side. She wanted to go to him, but Joe told her Angel was being prideful. He didn't want her to come to the hospital and see him in a weak condition.

Would he let her help him now? That night weeks ago in Allie's apartment when she'd bandaged and cared for him, he allowed her to help.

Charlie didn't care about Angel's pride at that moment; she needed to talk to him and hold him. She moved forward and the stairs creaked. Angel turned, looking her way. She restrained her movements, keeping her steps slow, rather than running to him, as she wanted to do.

She watched as he moved his hand from his side and a part of her wanted to smack him and tell him to quit acting like a child. He was in pain, and she only wanted to be there for him. Men could be so stubborn.

She stepped closer to him and spoke. Her voice was soft and she'd put it off as long as she could. She moved her hand out to touch his arm and began.

"I've missed you." It was a simple statement, but it meant a lot. "Can I get you anything?"

"No, I'm fine."

"Are you sure?"

"Yes, I don't need anything."

Charlie knew Angel was still trying to keep up a front. She was tired of this nonsense. Putting her hands on his shoulders she touched him. Letting her fingers softly move from his biceps to his shoulders.

"You look so tired. I know you can't be resting much on that old couch. Come upstairs and get in the bed where you can get some rest."

"I'm doing fine on the couch."

Charlie's temper rose, but she kept her voice low and firm. "That may be so, but you'll do better in my bed."

The smile that crept across Angel's lips let Charlie know what he was thinking.

"You know what I mean," Charlie's brow furrowed but she smiled as Angel laughed.

"Leave me alone. I need something to take my mind off this pain."

Charlie agreed, "Come on, you need to rest, and this time no arguments." Charlie could tell Angel was getting ready to say no. She leaned in, only inches away and whispered, "If you switch beds with me, I'll give you a goodnight kiss. I might even read you a bed time story."

This brought her the smile that she loved. The desire in Angel's eyes and the feel of his hands on her arms almost talked her into letting him kiss her now.

She watched him as he drew closer; another second and his lips would touch hers. She moved in and kissed him on the cheek. "Not yet," she whispered.

Stepping back she held her hand out, and he gave her a disapproving glance. After a moment he took her hand and they walked slowly upstairs. Charlie knew it was a small battle, and she could tell by the way Angel was acting that she might have won a battle, but by no means had she won the war.

*****

Angel could feel the pain from walking up the steps, but he knew the bed would feel almost as good as Charlie's kiss. Once in the room, he noticed the bed didn't look slept in.

His gaze moved to an empty chair, and he noticed a small Bible lying on an end table. He moved his attention back to Charlie as she pulled the covers back so he could get some rest.

When Charlie came to stand in front of him she gave him a soft smile. "Do you need anything before you lay down? Something to eat or drink?" Angel shook his head no.

"All I need is this."

Angel took Charlie by the wrist. She didn't fight him in the least, and it was a good thing, because he didn't have much strength. She moved closer to him. He felt such relief when their lips touched. It made him believe this ordeal was finally over.

This would be their first real kiss. Angel felt a deep longing inside when his lips met hers. Pain or not, he wrapped his left arm around her waist and while still holding to her wrist with his right hand, he pulled her closer, placing her hand on his chest.

The sigh that escaped her lips when she said 'Angel' brought on another wave of desire; so much so, that for the time being it drowned out the pain. He knew it would return, but he was going to enjoy it while it lasted.

Angel knew better than to deepen the kiss, but when Charlie didn't pull away, he lost some control. He tried to gain it back as he forced himself to slow down. It wasn't easy, but he finally found some restraint, pulled back, and rested his forehead against hers.

"Wow," Charlie sighed.

Angel laughed and straightened, looking at her. "I didn't mean to do that."

"I understand. I've got all these pent up emotions and I'm sure you do, too. I'm so glad you're okay. Leaving you alone with those men was the hardest thing I've ever done."

Charlie's touch was so soft. She let her finger trail down his cheek, touching him as if he was breakable. He wanted to tell her so many things, but he didn't know where to start. Angel closed his eyes and pulled Charlie close. He kissed her on the cheek and whispered. "You did the right thing. You went for help."

"I called the police as soon as I got away from Benny."

"Did he hurt you?" Angel used his right hand to make Charlie look at him. He believed her when she shook her head no.

"With the help of a homeless man and some answered prayers, I got away."

Angel cradled Charlie's face with his good hand, leaned in to kiss her again when she spoke.

"You know, it broke my heart that you thought I told Jerry you were an officer."

Angel pulled back and shook his head no. "I know you didn't tell him."

"But for a moment you doubted me. Angel, I would never hurt you."

"I know that." Angel looked down, but when Charlie touched his cheek he looked back.

"I'm not angry that you thought I told him, I just want you to know, you can trust me."

"I do trust you."

Charlie smiled, placing her hands on Angel's shoulders. "I want to hug you, but I don't want to hurt you."

*****

"I'll chance it." Angel smiled and closed his eyes as Charlie attentively put her arms around his neck and rested her head on his shoulder. She loved the smell of him, the feel of him; it felt so good to be in his arms. Charlie knew she could have stayed there for hours, but she also knew Angel needed to rest.

"This is better than any medicine." Angel laughed. "I want this every six hours, too."

"I think you need to lay down."

Angel hugged Charlie a little tighter. "I can do this lying down."

"Yes, but you're not going to."

"Party pooper."

Charlie leaned back laughing, looking him in the eye. "Sit down, you need to rest."

"If you say so." Angel relented, sighing as Charlie pulled back. Charlie waited for Angel to sit down, watched him grimace at the pain, and prayed he'd heal quickly.

Angel started to pull his shoe up to untie it, but Charlie shook her head no.

"Let me do that."

"I can manage." Angel started to lean over, but Charlie put her hands on his shoulders, looking down at him.

"Oh, no, you don't. I see that look in your eyes." Charlie's brow furrowed, "I'm going to take care of you, and you're going to enjoy every minute of it. You got that?"

Angel nodded, "Yes ma'am."

She bent down, taking off his shoes. "Want your socks off too?"

*****

"No." Angel felt awkward. Charlie put his shoes by the bed and sat beside him. As if it was the most natural thing, she sat close and began to unbutton his shirt. He swallowed and took a deep breath as he watched her. She was all business . . . helping a sick patient . . . but all he could think of was her touch.

He'd pulled his shirt out of his pants hours ago while trying to get comfortable on the couch, so he allowed her to push the shirt over his shoulders. He'd gone from an unwilling patient to a man who was totally dependent on the woman before him. Charlie worked carefully so she wouldn't cause him more pain, pulling his good arm out, then sliding the shirt off his other arm.

241

Even though Charlie's hands weren't cold, Angel could feel every little touch. She was sitting close to him, looking at his tattoo. Slowly she ran her fingers across the knife blade. Was she teasing him, or tempting him? Could it be she wanted to touch him? But she went to church!

She didn't explain anything, or even mention the tattoo. She only rose and spoke. "I should go unless you need something else. I'm sure you'll want to get comfortable."

Angel didn't want her to leave, but what could he do. "I hate to ask." He stood and unbuckled his belt. Without speaking she moved closer, pulling the belt out of the loops, and laid it on the chair. "Could you get me a glass of ice water and my pills from the table?"

"Oh, goodness yes. Anything you need, just ask."

"Thanks," Angel stated. The minute she was out of the room he slipped out of his pants, wincing from the pain, very carefully slipped under the covers and lay down. He looked at the other side of the bed longingly.

Was he having these feelings because he'd faced something traumatic, or was he thinking about being married because of his feelings for Charlie?

Sleeping with the same woman the rest of his life wasn't a problem. Matter of fact, it was something he looked forward to. At least, he wouldn't be lonely. He shook his head. Was he good enough for Charlie? His love life hadn't been that eventful, but he wasn't pure by any stretch of the imagination.

Now that he was older he was thankful he'd learned early in life that there were more important things than sleeping around. Repeatedly he'd been given the opportunity to be with women, but he'd said no. It was hard at times to keep his cover in place, and not sleep around, but he'd managed.

He valued his life. Maybe some of his mom's advice sank in after all. He knew marriage was about more than sex; it was about love and wanting to spend the rest of your life with that one person.

It was about sharing the good, and bad times, and staying faithful to each other. When Angelo Morganson got married, it would be for good. He just needed to find the right woman.

As if right on cue, Charlie walked into the room carrying his pain pills and a fresh glass of water. He could get used to this. He sat up and took a long drink and tossed back two pills. When he was done, Charlie sat the water and the medicine bottle on the table. "Do you need anything else?"

"Not that I can think of." Angel said as he leaned back.

"Are you sure?" Charlie reached out and touched his hair, pushing it back, smiling. He looked up at her as she pulled the covers around him.

"Is the pain bad?"

"It's rough."

"What hurts worse?"

"Here." Angel touched his side. Charlie nodded, reaching out to gently rest her fingertips over his hand. Closing her eyes, she began to pray. Maybe he should have closed his eyes, but he didn't. He watched her. Her lips moved but no sound came out. He couldn't believe his eyes when he saw a tear slip down her cheek, then another.

A few moments later she opened her eyes and smiled at him, "I'll be praying more through the night. I hope you rest well."

"Thanks for the prayer."

"You're more than welcome." Charlie hesitated, "I guess I should go." She rose, but he held onto her hand.

Once again, Angel didn't want Charlie to leave. When she smiled at him, he let go of her hand. "You can stay and read if you want to. The light won't keep me awake."

"Are you sure?"

"I'm positive." This won him a kiss on the forehead, and then Charlie moved to the seat and picked up her book and began to read.

Angel closed his eyes, trying to focus on Charlie and the fact that she'd prayed for him, instead of thinking about the pain he felt.

*****

Charlie hoped Angel didn't know how hard it was for her to read. She was doing her best to keep her eyes on the book instead of the man before her. Angel was so attractive, and that kiss . . . man, she'd never been kissed like *that* before! She peeped over top of the book now and then. Once he was asleep, she laid the book down and gave up.

Angel seemed to be sleeping peacefully, but she didn't want to leave. She crept down the stairs, took the blanket and pillow from the couch and returned to the chair. She laid the book aside and sat in the chair, pulling the cover around her. She propped the pillow up and sat for a long while watching Angel, until she fell asleep.

Chapter 41
Making Decisions

The next morning Nyssa walked down the hall going downstairs to put coffee on. She walked by Charlie's room, stopped, backed up and looked in. She couldn't help but smile. Angel was in the bed and Charlie was sitting in the chair. Joe came up behind her and kissed her on the neck.

"What are you doing . . . well I'll be," he finished his thought as he looked into the room.

Nyssa shushed Joe and they crept on down the steps and into the kitchen. "Do you think he's falling for Charlie?" Nyssa poured water into the pot while Joe took out the coffee.

"I don't know, but they don't need your match-making. Looks like they're doing pretty good on their own."

"Now and then some men need a push."

"No one ever pushed me."

Nyssa put her hand on Joe's arm, and looked at him, "What do you call that talk you and Daddy had?"

Joe furrowed his brow. "He laid out a few options. I don't see Charlie's dad being that involved in her life. Look how she's been living. Where is her family? Why aren't they in her life?"

"My point exactly," Nyssa kissed Joe on the cheek.

"Oh, no, you don't. I'm not getting in the middle of this," Joe stepped back, but Nyssa closed the gap, putting her hands on his chest.

"Why not? Angel needs someone to tell him how good a marriage can be, if you find the right mate."

"I think he might see a glimpse into that this morning." Joe pulled Nyssa close. "When he sees the smile on my face, he'll see it's not all bad."

"Joe!" Nyssa shook her head, but her husband's mind was on other things. She pulled away to get a coffee filter, but he came up behind her and began to kiss her neck. He slid his hands around her waist. "I thought you wanted coffee," Nyssa said teasingly.

"Can't I have both? You know we don't have much time alone, *and the kids are gone.*"

"Not a lot." Nyssa closed her eyes, smiling. An idea forming in her mind. She turned to Joe putting her arms around his neck. "Promise to talk to Angel about how good marriage can be, and I'll meet you upstairs with a cup of coffee and a smile."

*****

Joe knew there was a bit of blackmail going on here, but he didn't care. He kissed Nyssa; letting his hands show her what awaited her upstairs. He stepped back and smiled. "I'll take the coffee and the smile, but keep the robe on until you're in the room. Charlie or Angel might not appreciate our early morning antics."

Joe turned to go, but when Nyssa called his name, he stopped.

"*Joseph,*" Nyssa called in a singsong voice.

The smile on his face said it all. Joe stepped back to his wife, closed her robe and tied the sash in a bow. He took her hand in his, kissed her expertly, and then said in a husky voice, "The coffee can wait."

Four hours later Joe and Angel sat at the kitchen table playing a game of cards. The women were out picking up some medicine for Angel and getting some extra groceries for the house. Joe took a drink of soda and sat the can down.

He looked at Angel as he raised him two Oreo's and dealt himself two cards.

"I noticed you and Charlie switched beds."

"How'd you know? You didn't get up until ten."

"We were up at eight, but went back to bed for some extra marital activities."

"Two hours?" Angel looked at Joe. But the man only smiled and nodded, "Ah, the joys of married life . . ."

"And Viagra."

"Not yet . . . thank you very much." Joe laid down a full house. "But I was thinking . . . well, Nyssa was thinking . . . that I needed to have a talk with you. I agreed to do it, for reasons that aren't necessary to explain."

Joe guessed the smile on his face explained why they were having this conversation.

Angel shook his head no. "Well let me save you some trouble. Tell her we talked about it."

"That might work. But, I know tonight she'll be looking me in the eye and asking me what I told you. So listen or not, here goes."

Angel shrugged and looked at his brother.

"I'm sure you've heard me joking about being married. Well, I joke and carry on but I wouldn't take anything for my marriage with Nyssa. She's everything to me. I don't know what I'd do without her."

Angel nodded and Joe dealt another hand. "I understand what you're saying, but how did you know it would work out? And, why Nyssa? What told you she was the one?"

Joe shrugged and looked at his cards. "I don't think you can ever know it's going to work out. You put your best foot forward and hope things work out. Why Nyssa? That's easy. I wanted to spend every waking minute with her, and I couldn't keep my hands off her. I still can't."

Angel nodded and raised Joe one Oreo. "Was she the only one who made you feel like that?"

"Pretty much. We were good friends first; that helps. We had a lot in common. In the quiet of the night, when I was lying in my bed, she's what I thought about. She's what I dreamed about.

She's the only girl I ever dated that I wanted to do everything with."

"That makes things clear. But did you ever regret it?"

Joe laughed. "Sure I did. Nothing's perfect. There's times when she's mad and won't let me touch her . . . and I think what did I get myself into?

Then there's times, like this morning, when I wake up and look at her and think, 'why in the world did she ever want me'?"

"I wonder that too," Angel said with a smirk.

"I'd punch you if you weren't in so much pain already."

"I know. That's why I knew I could get away with it."

"Well, don't push your luck." Joe pointed his finger at Angel. He got up, got a glass of milk and sat back down and began to eat his winnings.

Angel became quiet and Joe knew he was thinking about Charlie in some way. "What's on your mind?"

"I don't know. I've been thinking, going over different scenarios about Charlie and me. We aren't even dating and I'm thinking about the long haul."

"That's a good thing. You're thinking things through. There's nothing wrong with that."

"What about church and praying and stuff? Does that ever get on your nerves? Does Nyssa try to get you to go to church all the time?"

"Not all the time. We've come to an understanding."

"What do you mean? You go every other Sunday, or so many times a month?"

"Nothing that detailed. I go now and then. I always go on special occasions, like Christmas and plays. But let's get something straight.

I may not show it, but I know I should go. I know Nyssa is the one who's doing what she should. Now, if you don't think that some day you'll manage to walk down that aisle and give your heart to God, *don't* get involved with Charlie."

"How can you say that, if you don't go? What's the difference?"

"There's a big difference. When you have kids, you don't want to be arguing all the time about if they go to church, or if they don't. You need to be in agreement with the person you're going to marry, about your religious beliefs.

"Marriage means a lot of work, a lot of give and take. You don't need to put obstacles out there that you know will cause you trouble. There'll be enough surprises along the way."

"I guess you're right."

"So," Joe began, "I know we weren't raised in the same house, and that Dad never was much for church. So what do you think? How important is God to you? Do you even care what denomination your wife is?

"Because that's important, too. I know this couple that divorced over Christmas. He was Jewish and she was Baptist. They thought for some reason they could make it work."

"I would want my kids to have Christmas. I know that much."

"That will narrow your field down some. Now do you believe the Bible? Do you think Jesus died for our sins and rose to live again?"

*****

Angel rose from his chair and went to the sink, feeling very uncomfortable. Joe turned in the seat looking at him, still wanting an answer. "I guess so."

Angel leaned against the sink looking at his brother. "How do you talk about all this stuff, like you're a . . . Christian?"

Joe shrugged. "When I was a kid I went to church every Sunday with Mom. I know it all. I was even baptized when I was ten, but I did it 'cause the rest of the kids did. I never meant any of my prayers.

"Maybe that's part of the reason I have trouble. I feel like, even if I do pray, He's not listening anymore."

Angel sighed, "Mom made me go some, but I didn't like it. To be honest, it kind of scared me. I didn't feel like I fit in and I didn't understand much of what went on."

"Well, there's a difference in fitting in and not believing that Jesus was real, and that He was God's son."

"I guess down deep I believe."

"Would you want your kids raised in the church?"

Angel thought about this for a minute then he shrugged. "Yeah, I would. But I'd want things explained to them better, so they wouldn't feel left out. I don't understand a lot of it myself. No one ever really wanted to explain things to me; they wanted me to do them."

"It seems you've given this some thought."

"I have, it was on my mind last night."

"Before or after Charlie helped you out of your shirt and pants?" Joe raised his brows up and down and smiled.

Angel shook his head. "Charlie stepped out to get me a glass of water, then I took the pants off. But wanting to sleep with her made me think on down the line."

Joe nodded, carried his milk glass to the sink, rinsed it out and put the glass in the drainer. "You're doing the right thing, thinking it all out. It's hard; so many things in a marriage, good and bad, come a little at a time.

"You're trying to imagine life five years or more on down the road. It's not going to be exact; you'll grow together little by little. It's good to know if you ever plan on going to church.

"But, you shouldn't *not* consider her in the running because you're afraid she'll want you to go to church."

"I see what you're saying. I do believe in God. I'm just not sure when I'll be ready to be on a first name basis with Him."

*****

"Can I ask you a question?" Charlie turned to Nyssa as they headed back to the house.

"Sure? Does it have to do with Angel?"

Charlie smiled, nodded, and spoke. "I've been studying a lot about being unequally yoked."

"I know; that's a tough one."

"Were you a Christian when you married Joe?"

"Yes. I asked God to forgive me for that. I fell in love with Joe. I didn't mean to. I asked God why did he allow Joe into my life if he didn't mean for me to marry him."

"What answer did you get?"

"I didn't get a clear answer. I just read the Word. I know I was trying to find a way to marry him. But I found this verse in Psalm 37:4 that says, *'Delight yourself in the Lord and He will give you the desires of your heart'*. My desire was that Joe be saved and be my husband. So I married him."

"I've read that verse too. I like Angel. He amazes me, and I think about him all the time. I can see myself spending my life with him."

"That's very important. We have to be ready for the good and the bad. I mean after the new wears off, so to say, there needs to be something real and concrete to build on. And, *trust me*, the new *will* wear off."

Charlie laughed. "I know that giddy love can't last forever, but even past that, I can see being with him. I can see us sitting on some porch getting old and enjoying each other. I know that sounds sappy."

"It does, but that's love. It's a lot of things. It's that brand new excitement when you see each other, it's that look in Joe's eyes when he holds the kids. Love changes as we do; it molds and bends to fit us as we grow older."

"I want a man who'll change with me, who'll love me when my hair's getting thin and gray. A man I can trust to be there through the good and the bad. How do you know when to put your heart out there to see if this is the one? Even more important, how do you know when you've found the right man?"

"I don't have a clear-cut answer. You have to have faith in your choices and your prayers. Nothing will succeed if you go into it with a bad attitude, or thinking it's going to fail.

"You look ahead and pray, knowing that God will answer your prayers. When things look bad it means it's time to build up your faith. Only God knows all the answers, and He doesn't always feel the need to tell us what they are."

"You're right there." Charlie laughed.

"Does that mean you have your sights set on Angel?"

"I guess it does."

"Then I suggest you start praying, and go after that young man."

Charlie nodded and smiled at Nyssa. As they pulled into the driveway she added, "That's exactly what I plan on doing!"

*****

That evening around six, Joe, Nyssa, Charlie and Angel all sat down for supper. The kids were still with the grandparents and Angel and Joe sat waiting as Charlie and Nyssa put the meal on the table.

They all held hands while Joe asked the blessing. Angel thought it odd that Joe didn't go to church, but yet he wanted his children raised believing in God, and he even said grace.

Angel looked down at Charlie's hand in his and wondered if Joe was right. Was he worrying about all of this for nothing? He'd done some hard thinking all day while lying and resting, reflecting on the kind of woman he wanted to spend the rest of his life with.

Angel didn't want to date Charlie on a whim. He knew the kind of young lady she was, and there was no way he wanted to hurt her.

She was the kind of person who was honest, compassionate and devoted. Charlie was the kind of girl you courted instead of dated.

Dates with Charlie would end with him getting a goodnight kiss at the door and going home, rather than waking up with her the next morning. Today he'd decided; he was willing to make a go of it, if she was.

Nothing was guaranteed. They might find out after a few weeks that they weren't compatible, but he wanted to know.

Charlie was beautiful. He was very attracted to her. He made up his mind he wouldn't let his youthful irritations of his family trying to pull, beg, or scare him into church, stop him from dating Charlie.

Angel knew it might not be easy pacing himself with Charlie, but he would try. As he heard Joe say 'Amen', he raised his eyes and looked at her. She smiled, and he didn't want to let go of her hand.

More than anything he wanted to be alone with her so they could talk. He knew her family was in South Bend, and he wasn't sure how long she was planning on staying in Chicago.

To Angel supper seemed to drag on forever, but he didn't say anything. Nyssa and Charlie laughed, talking about a Christmas play, while Joe and he sat enjoying dessert and a hot cup of coffee.

Dinner was *finally* wrapping up when Joe mentioned that soon Angel would need to go to the station to fill out some paperwork. Charlie jumped in, placing her hand on Angel's arm, shaking her head no.

"He needs to have more time to rest. Can't you bring the papers here? I'm sure riding around in the car would be hard."

Angel thought he'd feel less of a man if Charlie was to baby him. But now he was changing his tune. She could baby him as much as she wanted. Leaning back in the chair he used this moment as an excuse to be alone with Charlie.

"I think you're right. Sitting here at the table is making me tired."

"I'm sorry. I should have thought about that. Why don't you go rest on the couch."

As Nyssa began to clear the plates from the table and Charlie rose from her chair, Angel looked at Joe and winked.

Joe rose, too, and helped pick up a few plates. "Charlie, you help Angel; we can do the dishes."

"Are you sure?" Charlie moved to the back of Angel's chair, and when he rose, moved the chair making it easier for him to get up.

"Oh, yes," Nyssa interjected. "Joe helps with the dishes; with three kids around he's used to pitching in here or there."

"Ok. But if you need anything let me know."

"We will," Joe replied.

Chapter 42
Charlie's Angel

As soon as they walked through the door into the living room, Angel took Charlie by the hand. "Let's go to the family room. I want to have some privacy."

Charlie nodded, and Angel led the way behind the stairs to a back room. Angel knew the kids played in here a lot, but for now they'd have all the privacy they wanted. Joe would keep Nyssa busy in the kitchen and the kids wouldn't be back until later that night.

There was a snack bar in the back of the room, and several bar stools. Two pinball machines, a small pool table, beanbags of various sizes and a TV made up the rest of the room. Angel walked to the snack bar and sat down cautiously on one of the few stools that would support his aching back.

He held out his hand to Charlie, and she smiled moving to stand between his knees. Angel put his hands on her waist and pulled her closer. He watched as she gave him a shy smile.

"I want to ask you a few questions," Angel began.

"Sure," Charlie nodded.

Angel could tell being so close to him made Charlie nervous; this intrigued and pleased him. He rested his hands on her back and began. "First of all, I need to clear the air on a few things that I've learned about you. Ever since that night when you found me in the bushes I've been keeping an eye on you."

"Is that so?"

"Yeah, product of my work, and I find you intriguing." Angel smiled.

"Same here." Charlie gave Angel a shy smile.

"Well. I found out how you came to be here. You ran away from Benny, stole his gun, and some money."

When Angel felt Charlie tense, he shook his head no. "You're not in any trouble. I just wanted to talk to you about it. Do you plan on staying here? After the things Benny's done, you'll not have to worry about him pressing charges. But, if you do have the gun, it would be best to give it to Joe or me."

"I'd forgotten about the gun. The money's gone but I could pay him back. The gun's at Allie's old apartment. I can get it and give it to you. I don't want the gun. I took it because I was afraid he'd shoot me. He was very drunk that night."

"That punk! I'd like to put him away for a while."

"Benny will get his. But I have to admit; I'm glad things worked out as they did. What happened with Benny wasn't pleasant, but a lot of good things came out of it. If it hadn't been for Benny, I would have never thought about coming to Chicago and I would have never met you."

Angel's brow furrowed. "I guess you're right. But I still want to put him in jail."

"You might get the chance yet. Who knows with Benny?"

Angel smiled and tilted his head, studying Charlie. "Well, you're here now. Are you going to stay, or go home?"

"I like my job with Jerry. I think we can really do some good."

"So you're thinking about staying?"

"I guess. I'd think about it more, if I had a better reason to stay."

"What's a better reason?" Angel asked.

Charlie was hiding a smile. She seemed distracted by some imaginary lint on Angel's shoulder.

"Say, if I were dating a handsome young man whom I thought had potential, I'd consider staying on to see what happened."

"What kind of potential are you talking about? The kind of career he maintains, the money he makes, or something more?"

This time Charlie looked Angel in the eye as she answered. "A good job is important, but so is honesty, and good morals."

"You got anyone particular in mind?" He teased.

"I have one man in mind, who I think will fit the bill."

"I see. What are the pros and cons? What kind of chance does he really have?" Angel asked, smiling.

Charlie shrugged. Angel loved it when she was shy with him. He could tell she was having trouble looking him in the eye. She toyed with his hair, pressed out a wrinkle on his shirt and then seemed to be straightening his collar as she spoke.

"One of the pro's is he's gorgeous, and he's very interesting. I love to spend time with him, and his kisses leave me wanting more."

"That sounds good." Angel moved his hand and let his finger trail down Charlie's cheek, then straightened in the chair, bringing them closer together. "What are some of the con's?"

Charlie still wouldn't look directly into his eyes as she answered. "Some of the con's are; he doesn't go to church. I think he has a temper, there is this *dangerous* side to him that's a little scary, and his kisses leave me wanting more." When she was done speaking she finally looked him in the eye.

"How can that be a pro and a con?" Angel found it so hard to *just* hold her. His hands began to move as she talked about him. His right hand moved up her back; her long hair was soft against the back of his hand. His left hand flattened against her back and he fought to not pull her the few inches closer, so he could kiss her.

The word *dangerous* lingered in his mind as he looked at her. She'd dragged the word out as if it frightened her and intrigued her at the same time. This time she spoke to him directly, looking him in the eye, instead of pretending she was talking about a person who wasn't in the room.

"It's a pro because *your* kisses amaze me, but at the same time, make me forget who I am. *You* make me forget that there are rules I'm supposed to follow and adhere to."

"Does that mean I can't kiss you?" Angel waited for her to answer. At first she looked at him as if she didn't know what to say. Then something lit up inside her mind, and she tilted her head and asked him a question.

"What would you do if I said no, you can't kiss me? Would you honor my request? Or would you say no, move on and find someone else?"

Angel was surprised at his own answer that came floating into his mind. Of course he'd try, he wanted to know all about Charlie. He wanted to see what was going to happen. "If you say no kissing; then there'll be no kissing. But it wouldn't be easy," he added in a low tone.

He could tell his answer surprised her. The look on her face showed she'd not expected him to agree at all. She moved her arms around his neck and nodded.

"That's good to know . . . but kissing is allowed."

"Good." Angel started leaning in to steal a kiss.

"*But* . . ." Charlie began.

"But what?" Angel kissed Charlie on the cheek and then again close to her ear. She pushed him back and he complied.

"There will be some things that *are* off limits."

"I know," Angel's tone was soft as he confirmed he understood. "I'm well aware of what I'm getting myself into."

Charlie smiled and echoed his answer, "Good."

Angel waited. He wanted to show Charlie he had *some* discipline. The two of them stayed close. Charlie studied his features, moving her hand to trace her finger from his hair to his chin. "We're kind of laying our cards on the table here, so I want to say a couple of things."

"Sure. Go ahead." Angel could stay in her arms all night, but he had an idea she was going to get serious.

"I don't know what you're looking for at this point in your life, so I'll tell you where I am. I'm not telling you this to scare you off, or make you think I'm ready to get married next week. I want you to know that I'm not dating just so I can go out and have fun. I want what Joe and Nyssa have. I want to start

258

looking for Mr. Right," Charlie shrugged lightly, "I want you to know this is serious for me."

Angel nodded. "I know what you mean. I guess I'm getting to that point, too, where I want something more than a girlfriend. It'd be nice to have someone care if I came home at night."

"I'll care." Charlie kissed Angel lightly and then pulled back. "I'll even complain if you're late."

"Let's don't go that far," Angel smiled. He felt he was on the right track, but he was also unsure of what he was getting himself into. It could mean a long courtship and a lot of restraint.

As Charlie moved toward him, he felt desire well up inside. He knew as their lips touched, this wasn't going to be easy. She was everything any man could want. He'd bet money on the fact she was pure and untouched, in more ways than he cared to think about.

She sighed as he deepened the kiss. As she slipped her fingers into his thick brown hair, she whispered his name, "Angel".

Somehow he knew. From that moment on, he'd be Charlie's Angel.

We thank you for reading